MW01088336

Nightworld Shadows

By
Veronica I. Coldiron

© 2019 by Veronica I. Coldiron. All rights reserved.
No part of this book may be reproduced, stored in a retrieval
system or transmitted in any form or by any means without
the prior written permission of the publishers, except by a
reviewer who may quote brief passages in a review to be
printed in a newspaper, magazine or journal.

Prologue:

Bouncing the Super ball against his grandmother's head stone, Brent enjoyed the gentle wind whispering through his dark blonde hair.

"Do you miss me much Gram?" He sighed, liquid blue eyes welling with tears.

He continued throwing the ball against the headstone, hoping that she would hear it in the afterworld and shout at him to stop that awful racket. That would at least be something... something more than a hole in the ground that already had sod on top of it.

Helplessness overwhelmed him. His parents hadn't a clue as to what little boys really wanted... but Gram had known. She'd always known. His birthday was just a few days away and it would not be the same without her.

His mother and father talked about him in the distance but more importantly, they gawked at him.

Catching the ball, he rubbed it firmly in the palms of his hands. A slight sigh caught on his lips as he shoved the small orb into his pocket. Leaning against the stone slab that had separated them, he whispered:

"That's all right Gram. I'll be here when you come back. I love you... with all my heart." He glanced over his shoulder at his parents. They seemed so far away to him, their clothes dark and strange, flapping in the wind and silhouetted against the overcast sky. Gazing back to the head stone, he murmured even quieter than before.

"A bushel and a peck... you know the rest."

As he turned to go, a soft voice sounded in his ears.

"With all mine too... and a hug around the neck."

Brent stood motionless as the hair on the back of his neck rose on end. He dared not turn to look, knowing her well enough that this good-bye only bore good intent.

He smiled, taking his mother's hand. Brent was eight years old then and he went home to lie down on his bed, and weep. His ninth and tenth birthday passed in a terrible blur. Emptiness pervaded every thought. Each morning, he woke knowing that there would be no hope of going to Gram's farm on the weekends. Each day, he became less and less a little boy, more and more an empty shell... existing, but never really living.

A great weight rested upon his chest, constricting his breath. At times it hurt so that he wished someone would come to lift it away... to rescue him.

Tapping at the opaque shadows on the window of his upstairs bedroom, Brent gazed in quiet contemplation at the family graveyard on the hill. The very stones seemed to beckon from their station in the nightworld. Though he wished to deny it, he knew everyone would one-day wind up here. Yesterday, sweet yesterday called to him.

The sounds of his parents intruded upon his thoughts, as they argued downstairs... fighting about the same thing they always disagreed about... money. A polite frown tilted the corners of his mouth down as he listened to them.

Gram had always said that money was the root to all evil and whether that held true or not, money certainly had a way of fouling things up when it wasn't around.

Rising from his seat at the window, he took his time approaching the door. For a child of ten, he tended to move as though old age had stolen his energy. Bending his ear to the keyhole of the door, Brent heard his father's desperate plea to sell Gram's farm, followed by his mother's firm rebuttal.

"That farm was the only thing that meant anything to my mother besides Brent, and when she left it to him, she meant for him to have it! I won't let you take the one thing he has left of her over a few backed up bills!"

"Backed up bills Janet? Is that what you think this is about? This is about the inability to pay for our own home! What are we to do for him when he's hungry and hasn't a roof over his head? What then?!" Brent thought about what his father said. He understood it but like his mother, could never bear the thought of parting with gram's place. His mother's argument nearly rattled the door.

"Steven you're being unreasonably dramatic. We could always move to the farm. It might be hard, but at least there we can grow our own food... and there would only be utility bills to pay." Awful silence ensued as Brent's parents contemplated their situation. Janet's voice first broke the quiet.

"I'll just go back to work." She murmured, just audible enough that the boy could hear it from upstairs.

Even his father's deep sigh seemed to resonate through the stairwell.

4

"They must be right at the bottom of the stairs." He whispered to himself, pressing his eye even closer to the keyhole, though he knew it served no real purpose. He still would not be able to see them.

"You can't do that." Steven Price relented. "Brent needs you here. I'll... I'll work something out. Go to bed, dear."

Scrambling into bed, Brent dove under the covers at all speed, his feet kicking off the slippers just before he snatched the covers over his head. His mother began ascending the stairs, followed by his father. He knew that Dad would go on to bed, but Mom would come check on him like she always did after they fought.

She entered, the yellow aura from the hall light glowing all round her. For a second, she looked like Gram in her flowery dress and tall shoes as he peeped over the edge of the blanket, his eyes seeming almost closed so as to fool his mother.

"You okay puddin?" Her tender voice fell around Brent like a cool spring rain.

"I'm fine mom." He answered squinting against the persistent intrusion to feign having been asleep.

"Oh you're not foolin' anybody." She said, shaking her finger at him. "I know you were listening. But you have to understand, honey. Dad and I love each other very much. It's just that sometimes grown-ups have to argue to communicate with each other."

"Not me."

"Not me what?" She asked, plumping down onto the feather mattress beside him and brushing the hair from his brow.

"When I get married, I'm gonna marry the right person like Gram did and we won't have to fight. Mom? Did you ever hear her and Gramps argue?" Brent turned expectant eyes to his mother. His grandfather was barely more than a shadow in his mind. Though he had on many occasions tried to glean information about the family patriarch in a roundabout way, he had never been so bold as to outright ask about him.

"Oh, Sweetheart." She soothed, not bothering to tell him that her father had passed the week she was born. The admission of it was at times even more than she could bear. "You're gonna find out that when Gram and Gramps were around, things were a might different in the world than they are right now. There weren't near so many things to argue about. You'll see one day when you're all grown up."

"In that case... I just won't grow up." He stunned himself with the revelation but determined that there must, in fact be a way to keep from arguing with people.

Janet laughed for a moment, then recalling how much even she missed her mother, the smile faded.

"What do you suppose she wants us to do mom?"

"Who? Gram?" She asked.

"Yeah." Brent's biggest question to then had been if anyone thought she actually went to heaven but now, he found himself more concerned with what it could be that his grandmother actually wanted from him.

"I sometimes wish she could be here to help us son, to tell us what she would like us to do, but that just isn't possible any more. We're going to have to be strong and go on. Don't you think she would want it that way?" "I suppose." A gentle smile curved his lips. "Besides, I can't hear what she's saying from that far off anyway."

His mother chuckled.

"What a funny little guy you're turning out to be. Whatever are you sayin'?" Though she attempted to mask the concern, her tone trembled and chills raced over her arms. She hadn't forgotten that dark day at the grave, when he claimed to have spoken to his Gram. Doctor Taylor, the child-psychiatrist she took him to, had been able to do nothing with him in that regard. Janet straightened the covers as she waited for his answer. Slapping his arms down over the blankets, the decision to tell her everything weighed heavily on his thoughts. Brent's chest tightened. He wanted his grandmother back so bad it hurt.

"She stands out there on the hill sometimes at night," he ventured at last. "with her arms around Gramps and she waves for me to come there." His mother gasped.

"What do they look like, dear?" This was the first she'd heard of it. None of it made any sense and she began to ponder if there could be some sort of foul play afoot. There must be some explanation for the child seeing people in the graveyard at night. Even Brent's imagination didn't run that wild.

"Oh, she looks younger and happier than ever out there under the light pole waving to me like that."

Brent took a deep breath and sighed, thinking of the night before, when he'd last seen it.

"She seems so happy that I wonder if she even knows how hard it is on us since she left. Gramps doesn't even dare take his eyes off her. She's pretty as a flower." Janet thought about calling the doctor to come and check on the boy in the morning but decided at length to just try and comfort him this time. Doctor Taylor had said it was better to support him than to mock or scold him so she hugged him close to her, stroking his shiny hair.

"Brent, Gram knew how strong you were and she probably felt sure that one day you would actually let her go to Gramps and be happy. Baby, why can't you do that?"

He contemplated it in silence for a time. As she released her embrace, he looked at his mother wisely. "I suppose you're right. It's selfish of me to be mad at her. If she's really that happy... and I guess there's no doctor's visits or medicine there so she probly is... I think I can try to let her go."

Pride radiated from Janet's face. Her son was smart beyond his years. There could be no doubt about that.

'Wouldn't it be nice to have it all finally over?' she thought.

"Well you get yourself off to sleep young man. I love you." She kissed him on the cheek and added dutifully, "Dad loves you too." She straightened his covers again, rising to leave. As she opened the door, he felt compelled to agitate her.

"You're still a little mad with him aren't you?"

Her mouth formed a tight grin as she put her thumb and forefinger up together.

"Just a tiny bit... everything will be better in the morning. See if I'm not right."

"Mom?"

An angry sigh escaped her. He was prolonging the bedtime scene.

"What Brent?" "After I let her go... do you think I'll ever see her again?"

"I know you can. Just keep her memories in your heart all of the time and anytime you miss her, you can close your eyes..." here, she put her hand over her heart and closed her own eyes. Taking a deep breath, she found herself almost capable of smelling her mother's floral perfume before she finished. "and there she'll be. That's what I do."

"You could've saved me a few nightmares if you had told me that a couple of years ago."

"Ha. Ha." She jested. "Now get to sleep, boy. School tomorrow."

"G'night mom."

"Night." She whispered shutting the door and heading down the long hall to bed.

****

Brent lay there for a while, thinking of the possibilities of life and the unwilling depart from it. Even in his ten-year-old mind, he grasped that there was such a fragile line separating those living from the shadows of the nightworld.

The thought moved aside for a moment as he rose, making his way to the little rocking chair at the window. Scooting into the seat, he straightened the little plush cushion tied onto the rungs in the back before looking once more to the cemetery. Gram stood again on top of the hill, waving like always.

Brent whispered a quiet good-by… "with a bushel and a peck".

Eliza blew her grandson a kiss and his eyes fell upon Gramps, waving. Brent closed his eyes for a moment to remember them just that way. When he opened them again... they had gone. Only the vacant graveyard and the silent tombstones remained, bathed in silver moonlight.

Chapter One: Whispers and Shadows

[PART I]

A brilliant full moon left its luminous wake over the blades of grass blowing in the autumn breeze. Silver light danced on the fields of Brent's Grandma's farm, which stood on the other side of the family graveyard from his parents' house. The white plantation home loomed against the night-filled valley, a pale specter guarding its remaining earthly treasures.

Brent sat in a rocking chair on the second-floor balcony of the old house, remembering the last night he'd said good-by to Gram forever. Though a grown man now, the fancies of his youth remained embedded in his mind like a long-ago phantom wish.

His shrink once said that children commonly hold onto the past: especially when a loved one dies because they feel abandoned by that person. However, an adult who refuses to let go... well now, that was something entirely different.

Brent rationalized that if he let go of her completely, he might never see Gram again. He couldn't let that happen. He knew with certainty, despite the pleading of his therapists in the past, that what he had experienced as a child was real. He had seen her... and she was real. He clung to this notion despite even the near maniacal ravings of his mom, who begged him repeatedly to exercise some humanity and stop torturing her with her mother's memory.

He maintained the feeling that wherever he went, Gram was with him. He'd never known his Grandfather because he died the week after Janet was born. Brent had seen pictures of Gramps, but those old photographs hadn't stirred so much emotion as they did memories of Gram's pictures.

Heavy sighs became the dictate of the moment, as he sat thinking about his mother's pretty pleading with him to marry and have children right after college. It could never be said that he didn't like women, because he did... most emphatically. (His shrink had a field day with that point.)

It just seemed that all of the girls he had genuinely liked, and nearly worshipped sexually, were missing something. He tried explaining to his mother that he wanted to be certain about someone, but she had her own idea of how reality worked and there was no talking to her.

Remaining true to his love of contentment, Brent never argued with any of the women in his past. In fact, he refused to get involved enough for that to happen. He figured that when the right girl came along... he would know. Until then, his mother would just have to wait to be a granny.

Chuckling as he went to bed, Brent felt a tickle of emotion that had not visited him in some time... hope. In the back of his mind, the sound of its voice told him that tomorrow might bring some new knowledge of self-existence... that he might one day be the man that God intended him to be.

[PART II]

Morning dawned, glorious. Brent looked like a Greek statue standing on his porch. Watching the cows in the pasture, his thick, sandy brown hair glimmered gold where the morning rays of sun fawned over him. His tanned bare torso rippled in all of the right places.

The fact that he hadn't settled down with one of many women was a miracle: (not that the ladies hadn't tried.)

His steely blue eyes had been partially closed by the sun, his skin a little weathered by it. This was a side effect of his profession, veterinarian and farmer, which brought him out into the harshness of the elements.

It seemed the logical career for him. Until he began to make good money, he wouldn't be able to afford field hands. This meant he would have to know as much about animals and agriculture as he could. Agriculture had become his minor.

Returning to his seat, he sipped at a cup of black coffee. The back-screen door stood ajar and hearing the static of his old C.B radio in the front room, he smiled. Brent had been raised in the country in a time before computers were in every home and he and his friend Bubba had made a habit of C.B. radioing each other every morning since they were 12-years-old. Brent's 4+ years way at college hadn't made a difference. He fell right back into the practice almost the moment he moved back.

Brent sighed contentedly as the old pine floorboards of the porch answered the rhythmic movement of his chair with creaks and groans of their own. Bringing the cup to his lips he caught sight of an image, someone's shadow standing at the edge of his porch.

Throwing the cup away as he jumped, Brent jerked his head around to find himself alone. He had trouble getting his breath at first. Falling back into his chair, he calmed himself a little bit at a time. Seeing the cows grazing, he counted them to himself in silence to achieve a calming effect. His therapist said that when he had these spells, it would behoove him to sit down and count. At first, he'd keep time with his heart rate, and then slow down gradually so that his body would follow the count in turn.

His athletic body often worked faster than his brain, so catching a good pitch to begin counting could be trying sometimes.

As his eyes glinted nervously over the cows in the field, his heart rate began to pick up again. He only counted thirty head of cattle, which meant that two of them had gone missing.

Rising, his skin responded to the cool breeze chasing over him. Small crows' feet around his eyes tightened as he counted and recounted. He had been on Gram's old farm for more than two years now, isolating himself from the outside world. Those cows were like family.

After his eyes made the third pass over the fine fat beasts, he knew that Milly and Agatha were the culprits. He began running at the tree-line, looking into the woods for them as he passed the length of the barbed wire fence in a mad flurry of words. He called out to them as he passed over his shadow stretching out and disappearing with every new angle in the morning sun.

While they would normally reply with a faint "moo" or come trotting over to him, no such reply came just now. Randy, Brent's collie, followed close at his master's heels as he continued looking for the escapees.

Checking the fence for breaks, he continually glanced up and about for some sign of the cows. Both gates remained locked, no visible breach anywhere in the fence line.

He continued running, searching, the adrenaline coursing through his every fiber. As he made his way to the old red barn at the side of the house, he quickly grabbed the white cross-members and threw open its great doors. Peeking around in darker corners, he picked his way through the varied pitches of light and shadow. He hoped that he'd forgotten to let them out of their stall, but distinctly recalled patting Milly on the neck that morning.

Brent hated keeping them inside to begin with but in the mountains, predators were many and those cows were his kin.

He wondered if maybe the silhouette he'd seen had been one of them getting by him. His feet crunched in the brittle hay strands as he headed for the open door... and daylight.

The darkness of the old structure made offense to the nose. Dampness lingered, the enclosed feeling bringing up foreboding images. They flashed in and out of his mind so fast he couldn't even distinguish what they were meant to be.

His pace reflecting obvious discomfort, he tried to get out of there as quickly as possible. Emerging the darkness, the brilliance of sunlight blinding him temporarily, he suddenly remembered his favorite picture of Gram.

"I remember." He whispered, letting the words fall from his lips, unexpected and almost dreamy in nature.

The memory brushed his consciousness so discreetly, that he dwelt on it for a moment. He could almost see her sitting on the very porch he'd been on that morning. In this photograph, she'd been very young and beautiful. He could have drawn the picture himself just then...

Sitting in a rocker in a pink dress with little yellow flowers dashed on it here and there, she'd looked to be breastfeeding a baby. That moment seemed to be captured by someone coming out of the back door.

Brent recalled this photo so well because it showed Gram with the inner glow of warmth one only achieves as their every pore emanates complete adoration and happiness.

'*Did Gramps take that picture?*' He wondered.

Standing in the sun, he smiled, thinking of her with a special kind of loneliness in his heart. Then he thought he heard faint mooing coming from somewhere at the side of the house.

As his spirits lifted, he freed his mind from the vision for the time being and trotted around the side of the barn, where he had a clear view of Milly and Agatha at the top of the great incline, eating of the grass in the family graveyard.

"Milly! Agathaaaah!" He called out to them as he ran up the side of the hill. Clearing the horizon with a smile on his face, Brent came upon the thought that he had not been to the grave since he was eight years old... and the happiness dissipated. All of the happiness about finding the cows left him and his heart sunk. The cows lazily walked amongst the graves, but not over them. As he called them, they looked at him with a dumb expression for a second, and then went back to eating the daisies on the hillside.

"Come *here*!" He ordered in a more authoritative voice. As he did this, he thrust his pointed index finger to the ground at his side, in a very forceful manner. Neither of them so much as turned their heads to look at him and his patience grew thin.

Part of him wanted to go out there and slap them good with a big stick across their backsides, but fear gripped the child living inside of him. He dreaded to enter the place where dead folks sleep, and worse ...where he left his Gram.

Groaning, he walked over to the woods bordering the area and snapped off a long switch. He stormed over to where they stood and raised the stick only slightly letting it come down with a small sting upon Milly's behind. The animals let out a loud "MOO" and began to trot down the wrong side of the hill. Their udders sloshed, the brown spots of their coats catching in the gold sunlight as they tried to get away from Brent.

"No!" He shouted, running to get in front of them. "Git yourselves back over that hill, you stubborn old ninnies!"

Gesticulating all over the place with his arms to try and get them to go, he finally convinced the confused creatures to turn back.

"I'm completely exhausted already and it isn't even eight o'clock in the morning!" Brent complained aloud.

Wiping the sweat from his reddened brow, he began walking up the emerald green hillside after his crazy cows. As he reached the horizon, he found that they had disappeared.

Turning, Brent looked toward his parent's house nestled against the valley on the other side of the hill. Their car wasn't even home. If this was some kind of prank he didn't like it. But who could do such a thing? He lived like a hermit. No one even knew him to play pranks on him.

Walking to the other side of the graveyard, he found himself hoping that maybe the cows had stopped to graze on the other side of the hill. As he stood gazing down, he found nothing there but glimmering grass, emerald strands waving without care from behind plump golden dandelions.

Making a mental note to take out the spreader later and put down some weed killer, he raised his head to look across the property as far as he could see from there. His shadow lilted across the yard in the high sunlight rising behind him. The statuesque house basked in the golden rays, its shaded porch barely lit by the sun. The dazzling white of the new paint job Brent had put on it shone like water in the attention of the morning glory. The stark contrasts of the old house stood out in his mind as his gaze shifted up the backside of the old structure.

The window where he sat every night, looking out at the graveyard with the unnatural want to be cared for by his Grandmother called to him, making him laugh at himself. Brent embraced the cool breeze, which made the sweat droplets on his skin seem swallowed back by his body. He could just smell the lavish scent of lilacs and a faint smile drifted pleasantly to his face when... someone whispered his name in his ear.

Snatching around to find himself alone yet again, his knees weakened. His whole body rippled chills like a shock wave over his skin as he ran frantically from his spot in the hills. He didn't stop until he reached his back porch, where he readily fell to his knees and lost consciousness.

****

A warm golden feeling invaded his limbs. Opening his eyes, Brent groaned. His mother stood over him. Smiling, she smoothed his brow like she had when he was little.

He sat up in a flustered hurry, still befuddled by the morning's events and began screaming at the top of his lungs for someone to make it stop!

"*What* Brent?!" His mother asked in her soft southern drawl. "What do you need us to stop, hun?"

As if brought to consciousness with those words, he got quiet before answering in the only way he could.

"I don't know. God, mom... how did I get here?"

"Your daddy and I decided to drop in and see if you wanted to ride into town with us for some supper. We found you on your knees in the back yard with your head on the steps. Doc Broil is here. Do you need anythin' before he talks with ya?" Janet pushed strands of salt and pepper hair away from her eyes as some of it had slipped out of the beehive hair-do she'd been so proud of in the past.

"No mother." He grit his teeth. "Just let him come in so I can get back. I've got a couple of cows missing and I have to get home to find 'em."

"They wasn't any cows missin', hun." She spoke in such a tone that indicated she might think he had lost his mind.

Brent went on the defensive.

"Yes there *were*!" He shouted.

"There's no need in shoutin' son..."

14

"Well stop acting like I don't know what I'm talking about ma!"

"It's not that son, it's just that your daddy took 'em all back into the barn while I was helpin' the doctor get you safely into the back of his car. Dad says they're all there. He could've miscounted though I 'spose. How many cows should ya have now anyway?"

"Thirty-two." He said ruefully.

Her need to over-mother him could be quite trying at times, but he knew she meant well. Her gaze bored through him, so that he felt an explanation might be in order.

"I noticed two of them missing this morning and found them up there in the graveyard. Then... when I went to get them they wouldn't listen to me! So there was this stick and I slapped Milly with it to let her know I meant it! Then they ran to your side of the property line and I had a time waving them off so that they would go back through the graveyard and get down the hill, where I could get them back into the fence. They were walking a little ahead of me so they got over the hilltop first, and when I came over...they weren't there. Then this breeze... and someone said my name and I was running crazy through the tall grass... and when I came to the back porch, I fell down, and now I'm here."

Brent had attempted so hard to say everything in one breath, that he thought he would pass out. Once he regained control of himself, he sat staring at his mother with his arms folded across his chest.

Janet's right eyebrow arced. She had always done that when he lied about something as a small boy.

"*What*?!" he shouted again.

"Nuttin." His mother grinned. "I'll have a talk with Dad and I'll send in the Doc. I'll probably go call Doctah Taylah too..."

"Oh, for crying out loud! I'm not crazy mother... maybe tired and disillusioned, but I do not need a head shrinker!"

"Whatevah." She left him with a flippant smile as she departed. Brent hated being thought of as a child, but he talked himself down with reminders that they were his parents: (no matter how ridiculous they could be at times.) As the doctor made his way in, soft blue eyes peering over the rim of thick spectacles at Brent, he had that same "I feel so sorry for you" look on his face that his mother had just left with.

"Spare me the pity Doc. Just give me the prognosis so I can get the heck out of here."

"Have you even tried to move, boy?"

Brent looked surprised, almost bewildered to the point of speechlessness.

"That's what I figgered. You won't be goin' anywhere for at least a week. You sprained your ankle. Strained the lower lumbar regions too. Yore bad enough off that I'm prescribing plenty of rest and relaxation for at least seven days. These," He handed him a bottle from the magic black bag of doctor tricks. "These are your painkillers. Take two with each meal three times a day."

"I don't think I need these Doc. I can't feel a thing... really."

The doctor's laugh was cynical, however infectious it could be on the right occasion.

"Of course ya don't son. I already gave you a shot to kill the pain but believe me, when it wears off yore goin' ta need those. Now I'll drop in on you in a couple of days. I don't usually make house calls, but yore maw was so worried I didn't see any way out. So, you take care. Bad enough I have to drive this far as it is... I don't want to be makin' any unnecessary trips. Okay?"

Brent nodded, a near reluctant sneer on his lips.

"Thanks Doc."

"Yore welcome. Call if you have any questions about the medication or if you just need some normal conversation for a change." Doc Broil had been ministering to Brent, (and to his mothers' worries), for several years and he favored this young man almost as he would a son.

Brent 's grin stretched across his face like a thin strip of elastic as he chuckled, waving the good doctor a hardy good-by.

End of Chapter One

Chapter Two: Death and the Doppelganger

Vermillion streaked over his victorious hand as it stretched toward the dark horizon. Dawn approached, as he moaned with warm satisfaction, her essence wafting over him in the cool air.

His erection slowly faded into the abyss of his soul as the light in her eyes, dimmed. She lay breathless in his arms.

'*Bitch*' he thought. '*Wasting time with pleas of mercy*.' Had anyone taken mercy on him? '*No*'. He thought not.

This one fought him. He picked at a coral colored fingernail lodged in his side. His pale graying skin shuddered against the object as it emerged his body. The orange, chute-like hairs of his back stood on end. With eyes blazing in fulfillment, he looked upon his prey. They all wanted him but once he had them, he made them pay. He would extract a toll on all of them for impersonating her, his only desire.

Gazing to the doe-like lady with her back arched over a stump, he smiled at the breasts, firm as they pointed toward the treetops. Her lifeless stare fired guilt at him, invoking a tickle of remorse. Her silky, pale skin shadowed against the night, made a grim reminder of how his appearance bound him to the darkness. A tear formed in his eye as her delicate hand dropped to the ground.

Had he wronged this woman? His mind cleared as he thought of how devious the last woman had been. He smiled a devilish smile.

No. It was impossible to wrong a woman. They were all relentless bitches. He would kill any vision that brought a memory of her back to haunt him. With this one it had been her perfect youthful skin, fragile as a lily in morning dew; so soft, so supple, so beautiful with her blood and his semen dappled upon it.

He ached all over to feel her pressed against him… the beauty of her ghostly pallor held tight against the dim colors of his damaged body. His jagged, toothy grin glinted in the full moon as he wailed with satisfaction. Then the eerie feeling of her gaze captured him again. He could no longer bear to have her watch as he pleasured in her demise.

17

Looming above the stilled figure, now a mere shadow of the passion he had taken from her, hatred pooled deep within him. She had caused him to do this to her. Sliding his clawed fingers through her flaxen hair, he marveled at it. The straight shafts shimmered in the dappled twilight, which penetrated the shadowy trees. He thought how soft the hair was, how like moonlight it was…not like hers at all.

Hers had been the color of midnight fire. He sighed, thinking of those auburn tresses as he held the heavy head in his hand. He looked into those blue spheres. They were so like hers in shape, but not green as his lovely's eyes had been.

Why couldn't this be her, his vengeance exacted? What was wrong with this woman? Didn't she know how he needed for her to be the one? His breath quickened within him. Hateful stares lost themselves in the expressionless visage. Its every contour seemed etching madness into his heart with an uncaring smile. She taunted him even in death, her face so pallid it cared not for his misery.

How dare her! She had prayed for him too… most annoying habit.

It enraged him to insanity so deep; he scarce recognized that the body fell away, the head still resting in his hands. Pink light filled the sky as he sat, blood streaming over his hands and legs, warmth spilling into every precipice of his soul. A vision appeared; soft, floating in from clouds on the neon horizon. Beholding the green knoll where she rested, his heart filled with longing. Dropping the object in his hands, no longer able to formulate what it was even that he had been holding, he skulked away to rest.

There was hunting to be done and for now at least, he could sleep.

End of Chapter Two

CHAPTER THREE: Bovine Bull

     With the weight of the yoke fully upon her back, Alyssa groaned.

     "Why'd you do that Carlos?" She sighed looking at the bull, who now lay in the fields crying like a giant's child. Patting softly at his big muscular neck, she marveled at his soft, blue-black fur. There had been a time when "*Carlos the Magnificent*" won prizes for her Aunt Edna, but since his illness in the past spring he did little more than pull a plow. To Alyssa's current thinking, even that hadn't been anything to write home about.

     She stood up in the field, gazing through the sweltering heat in the direction from whence she had come. The rich, browns of the fresh tilled earth faded into deeper shades within crevices of blackness, vapors of heat radiating up off the land.

     "*Hottest summer in history.*" She muttered, mimicking the radio news broadcaster's voice she had heard that morning. While shaking her head and thinking how stupid she'd been to bring Carlos out on a day like this to begin with, she kneeled over the whining animal and petted him softly.

     "I'm sorry Carlos." She groaned, knowing she'd have to leave him out there alone for a bit. "I shouldn't have brought you out today. I don't know what I was thinking."

     But she did. She had reasoned it out that morning. The doctor had said Carlos needed to feel useful. He would have to stay active or he would become stagnate, grow old fast and die. All the same, the idea she'd entertained of putting a yoke on him this morning didn't make much sense to her right now.

     Alyssa took the red and white bandana from her hair, using it to wipe her brow of the sweat that had begun to pour from her forehead and down her nose. Light reddish-blonde hair clung to her shoulders in heavy, damp curls and she quickly put the bandana back into place to keep the heat off her neck. Even though she hated to leave him, she knew that if she didn't go for help he'd be worse off with heat exhaustion than with a twisted leg. Alyssa stood up smiling at Carlos, then her gaze shifted across the lumps of deep brown dirt beneath her feet. Staring at the hole where Carlos's hoof had fallen, she thought how it looked almost as if someone had made the hole specifically for him. It was just the perfect size.

Grumbling with discontent, she hoisted the big yolk farther onto her back. The farmhouse stood over a mile away and she couldn't even see it from there.

"Hope you know how much I 'preciate this… you big baby." She pouted. Whining heavily, Carlos seemed to answer Alyssa as she started for the house, bobbing under the yoke while she scurried across the field with as much vigor as she could muster.

By the time she reached the back door her breath came in short gasps. The sweat poured over her so that it took her a minute or so to get the yolk down onto the porch and make her Aunt Edna understand what had happened.

Edna didn't waste a minute. She quickly picked her cell phone up from the table and called Janet Price.

"Hello. Janet? Yes. This is Edna Johnson ovah at the Biggman Ranch? Yes ma'am, from church. My own veterinarian is out on holiday right now and we have a small problem. Didn't you once tell me that you had a son who had become an animal doctor? Well… he wouldn't happen to be around, would he?"

Alyssa listened to the calm drone of her Aunt Edna's voice. The heat still radiated from her skin so that she thought she'd pass out in the floor. Edna didn't seem interested in whether she was okay or not. She had kept her wits enough to stand there and chatter away like there wasn't anything wrong at all.

Pulling a pitcher of water from the refrigerator, Alyssa's hands shook so bad she nearly dropped the glass she planned to pour it into. Falling into her chair as she drank the cool clear liquid, the heat dripped away and she relaxed a little in her chair. Then, wiping the sweat that had been dropping from her forehead onto the red gingham tablecloth, she heard something that really rattled her.

"Well it's not that he's valuable or anythin', but we *luuv* 'im, and he does help in the field when Alyssa's able to come in from town and strap a yoke on 'im." Her aunt laughed casually and Alyssa clinched her teeth together so hard she was sure that even people in Hong Kong could hear her.

Carlos *was too* valuable. And besides… *she* loved him and that in itself made him valuable to her!

"Certainly. Well thank y'all Mrs. Price. Yes, I will and y'all do the same. Thanks agin. Yes. Mmm. Bye."

Alyssa stared at her aunt as if to say "Well?"

"Oh don't look at me that way Lyssie. Janet is sending her son ovah to have a look at Carlos. Were any of the field hands still out yonder with y'all?"

Alyssa wanted to say that there were field hands out there with her, but lunch had crept up on them. On Saturdays, the men always left at lunch. She and Carlos had been out there alone… a real "no-no", in her aunt's book. Alyssa shook her head, much to Edna's dismay.

"Well…" her aunt responded sharply. "why don't you go on out and find Jack? He needs to get out there to Carlos with some water. It's near a hundred and ten degrees or bettuh out yonder today and you're lucky you didn't pass out with heat exhaustion yourself! I do have hired hands to do this kind of work Lyssie. I don't need you to come."

"But Carlos does. If I didn't come out here at least once a week, he'd think I didn't love him. And besides… he wouldn't get enough exercise either."

Her aunt folded her arms across her chest and looked at her niece with some distant happiness.

"Oh I know. '*He's getting too old to be playing around with a lonely little girl*'." She snipped quoting one of her aunt's most common sayings. "Maybe I *do* come out here as much for me as for him, but I don't have anything else to do on the weekends."

"That's because you don't *do* anythin' else deah." Her aunt said sitting down across the table from Alyssa. "Look at you." she gestured toward her niece's clothes, her gaze softening as she looked at her.

Alyssa looked down at herself. Admittedly she was no prize today, but there wasn't much point in wearing anything too becoming while traipsing across the fields with that over-grown-son-of-a…

"You're a beautiful girl", Her aunt interrupted the train of thought. "but you dress like a boy and you won't let *any*one get close to ya. It's high time you got a life of your own." Reaching her fragile hand across the table, Aunt Edna squeezed at Lyssie's fingers.

"What would yore mama think if she had seen the way I let you turn out?" With heat rushing to her cheeks, Alyssa fluttered blond lashes down over two large green eyes, her gaze shifting to her lap. She batted back some tears, which were blurring her eyesight and her hands fidgeted nervously.

"I think I'll go to Carlos maself!" She answered as she pulled her hand back from her aunt, standing up so fast that the chair wobbled back and forth and nearly fell backwards.

"You can't do that." Her aunt protested. "Someone has to show the doctor how to get out there to 'im!"

"Stand on the back porch facing the sun and go straight for a mile!" She snapped. "Y'all can't miss us!"

Storming out, Alyssa went to the hose to fetch a bucket of water for Carlos.

Edna found herself standing alone in the kitchen, and just threw her arms up over the whole affair.

Walking across the field in the sun, Lyssie yanked a plump carrot from its earthen bed to feed to Carlos and wiped the dirt of it onto her overalls. She could not help but count the seconds until the doctor would finally arrive.

****

Brent's mother pressed the directions to the Biggman Ranch into her son's hands and planted a dutiful kiss on his cheek.

"Mrs. Johnson is vera nice. She inherited her daddy's farm when she was vera young. Now, she runs a tight ship so if yore on yore best behaviah, you might be able to keep working for her." Janet straightened the collar on Brent's soft blue denim button-down before going on. "They's money to be had at that Biggman place and they's no reason you couldn't be earning some of it. How's that ankle deah?"

Brent flexed it for her because he knew just telling her wouldn't be convincing enough. He had already stayed with her a whole two days extra to keep her off his back. He couldn't have been happier to receive the call about the bull and had absolutely no intention of returning to his mother's. It had been extremely nice of his papa to send Jim around to tend the livestock but he held to the notion that no one else could tend to his "babies" like he could.

"Bye bye mother." Brent smiled oozing sweetness from his grin as he pecked her on the cheek.

She instantly grew flustered by his attitude.

"Yore not coming back, are ya?" She questioned, genuinely worried.

A noise from the stairwell broke the silence between them as Harvey bumped the banister bringing Brent's satchel down the stairs.

"Brent!" His mother exclaimed with wide eyes.

He grabbed her and hugged her tightly.

"Come on now mama. You didn't think I was going to move back in just because I sprained myself, did you?"

"No. I guess not." She sniffled, trying to muster some sort of adult dignity. "I'll come 'round tomorrah to check on ya, yungun."

Tempted by the notion to explain why her visit would not be necessary, he opened his mouth but nothing came out. He knew she wouldn't listen anyhow, so he kissed her on the top of her head and went out the door without a backward glance.

****

Having gone back to his farm to gather his tools and rescue equipment, Brent began the long drive up into the twisting turning roads of the mountain, hoping to discover the Biggman place. Most of the roads were rarely used that far up and he had a difficult time maneuvering even *his* jeep along the tight twists and turns of them.

With each new curve came a stiff jerk of the wheel from the holes in the mountain asphalt. Chuckling at a private joke that Harvey had told him when he took him home, Brent thought what a lovely day it turned out to be and reveled in the sight of the dappled sunshine coming in between the forest trees above the road. The scent of pine delighted him as his mind roved over the serenity in the air. Even the heat couldn't mess this day up for him. He had left his mother's house. Yes sir. No complications. No fussy women to argue with, no clients complaining. Once he took care of this little "problem" he would return home and look through that old trunk in the attic. He had to find the picture of his Grandma that jarred his memory so hard last week. He didn't know why the matter took such precedence... it just did.

Curiosity made him question why he remembered that particular photo so well. If he could just find it, he might understand better why he remembered it with such vividness. It didn't make any logical sense, but then neither did a lot of things... like why anyone in their right mind would have an over-the-hill bull out pulling a plow on a scorching day like this one anyway.

He chuckled over his mother's words *"she runs a tight ship."*

Shaking his head, he thought that surely the woman couldn't have been too bright if she had actually done this to that poor bull. His Jeep idled outside the wrought-iron gates with the big "B" on each side. As he reached for the buzzer to get some attention, the gate eased open.

He shrugged and drove on through, breathing in the scent of Magnolia trees that lined the massive cobblestone drive like advance guards at a Queen's Palace. Pulling into the driveway in front of the sprawling Southern estate, Brent could see Edna Johnson standing on the porch.

The afternoon sunshine sparkled in the silver highlights of her hair. A soft old-fashioned purple dress with pink flowers all over it in a very busy print, made her look like a freeze frame from some earlier year beneath those huge white columns of her porch. Brent got out of the jeep and walked to the old wooden porch in his laid-back sort of way, swinging a hand out to the elderly woman.

"Mrs. Johnson?" He queried, as she offered a firm handshake.

"That's me!" She chimed in a melodiously thin voice. Brent cast a casual smile as he looked up at her. She seemed a nice enough lady and as they struck up a conversation... he liked what he learned about the woman. He learned that it was no fault of Edna's that the bull was out in this weather, and she had made mention of the cows remaining in the fields at night during her description of the farm and its capability. This perplexed Brent. "How is it that you can live this far up in the mountains and not have predator trouble? I mean, I have to put my cows in the barn at night to keep the wolves and mountain cats out. I lost two cows last year before I started moving them to the barn. How do you manage?"

Edna grinned, turning to the side of the porch. Placing two fingers in the corners of her mouth, she whistled in a shrill octave that reminded Brent of his big city nights during college, when cab fare was the only way out of driving drunk. He found the hair on the back of his neck rising as a large silver wolf came wandering from the corner of the house. The creature's amber eyes flashed all over Brent, making him uncomfortable. The canine licked his chops as he went to Enda and sat at her feet.

Edna replied with a smirk.

"This is Atilla. Keep a predator happy, Mr. Price...and you have no problem." She winked.

A slow smile spread across his face. His mother had been right about Edna Johnson. She knew a great deal about her farm and the proper running of it.

As she pointed him in the direction of the bull, Brent made a solemn promise to chastise her niece properly for doing such a silly thing as to go out into this heat. As he went across the fields shaking his head and muttering about crazy women, a deeply enhanced smile curled the ends of Edna's lips. Watching after the young man, she wondered if perhaps fate might be more responsible for the events of the day... and *not* Alyssa's stubborn streak.

****

Brent came stomping across the fresh tilled ground like a God delivering thunder to the sky, as the big body appeared like a mirage in the sweltering heat. The land leveled out and as it did, he could just make out the figure of a girl sitting next to the bull. Speeding up his pace, he quickly knelt beside the beast as he reached him.

"Has he had any of that water?" He asked, pointing to the bucket that looked to be nearly full.

She shook her head no.

"Why?" He asked as he examined Carlos's swollen ankle. "Isn't he thirsty out here?"

"This is the second bucket. He drank the entire first one in one big gulp." She explained. "so, I went back and got him some more, but he didn't want it."

Brent looked up at her questionably and then back over his shoulder in the direction from whence he had come. Had this little lady made that trip twice already?

"You made two trips already huh?" He asked, doubt actually breathing within his voice.

"No." She answered knowing she had made three.

"Ahh." He grinned teasingly as he felt at Carlos's leg. "But you said you got two buckets of water. Was there one already out here then?" He had rather hoped there had been. At least that would mean she wasn't a complete idiot.

"No." She smiled. She owed him no answer and had no taste for his insinuation.

Brent shrugged it off, deciding that it was better not to get into it with a woman he didn't even know. He didn't let women he liked bait him into an argument and he wouldn't let her do it either.

He frowned as he fiddled with the leg.

"What is it?" She yelped jumping to the animal's side, a small tear trickling from her eye.

'*Maybe there's hope for her yet.*' Brent thought.

"There's nothing to be upset about Miss..." He looked at her wedding finger to find it bare.

"Johnson." She supplied.

His stomach filled with retarded somersaults. Never had any woman with such a poor attitude gotten this much of his attention. Though he knew his thoughts were unwarranted, the more he looked at her, the more his stomach tickled. He wanted to kick himself for this ridiculous feeling about a little slip of a girl in boy's overalls and a rag on her head. Sparkling emerald eyes filled with moisture gazed back him as she waited for an answer and it was all Brent could do to speak. In a moment, he got his voice.

"Well I wouldn't worry too much. He's just twisted it some. We'll give him a few aspirins and wrap this up nice and tight. If we can convince him to get up he could walk back to the barn very slowly."

"Are you sure?" she asked, breaking the gaze and petting the black fur with slow, sympathetic strokes.

On first instinct, he thought to snap at her for questioning his expertise, but then he could understand her concern. He had behaved a lot worse when he thought Milly and Agatha were in trouble.

"Sure." He answered in comforting tones. "It isn't anything at all. Most of the swelling has gone down. Really, he should have already tried to get up on his own a long while ago."

He watched her fawning over the animal like its natural born mother and grinned fiercely at her. She was weird enough that he actually found her interesting.

"Although I can see why he didn't." He added.

She shot a hurried glance over to him and answered in a smart way.

"Shouldn't you be wrappin' that famous leg or doing sumthin' constructive?"

He smiled, fully content in watching her worry and tend to that whining, over-indulged bull.

"I was." He flirted.

Blushing, she merely turned her face away without further comment. Nervousness made Brent chuckle as he reached into his bag and pulled out some bandages.

Wrapping the animal's leg tightly, he slipped Carlos a few aspirin with her help and asked the young lady to try and coax Carlos into getting up. Alyssa rose, dusting herself of the debris and walked in front of Carlos so that he could see her without struggling.

"Come on sweetheart." She smiled patting her legs as though she were beckoning to a small lap dog. "Mama's got a big pretty carrot for you." Her voice was thicker than molasses in January as she dangled the dirty carrot back and forth. She sounded more like a worn-out record than she did a human being, and Carlos only snorted at her.

Brent found himself near hysterics laughing, when she looked down her nose at him.

"I don't see what's so funny about this! You *told* me to call 'im"

"I'm sorry." He giggled. "I'm not laughing at you, really. I have my cows on a first name basis with me and I call them too... but not like that." He continued to laugh at her. He didn't intend to upset her, but the hilarity of her pleading with that creature overwhelmed him... especially given his own recent difficulties with cattle. In fact, he laughed so much that he hadn't noticed her anger. She moved toward him with fluidity and prowess, a very endearing look playing about her face. The instant he looked up at her, he felt the blood rushing to his head so quickly that he immediately stopped laughing.

She had the most beautiful pale green eyes with little golden flecks of sunshine playing in them. He took on her beauty for only a moment, when she reached out and kicked him right in the shin.

"*Yow!*" Brent screamed as he jumped to his feet holding his shin. "What in the *heck* did you do *that* for?! Have you lost your mind?!"

"No. But I can't say that I like yore attitude Mister, and I'll thank you kindly to take yore pay from mah ant and git out of here. You...You jerk!" Alyssa started for the barnyard, throwing her arm up for Carlos to follow her but when the stubborn animal wouldn't get up, she grew furious. Her whole body radiated a red energy that would have engulfed up the entire universe if it were to shoot from her eye sockets.

Brent let go of his sore leg, (that had been beat up quite a lot lately), and gathered his things to go. As he slung his bag onto his shoulder and dusted some dirt from his jeans, he looked back at her begging that dumb bull to get up.

"It's your own fault." He grumbled. "You've spoiled that creature rotten and he doesn't have any will power because of it. He's not some mutt you know... he's a bull. He has pride and he cannot be treated like a lowly house dog."

Alyssa didn't much like the implication of that. "Will you just shut up and *git* all ready?!" She seethed.

Brent laughed, knowing she had gotten his meaning and headed back to the farmhouse with every intention of reporting to Edna, that her niece had just behaved like a hell princess.

****

By the time Alyssa got crazy Carlos back to the barn, night had fallen and Aunt Edna stood at the entrance tapping her foot with anticipation.

"You get that bull put away, missy, and *git* yourself into this house! You got a *lot* of explainin' to do." Alyssa breathed a regretful sigh as she watched her aunt storm up the back-porch steps.

27

"See what you caused Carlos?" She whined as she put her forehead to his. "Why can't you watch what yore doin'?" She blamed the whole affair on him, but honestly: she hadn't stopped feeling guilty about kicking the handsome young doctor like that. It didn't help her spirits any that he told on her. She smacked Carlos lightly on the behind and herded him into the stall.

"Good night sweetheart." She said, kissing him on the forehead as she started out of the barn. "I hafta go find out what all that awful man told about me."

Weariness clawed so heavily at her from the day's events that every muscle in her body screamed for a hot bath and liniment. Still, she knew she wouldn't get past her aunt without some sort of explanation. She dreaded every step up the back stairs. As her hand tried at the knob, the door swung open. Edna Johnson stood like a mountain in the light of the kitchen.

End of Chapter Three

CHAPTER FOUR: Truce and Warfare

"But Aunt Edna please. You don't think that I..."

"Hold your tongue." She snapped pouring out a cup of decaf for both of them.

"And *no*, I *don't* think...I *know* you did something unbecoming out there because that poor boy wouldn't even take my money this aftanoon! He seemed worried 'bout you; and said that if you couldn't get that mule headed bull of yores to mind, I could call 'im back and he'd come out here with a pulley to hoist 'im up for us!"

Alyssa breathed a sigh of relief upon hearing that he had not told on her. She had been sure that he would, but since he hadn't… why ruin it?

"I don't know what's so bad about that. In fact, it sounds like a very professional assessment of the situation to me." She said stiff lipped as she took a sip from her coffee.

"You weren't here to see the look on his face, Lyssie. I know you did something awful over that stupid bull. If this neurotic behavior doesn't stop, I'm afraid I won't have any choice but to stop payment on your apartment rent, sell Carlos and keep you here, so that I can keep a better eye on ya."

"Oh you wouldn't! You *couldn't* Aunt Edna!" She cried. She and Carlos had been together since childhood! That place wouldn't be the same for her otherwise... and to live on that awful farm? She couldn't bear the thought. It was a wonderful place to visit, but she didn't want to *live* there. She couldn't continue to work in town if she lived that far out... why it wouldn't be practical even.

"Aunt Edna… please."

"I don't even *much* want to hear it Lyssie! That young fella is coming back in the mornin' before church, and you will be here to apologize or ahm going to do everythin' I said."

"But Aunt Edna! I have to be in town tomorrow. You knew I was leavin' in the mornin'! I just have to get some shopping and some housework done before work Monday morning. I can't possibly stay here! I'll nevuh get everythin' done! Besides... I told you. I didn't do anything to him!"

"And ahm the Queen of Spain!" She tapped her foot repetitively at her niece, her foreboding brow telling Alyssa that she had no choice in the matter.

Her aunt had obviously made up her mind so Alyssa would cooperate, or she would never get back to what other people considered to be a normal life.

"Oh all right." She hugged her unsuspecting aunt, who she supposed was right anyway. "I'll stay. I'll even go to church with you tomorrow if it'll make you feel any better. I've got a dress with me. I suppose I could stand to let things go once in a while. Besides. I've been meaning to treat mahself to a little break. This might just be the right time for it. I'll apologize even though I don't know what for."

Edna let go of a relieved sigh, despite the defeated feeling that made its way into her heart. About the time Alyssa had gone half way up the stairs Edna called out to her in a sweet voice.

"What did you do to 'im Lyssie? He didn't seem so much in pain as he did rattled by something. I'm not mad. I'm just genuinely curious."

"He was acting like a jack-ass, so I kicked him in the shin. I didn't mean to..." She defended herself as her aunt's face fell. "But he was being rude and unprofessional about the whole thing... and besides, he was laughing at me." she pouted. Edna sucked at her teeth in a disgusted manner and turned to go to her room for the night. Maybe fate was going to need a little shove after all.

****

Brent tumbled into his back door, throwing the keys on the table in a fit of fury. How dare that girl do something so mean to him! He was just trying to help! It wasn't his fault that she made an idiot out of herself! He fumed about not tattling on her, but his mother had asked him to be on his best behavior. Despite the fact that he wanted to throw that girl over his knee and whip her, he had managed to keep his head straight.

He had never been so rattled by a woman, (other than his mother), as he had been by her. "Who does she think she is?" he grumbled to himself. He snatched the refrigerator door open and cursed as two or three cans of soda dropped out of it.

Picking one of them up, he thumped furiously at the top so that it wouldn't spew all over the place when he opened it. Then, as he pulled the cap, he held it over the sink in case it did decide to spill anyway.

Still sucking at the foam frothing out of the top of the can, a shadow moved in front of him.

His face darted upward. He thought he had seen someone standing right in front of him on the other side of the window at the kitchen sink.

He gasped for air, dropping the can into the sink and staggered back a few feet before he realized, his own reflection had frightened him. He patted at his chest softly, calming himself and sat down into the chair, once again counting the amount of times he could hear the sink leaking from the washer where the water came out. Once he got a hold of himself, he remembered that his imagination had caused a similar fit only days ago, and he began to worry about his cows.

Breathing deep, he got up. Fishing a flashlight out of his junk drawer he clicked it on and started out to back door to have a look around in the barn.

His sore shin ached as he stalked across the wet, mossy grass that grew between the house and the barn. Anxiety that the Johnson girl had caused still gnawed at him, and it put him in a foul temper. He strained heavily at the door, but managed to get it open without doing his back any further damage as he peeked inside. The cows were in the dark, but Agatha was snoring.

He smiled fondly in the absence of light, knowing that snore better than he did the sound of his own voice. As he drew the doors back to a close, he began to wonder what ever possessed those idiots to go up onto the hillside like that. Making his way out of the barn and into the night, Brent found himself trotting back into the house.

If the truth of it were known, being out at the barn at that time of night, thinking the kind of thoughts he had been thinking, set his spine into fearful twinges.

Once indoors again, he abandoned whatever hope he'd held of regaining his day. He had to go to church in the morning and that frightful girl had ruined his plans. If he did find the picture he'd been thinking about, it wouldn't make him happy anyway. The only consolation there would be for him tonight was some small possibility that the girl might still be begging that stupid creature to come with her.

He heard thunder in the sky and grinned. Wouldn't it serve her right to be out in a storm arguing with the animal that she was responsible for spoiling in the first place? Brent laughed out loud, the sound so odd in the quiet house, that he shook his head of the silly thought and went on to bed... equally sure that the capable Miss

Johnson wouldn't be left all alone in a field that her aunt was responsible for.

****

Sunday dawned bright and early for Alyssa, and while she always got up before dawn, she was especially tired this morning. She'd had a fitful sleep with tender dreams of that mouthy man she had met, and spent most of the night trying to straighten it out. Tossing on a pair of jeans and a sweatshirt, she glanced quickly in the mirror on the dresser. She still fluffed at her soft strawberry-blond hair when out of the corner of her eye, she saw the dress she had made promises about the night before. A discontented groan escaped her much the way it had when she'd tended to Carlos the day before.

Was that her that promised to stay for church today? Then she shuddered, remembering that she had told on herself when her aunt set that trap on her.

"Jeez!" She muttered as she got up and went to take a shower.

Realizing that there was no way out of this apology, she had still noticed him looking at her. While she was virtually unknown to men in the physical sense, she had seen that look on one before. If there was to be an apology made... he was going to make one too. She knew that if she put herself together properly, she could arrange a real show of beauty, that would set him apologizing for being such an as...

"Lyssie?" Her aunt called from the hall, breaking her concentration. "You ready child?"

"Almost." She nearly cheered as she looked at herself in the mirror. True beauty was a thing of rarity in the world to her opinion. Still, when putting her mind to the task she could fake it rather well.

To her thinking, she had a long, crooked nose. Her eyes were too big for her head and her skin was too white and freckled. But today, even Alyssa was pleased with how she looked when a faint thought drifted through her head. A playful smile wafted across her face as she began to make a transformation back into the sweaty, funny looking woman who had kicked Brent in the first place.

****

Aunt Edna stood downstairs on the front porch cursing her niece under her breath, as the young man had arrived and gone into the barn to see about Carlos quite some time ago.

"Where *is* that darn girl." She fussed looking at her watch.

"Right here Aunt Edna." Alyssa chirped as she glided past her aunt with a peck on the cheek, and headed toward the barn. Edna could

32

think of nothing to say. Alyssa looked as though she were going to spend the day working on the farm. She was certain that she had showered and perfumed herself earlier, because she could smell the soap and shampoo from the hall.

"What on Earth is that young'un up to now?" She drawled in wonderment.

****

Brent soothed Carlos as he peeked around him to the injured leg. The swelling had completely gone down and the bull seemed to be fine. As a matter of fact, he seemed down right frisky, which was hardly what one would expect from a bull that had laid on its back begging for attention not even twenty-four hours ago. Alyssa saw Brent soothing the hair back on Carlos's head and began to regret her choice of apparel.

He certainly seemed warm and caring, standing there talking sweet the way he was in that low, condescending tone he had used when he was trying to reassure her yesterday.

"He's quite taken with you." She said with a smile that stretched like a broad snowy river across her face. Brent hadn't realized that she had come up behind him. He didn't care for people sneaking up on him like that.

"At least someone is." He scowled. He regretted it the moment the words passed his lips, because they seemed to light up her face.

He pushed past her to leave the barn, the bottom half of the door to which she still hung over swinging wide in front of him. Their eyes met and Brent defeated the urge to say anything as he turned to go.

"Hey!" She called out from behind him in a casual manner. "Doctor Price?"

The title crept up his body like a line of ants looking for food and he turned to her with a sour look on his face.

"I'm sorry about yesterday." She said in a genuine way. "I've been going through some... weird times and I guess I kind of took it out on you. I'm *real* sorry. If I can do anything to make it up to you... and thanks for Carlos too."

She added quickly realizing what she had said brought the interest back into his entrancing blue eyes.

He smiled down at her, admiring her regal features. He wondered what color her hair was under that bandana and had to struggle to remember what he was going to say.

"Salright." He murmured. "I'm sorry too."

The pang of triumph rang through her like a china gong.

"I guess you could say I'd been suffering some pretty weird stuff myself lately. Anyway." He continued trying not to admire her lovely imp like face. "Carlos is going to be fine. Walk him once a day for a week and take the bandage off daily to check it. If he seems irritable when you remove it, he probably just needs it as a mental crutch for a few more days. Don't baby him too much." He grinned wagging his finger at her.

"I won't." She smiled pumping his hand playfully. "Thanks doc."

"Don't mention it." He replied, raising an eyebrow at her handshake.

As he passed the front porch to get in his jeep, Alyssa dashed past her aunt and back into the house.

"You goin' to church today doctor?"

Alyssa heard her aunt from inside the house and froze in her tracks. She hoped like crazy he would say yes.

"Every Sunday Mrs. Johnson."

"I knew you looked familiah young man. It's one thing to see you in church and something different here. I knew that I knew you from someplace else... I guess now I know where from."

He grinned as he cranked his jeep.

"Well mother doesn't really want anyone at church to know who I am either, so let's keep that between you and me." he answered, winking at her.

Edna pretended to be locking her lips and throwing away the key as Brent drove off into the pinkish rays of dawn. Edna was so busy watching him drive away in fact, that if Alyssa hadn't brushed up against her she wouldn't have known she had arrived.

She turned to see her niece wearing a lovely sleeveless, powder green dress that, while it didn't reveal anything, it didn't hide anything either. She had curled her hair so that it hung in beautifully spiraled strawberry blond locks, which went sprawling over lily-white shoulders as a waterfall does to a spring.

Edna gave a satisfied smile of approval. Now that the young doctor had Alyssa's attention, she could relax and let nature take its course.

****

The little white washed church nestled against a country glen, yellow highway rye swaying all around and a small picket fence embracing its yard. The red Georgia clay supplied an ample drive for the vehicles that came in, parking in the downy grass. Soft wispy hues lit the afternoon with gentle sea shine colors. Alyssa and her aunt walked through the barnyard-red double doors of the old wooden shack church and were greeted by many of Edna's old cronies. Many of her friends played bridge and quilted with her so they had a lot to catch up on from one week to the next.

Alyssa marveled at the blue hues of the hair, the busy flowered print dresses, heavy support stockings and the orthopedic shoes. It was bad enough that the polyester dresses and flowered hats looked like rejects from a Norman Rockwell painting… but orthopedic shoes? The two of them made their way to one of the pews mid-length through the church and Lyssie flipped her hair over one shoulder, just managing to keep from turning around to look at the good doctor.

She'd passed by him where he sat when she came in, but refused to give in to the thought of looking at him or *for* him.

Fidgeting in her seat, Lyssie took one of the tattered hymnals from the antique pew in front of her. As the service began with a hymn, she flipped through the yellowed pages, her aunt nudging her in the side with her elbow.

"He's looking at you." She kept saying.

The hymn ended on a shrill note, which caused Alyssa to wonder why everyone in church tried to sing in an octave higher than they were able to.

As the reverend asked the congregation to be seated, two little boys from the youth church brought the offering plate around. Edna began elbowing Alyssa again. This pattern continued throughout the sermon and at length, Lyssie decided to put a stop to it.

"See? I told you." Edna whispered as her elbow jolted her niece once more. "He's looking at you again!"

"That's because he doesn't know who I am Aunt Edna. Now if you'll give my sides a break, I might be able to walk out of here in an upright position."

The elder woman grinned.

"Well I don't see how, *'Little Miss Shin Kicker'*."

"Oh Please." Alyssa whispered in her best *'I don't care'* voice, the tone of which seemed to work on everyone but her aunt.

****

Brent had originally sat in his spot at the back of the meeting hall as always, but when he saw Edna Johnson come in with such a lovely girl at her side, he had inched closer one pew at a time since the service started.

This desperate attempt to see if that glorious creature was really Miss Johnson the bull tamer might make his intent obvious, but he didn't care. He hoped it *wasn't* her, because he would be able to start out with this girl on a clean slate, but if it *was* Miss Johnson ...oh boy!

He tried not to be so obvious as he peeked over at the side of her face and the back of her head, but he could see the awareness of him all about her.

Despite his belief that it was she, he continued to hope he had made a mistake. If it turned out to be Miss Johnson and she *caught* him looking at her? She'd definitely make him pay. This much, he was absolutely sure of.

The young lady turned to talk to Mrs. Johnson and at that moment, certainty overwhelmed him. It *was* her.

His whole body cringed at the thought of the start they had gotten with one another. It almost didn't seem fair.

Though he found it difficult to refrain from appreciative glances at her radiant appearance, he had been much more at ease with the little rag-headed farm hand he had spoken with that morning.

He had to keep cool though. If he acted like he didn't see her, she'd know he was thinking about her... and he couldn't have that. He'd have to socialize the way everyone did after church but he didn't have to like it. That hardheaded girl had already gotten on his nerves once and now she was inadvertently doing it to him again.

He wanted to look at her, knowing he shouldn't do it now that he knew who she was, but he couldn't help it. He had to sneak a look. Her rare beauty captivated him. His eyes veered over to the right at the pews in front of him and she was looking back, smiling.

It was all he could do to keep from jumping and looking the other way but he managed a polite, uninterested smile and she promptly turned back around.

****

"Oh dirt!" Alyssa pouted.

"What is it dear?" Edna sat up at the sight of disquiet settling in on her niece so suddenly.

"Nothing."

Edna cast a stern sideways glance at her niece.

"Well poop. He's not the least bit interested, Aunt Edna. Who could blame him? Me. Little Orphan Annie with stringy long hair, freckles and a hose nose. I think I had better stick to my Carlos. At least he's always interested."

"Yeah." Edna remarked. "Interested in food and pampering."

"Well what's so different about men?"

Her aunt turned and waved at the disturbed doctor, then winked back at her niece.

"Men like something to look at too, and that's about it dear."

"Then I had definitely better stick to Carlos. He doesn't care what I look like."

"I'll not listen to you degrade yourself at a Sunday sermon Lyssie! That's quite enough."

The elder woman had to catch herself from yelling.

For a moment all eyes were on the two women down front.

Though the preacher had been upended by the oration for a second, he went on, ignoring the noise with a grating look to the two ladies.

Alyssa pouted again and Edna began to feel guilty, so she decided to lighten the air between them.

"Besides. I suspect Carlos *does* like the way you look," She whispered, "cause I never once caught him a lickin' Jack the way he does you."

They both laughed in such a way that made Brent certain they were talking about him, but he dared not let it show that it ate away at him so much.

****

After the service, everyone milled around talking in polite social tones while waiting for an opportunity to tell Reverend Davies what a lovely sermon he'd given, but Brent and Alyssa had the same idea. Neither of them wanted to be confronted by the other so they secretly, separately started planning a course of action to get out of there.

Alyssa excused herself when Edna made her way over toward Brent's mother.

Lyssie had complained of a headache and made for the exit. She kept a watchful eye over her shoulder for the dashing, but unnerving Brent Price and, not having seen him, she reached for the knob.

Instead of grabbing a cold lifeless protrusion like she expected, she felt something warm and firm in the palm of her hand. She didn't dare look right away. It took a second before she even could decide what to say if the hand she felt beneath hers belonged to Dr. Price. She peeked over at the person whose hand she held with just one eye open and discovered that her worst hope had come true after all.

Seeing him here reminded her of seeing a painting hung in an off-centered position, or in the wrong place on a wall. It seemed that there wasn't anyone in the room at that moment but them and their eyes met in a way that only movies and great poets could have conveyed.

Dumfounded by the way his liquid blue eyes danced with pleasure; Lyssie trembled as he gazed at her. Compelled to stillness at the warmth of his touch, the flesh of his hand hot against her own, she thought for a moment she might drool. Though her mind screamed at her to let go of his hand, her heart begged and pleaded with her to lie down and submit.

The very thought of submission enraged her... not with him, but with herself. He was *just* a man. It did not make him better than her. And besides, he had done nothing to earn her affection so she refused to give in to ridiculous wanton needs.

Snatching her hand back as if she thought certain she would contract coodies, Alyssa winced as she snagged her fingernail on the latch that hung between the doors.

"Ouch!" she yelped as she closed her other hand around the scrape.

"Let me see it." He commanded in a professional manner.

"No. It's *yore* fault I did it in the first place!" She retorted half out of pain, half in anger.

Brent shook his head smiling and reached out to take her hand.

"Come on now Miss Johnson. You're making an awful big deal out of nothing and I can't say that it becomes you. I am a doctor of sorts. I'd like to look at it... uh, seeing as how it's my fault and all." He added, the sarcastic lilt of his voice making her aware of the fact that this wasn't flirting.

Not much liking his tone, Alyssa sucked at the little bit of blood at the tip of her finger. Brent watched her sucking her finger that way and felt strangely aroused by the whole ordeal. Her soft pouty pink lips were so sensual with*out* the implications his mind added to her actions: that he could hardly contain himself. She broke his stare.

"Oh alright. Here." She said thrusting her hand into his, wrist upward, for his inspection.

"At least now you can see it without the blood getting in the way."

Her soft hand felt so good in his that he thrilled to touch it, but managed to keep his wits enough to be decent about it.

"Well." He said with a wry look as he pushed her hand back to her. "I think you'll be alright. The latch isn't rusty so I wouldn't think you should have to worry. Just make sure you wash it out good when you get home and put some antibiotic ointment on it. It should clear up in a few days, although I'm afraid I can't say the same for your fingernail."

Alyssa snapped her hand up in front of her face to view the lovely salmon pink color her nail technician had applied the day before she left town. It was her favorite nail color and until that moment she hadn't realized that she'd broken a fingernail.

She groaned.

"I hope Patty can fix this up."

"Patty?" He asked.

"My nail stylist in town. It's broken pretty low though." She grimaced at the nubby looking fingertip.

"Let me ask you something, Miss Johnson. I was just wondering how a young lady such as yourself could keep such nice attractive looking nails... what with bull taming, plowing and running five or six miles a day for water?"

She detected a note of cynicism in his tone, but determined not to give in to him again. Edna would pop a blood vessel if the two of them had a fight in church, in front of *"Gawd and everbody"*.

"Acrylic." She tapped at a fingernail on one hand with a fingernail from the other to illustrate the strength. "Not that it's any of your business." She added.

Brent's temperature began rising again and he didn't much like the way it affected his temper.

"You aren't much of a sport. Are you Miss Johnson?"

"Look." She was dismissing him. She'd had enough. "Just send me a bill okay?"

"This one's on the house." He grinned from ear to ear. At least he wasn't alone in the world where that horrible flustered feeling was concerned. "But I must admit..." He had to raise his voice on the last bit because she turned the knob and hurried outside to get away from him.

" The bull made a better patient!"

****

Alyssa almost hadn't uttered a sound all of the way home and Edna couldn't bear the silence any longer.

"What's wrong?"

"Oh nothing."

"Yeh right! You haven't said a word since we left the church and you've shredded those tissues to pieces!"

Alyssa turned a gloomy glance down at the floor of the car. The papers littered the floorboard all around her feet and ankles. While she had done it in an unconscious effort to relieve tension, she betrayed her secret thoughts.

"Alright. Here it is. I'm thinking about staying on a week..." she had to put her finger up to keep her aunt from getting excited "but *don't* go getting excited you old busy body. I'm staying because Doctor Price says that Carlos will need some walking attention and you and Jack are too busy to manage it."

Aunt Edna chuckled in her hope that her twenty-two-year-old niece, might finally be turning into a young woman and not some transvestite. She laughed out loud at her own thoughts.

"Don't laugh! And don't think I didn't know what you were up to either because I do. And I don't like it one bit. So just cut it out. Dr. Price couldn't possibly offer me anything I don't already have. So there."

"Cept a life... and some passion." Edna quipped. She could see a flush of rage flooding over Alyssa and she smiled before clamming up. At least she could rest assured that little Lyssie was having some grown up emotions beyond that stupid bull and she wouldn't question her now... even if she did seem ticked off.

****

Raking gnarled claws across his dry, gray backside, he winced at the beautiful pain it caused. It had itched so badly! He then picked at his teeth, his other fingers thumping the bones of a pigeon he had burned for dinner the night before. No meat left on those bones. Maybe he'd sneak into town and see if he could raid someone's pantry. Swiss rolls and ding-dongs beat the heck out of pigeon meat any day.

Stretching, he took a deep breath and smiled as the scent of death wafted across his nostrils. It was time he rid himself of this one. He had finished using her anyhow and she wasn't pretty to look at any more. He hobbled impish-like over to where she lay in his cave, his bent frame moving in a strange gait through the shadows.

Wincing at the bruises on her pelvic area, he wondered if he'd really pounded at her that hard. He snickered in a low gruff voice. He had taken more pleasures with this one than he had with any of the rest. This body was almost the perfect replica of "hers". He would take a look at it, thinking to dump it and then change his mind… wanting to fuck it just once more.

The orange hairs of his skin began bristling again, an erection beginning to shove at his tortured mind. He looked at the body. Still, it was gray almost. But so like her. He pushed a little closer, almost afraid to move it because it would surely smell… Then the oddest thing happened.

He could see "her"! He closed his eyes, honing in on this vision. He could not tell where he stood at the moment…but there was his "lovely"!

She wore soft green, surrounded by a halo of light… and she was sucking at her finger with a pout that sent chills up his spine.

He opened his eyes to the hallowed eyes of the withering corpse before him, and shuddered. Nothing but the "lovely" would do at this moment. He wanted her so much. He squatted on the floor seeking out what portion of manhood he had left. He closed his eyes where he envisioned her sucking at that finger, surrounded by light like the angel she once was. With gradual progression, his body quivered in ecstasy as he bobbed, rhythmic motion setting his soul free from want… if only for now.

End of Chapter Four

CHAPTER FIVE: Match Makers Unlimited

Standing in the middle of her aunt's living room, Alyssa breathed deep, relishing the smell of the ham roasting in the oven as she looked toward the kitchen. Soft light from the old chandelier cast yellow shadows on the wallpaper in the kitchen, warming the look of the room.

"Aunt Edna?"

Yes?" Her voice touched Lyssie with warmth, at times reminding her of Christmas morning as a child. She couldn't help reflecting it with a happy smile.

"Would you like me to come in and give you a hand?"

"Thanks dear, but no. I jes' 'bout got it wrapped up. What'd yore boss say?"

"Oh: you know." She grimaced, plopping down onto the white French provincial couch. Poking through a gardening book that had rested on the oval end table, Lyssie smiled.

"The usual stuff. *'Just be sure you're back in a week, and don't expect another vacation this year neither!'*... and yak, yak, yak."

She complained using her hand to imitate a mouth.

Edna came to the doorway wiping her hands on a dishtowel and grinned at Alyssa.

"I'm glad you decided to wear something decent tonight."

Alyssa looked down at her jeans and yellow angora sweater with a curious smirk. Then, looking back to her aunt, she put the book down onto her lap.

"Why's that?" The tone of Alyssa's voice was such that Edna gave a second thought to telling her about the plans for supper, but... no point in prolonging the inevitable.

"Oh alright. Ya got me. I invited Janet and that charmin' son-a-hers over for supper tonight."

Betrayal! Lyssie had never been so let down in all her life.

"The vera idea!" She snuffed with indignation.

"Oh you're not foolin' anybody gal. I saw you two at church today; and whethah you noticed it or not, there was some kind of chemistry between you."

"Yeah!" She raised her voice, but she dared not yell at her well-intended aunt. "Like a wart on a toad!"

"I should think it was more like a match to gasoline. I ain't seen a fire like that on a woman since I was a young thing myself and I won't let you deny it... for whatevuh reason. This might just make you happy! Although at this moment, I can't see how anythin' could please the likes of you!"

Edna stormed back into the kitchen and Lyssie leaned her head into her hand. She never meant to upset her because Edna had always been there whenever she needed anything.

She just couldn't stand the thought of eating dinner in the same room with that unsettling man, much less at the same table. He might look her way, smile a certain smile, make a certain remark and she'd be too far gone to come back. She'd never be able to keep herself from looking at him like some sort of starved puppy.

The concept of getting her aunt to understand that without admitting her feelings, might be difficult. Having decided to go in and make some attempt at an apology, Lyssie laid the book down and cautiously approached the kitchen.

"Aunt Edna?" She said peering around the edge of the doorway as if entering whole-heartedly would be like bringing an escaped prisoner into a trap.

"What?" The soft-spoken reply had been unexpected as the elderly woman stood over the plump, juicy ham on the counter.

"I'm sorry. I have no idea why you put up with me, but I'm awful glad ya do. I promise to behave myself tonight."

Edna looked at her in wonderment.

"I swear, Lyssie. The way you're a carryin' on, you'd think I had paired you up with a midget or some kind of leper or something. He's a doctah for goodness sake."

"You of all people know that money and social standing isn't everything..." She was going to throw her aunt's own words at her from the years she had spent preaching them to her, but Edna wouldn't let her. She put her hand up to the girl.

"I could see it dear if he was unattractive, stupid or even down right mean, but he's a handsome boy. He's responsible. He owns a farm. He's kind and vera intelligent. Yore not even givin' 'im a chance."

"A chance at *what*?!" She caught herself raising her voice again after having made up her mind she wouldn't do that anymore.

"I'm sorry. I won't do that again." Discord never entered Edna's mind, however. In fact, she laughed at Lyssie.

"You and your maw. You don't know how much you remind me a her when you blow up like that. She may have married into the Johnson Family, but she was as much my sister as anyone could be.

You remind me so much of her at times, Lyssie, that I don't know what to think."

Alyssa shook her strawberry locks, folded her arms across her chest and looked at her aunt with a stern but playful expression.

"Don't you go a changin' the subject like that. You've been plottin' behind my back and I want a solemn promise that there won't be no more match making!"

She raised her fine aged hand over her heart.

"Cross my heart. Now go on and clean up for suppah. The Prices will be here in an hour."

"But dinner isn't for two hours at least. What are we supposed to do with them in the mean time?"

"Well Janet and I are in the same quilting class and we decided to have some tea on the porch and compare our projects. I figure the men will probably talk sports since Jack will be here."

"Jack! Jack's been here ever since I can remember, and we have never invited him to eat supper here! Why now?"

"For heaven's sake Lyssie! I knew you would probably sit with us wimmin, so what were a father and son going to talk about that they hadn't discussed already?!"

Alyssa groaned.

"All right. But I'm warning you." She wagged her finger as she went to the stairway, *"No more match makin'!"*

"Okay okay. Now shoo gal!"

Then Edna said quietly to herself …

"Hopefully I won't *have* to do anythin' after tonight."

****

If Jack had been early so that he could help set the table, the Prices were fashionably late. Mrs. Price had done a reasonably fine job of making excuses for her husband's absence. In truth, Alyssa suspected that he knew about the little old lady match making party that was really going on, and refused to be an accessory to it. Dinnertime came on them when the Prices arrived and naturally, Janet ran off into the kitchen to help put finishing touches on the elaborate meal.

Alyssa sat on the big antique couch, her legs crossed, reading a cross-stitch book and trying to look involved.

All the while, Jack tried to pick Brent's brain of medical knowledge that might be useful to him around the farm. The big man made a picture in Lyssie's mind of what Paul Bunyan would have looked like at age sixty.

The warm, fur lined cap had come off and oversized fingers twisted at it as he listened, intent on remembering what he heard. Though a flannel shirt peeked out from under his good overalls, even a novice eye could see that Jack had donned what he considered to be his best clothes. His gray beard had gone a little scraggly since the harvest had come in but his blue eyes twinkled with the new knowledge.

Brent was extremely gracious, answering every question with great enthusiasm, although Alyssa was certain that he didn't come half the way up the mountain to talk shop.

She wondered if he knew about the little matchmaking scheme, or if he was as much a victim to it as she was.

'*Some victim.*' She caught herself visually adoring him.

Then glancing back to her book, she became angry with herself for submitting again.

She occasionally glanced up to snatch glimpses of the handsome doctor and admired most of his features. His eyes were close together, but not so much so, that he was cross-eyed or anything: just enough so that he always appeared to be thinking about something other than what seemed obvious.

His hair glistened in the dim lamplight. Soft sunshinelike hues set off his golden skin and Alyssa had to mentally labor at keeping her eyes off of him. As for his body... well let's just say that his was one of the most attractive she had seen... firm, and strong. The size of his forearms indicated that he worked hard for a living and though the large hands seemed hard and calloused, Lyssie wondered if they could turn to velvet in a touch. He didn't fancy himself up for the occasion or anything. He had worn blue jeans and a casual short-sleeved button-down shirt, of a soft baby blue color that set of the glimmer in his eyes perfectly. He had shaved and cologned though, so maybe he *did* know what was going on. The contrasts of her own interest in this man were so ridiculous... one minute liking him, the next minute hating him; that she didn't know *what* to do with herself.

Jack obviously enjoyed his part of the conversation and had been about to tell the doctor so, when Edna emerged from the kitchen, glowing with a maternal happiness. Her expression caught Alyssa off guard.

"Dinner is served."

Everyone got up, stretching and straightening their clothes, and walked into the dining area. Alyssa cast a questioning glance at her aunt as she passed by en route to the other room, but as soon as she got to her seat, she knew what it was all about.

The best country blue pattern of china donned the table and a tall, sliver candelabrum lit the middle of the big cherry wood dinette. The sunny yellow candles sent their light dancing across the setting.

Edna had elongated the table by adding the extra leaflet that went in the center and the entire room, with its fresh cut flowers, antique doo-dads and little frilly napkins set the stage for romance.

Alyssa grimaced at her aunt when she was pretty sure no one could see her then took the seat that Dr. Price so willingly pulled out for her. At first, Lyssie was thankful there wasn't much talking, but as the bellies filled, a comfortable feeling seemed to settle in on the bunch and a little casual discussion about the weather was soon under way.

The next thing she knew her aunt began referring to her by her nickname, which wouldn't bother Alyssa so much except that it was too familiar for strangers. Eventually, her aunt went to telling ghastly stories about her childhood and worse: the pimple years.

Lyssie refused to give anyone the satisfaction of blushing, so she smiled at the humiliating onslaught, pretending not to care.

She nearly jumped out of her seat and left the room however, when Edna told about her falling in cow flop in front of her first "beau". Fortunately, Brent interrupted with something he had learned about healthy cow flop, being important in assessing an animal's medical condition. She blushed, grateful that he had interrupted the story, but not entirely certain it had been deliberate so she maintained her sense of dignity without a "thank you" glance.

When it finally came time to get up from the table, Lyssie started piling dishes to carry into the kitchen, but her aunt wouldn't hear of it.

"Now now. You young folks just go on out to the porch and sit a spell while us two old cronies take care of the clean up."

Alyssa cast a frightened glance at Jack.

The tall man rose, heading for the door with an apologetic look and jingling the keys in his Sunday go to meeting overalls, whilst clopping over the hard wood floors in his work boots.

Lyssie cast a desperate look in Brent's direction and, noting the smug smile on his face, she refused to spend the first minute alone with that awful, pig headed...

"I wouldn't *heah* of it dahlins." She said in her thickest southern drawl as she grabbed her dear aunt's soft bluish white hand, squeezing as hard as she could without inflicting too much pain.

"You two dears have done so much already, that I wouldn't dream of imposing on you further."

Alyssa shot a look over at Janet Price and smiled. The woman looked like cornered animal as she witnessed their schemes crashing to an abrupt halt.

"What a nice idea." Janet smiled, nodding. "We do have a few recipes to exchange, and I have a new quilt pattern to discuss with you Edna... perhaps Brent..."

"Would love to walk y'all out to the porch and fetch your things!" Lyssie added, grinning over at Dr. Price, who had begun studying the women like interesting bugs. Brent was taken by complete surprise.

While he didn't want to run and fetch a bunch of quilting supplies from his mother's car, he could see that there wasn't much chance of being alone with Alyssa either. She obviously found him repugnant. She had been looking at him all night as if he was diseased or something.

"I'd just love to." He lied as he went to their end of the table and offered each of them an arm.

'*There is a God*' Alyssa thought.

Watching them go, she could have sworn that she saw a rejected look from over Brent's shoulder. Had she been wrong about his passiveness? Did he really like her after all? She shook her head of the crazy thought, clearing the table so that she could get the kitchen tidied up and go to bed. Surely the guests would be gone by then.

Not only did she refuse to have Dr. Price forced on her, she refused to let someone force her on him either. He did seem like a nice man, but there was no reason for him to have to be nice to someone he obviously didn't like.

****

Alyssa hummed a church hymn to herself, thoroughly enjoying her dish duty. Working in the kitchen always relieved her of some anxiety and if she hummed or sang, that usually helped some too.

Brent walked quietly up to the doorway of the kitchen. He breathed in the sight of her as she swished the dishes with a yellow rag that matched her blouse and sang melodiously to one of the hymns from the church service that morning.

A faint smile drifted across his face.

She was everything he'd dreamed a woman should be... except that she seemed to like to argue, and he hated it.

His face lost any expression at that thought and as he stared at her blankly, she got the sneaking suspicion that someone had snuck up on her. Spinning around, she dropped a plate into the floor.

The fragments from the expensive dish shattered into little pieces. He bent and apologized while helping her get the shards up. Alyssa had been so worried about the serving dish that she almost forgot that she had been mad at the doctor.

He still held the dustpan for her and she stopped sweeping for a moment. She looked down at him with those dazzling green spheres glittering with anger.

At the first sign that the broom had stopped, Brent looked up and, seeing the witch's brew bubbling up within her again, he looked back toward the floor shaking his head.

"You're going to start yelling at me again aren't you?"

Lyssie hadn't realized that she'd ever really yelled at him to start with but as she thought about it, she realized that she hadn't even once been civil to this man. Maybe he wasn't so bad.

Maybe she was just the kind of person who brought out the bad in everybody. Look what she had done to Aunt Edna over the last few days. She had been barking at everyone like an over-zealous guard dog... and she didn't like it.

"I'm sorry." She said, the meekness in her tone a welcome thing to her dustpan holder.

Brent couldn't believe his ears as she pushed the rest of the glass into the dustpan. Looking up into her face from where he knelt, he thought how, for all of her strong points she looked small and vulnerable just now.

Rising, he went to dump out the debris into the garbage bin, while trying to think of something to say that wouldn't spark her anger. Then, she added to her previous statement.

"What were you standing there like that for anyhow?"

Brent smiled. At least her tone was more emphasized now and less like a dying animal.

"I was sent after a tray of tea that your aunt already prepared and when I heard you singing, I enjoyed the quality of your voice so well that I didn't want to stop you."

Alyssa blushed and pointed to the tray, sitting on the table.

"Thank you... and it's over there."

He looked at the tea tray and went to pick it up. Every step put him a little closer to leaving the kitchen and he was just beginning to get through her defenses. With no real reason to stay, he had to begin his task but hoped that she would give him some reason to stick around a while.

The little porcelain cups rattled as he handled the tray, nervous about dropping it or spilling tea on the lacey doilies on the tea service. Alyssa went over to take it from him.

"Like this."

She showed him how to hold the tray like a professional. She'd spent a few years waiting tables before finishing her accounting degree and working her way into management. As she took it, she placed one hand directly under the middle of the tray, scooped it up next to her head and used the other hand to steady it as she walked with it.

"Here ya go. You try."

As she pushed the tray at him, their hands touched.

Normally they would have brushed hands like at church that morning and exchanged rude remarks, but now: Brent held her hand tightly and put the tray down on the table.

He drew her to him with his hand clasped to hers and slid his arms around her dainty waist, gazing down into those glittering jewels. His mouth pursed as his head drifted nearer to hers. His throat went dry with the thought of actually kissing this miraculous creature.

Alyssa's head sagged backward, her eyelids lowering.

She could scarcely get any breath at all and her heart pounded a path inside of her at a rate of ninety to nothing as it skipped beats here and there. Her mouth became as dry as a whole piece of cotton, and tiny tears attempted to break free of her eyes.

Never had a kiss bore so much passionate promise to her tingling body, and she lost her breath with the anticipation of it. Her arms floated around his neck as she ran long slender fingers through his thick hair.

Elation filled Brent to have gotten this far without being kicked and he could almost taste her lips when the two older women burst into the room, talking. Brent shoved Alyssa back so hard that she nearly fell over the kitchen table when her right side bumped into it and the two older women, who had given up on the match making, had decided to go and get the tea for themselves.

So now, they both stood there gaping at the younger people, making apologies as they practically ran from the room to take their quilting back up.

Dizziness spun Lyssie for a moment and she giggled, one hand clutching the table, the other holding her head.

Brent had as yet to catch his breath.

They looked at each other longing to reclaim the moment, and then started laughing and recounting the stunned look on the faces of their elders once they got what they actually wanted.

"You knew too?" Alyssa giggled.

Brent's laughter had subsided somewhat and he smiled at her.

"I must confess, that until I saw that ugly face you made at your Aunt Edna at the dinner table, I thought you were in on it too."

"What?"

Alyssa said, having lost all of her cherub-like giddiness.

Brent realized that he'd managed to stick his foot in his mouth again and rather than bait her into an argument, he pushed himself between the table and the wall so that she couldn't kick him again.

"It doesn't matter what either of us thought then. Now does it?"

He gave her a shy smile from behind the table and Alyssa couldn't decide whether to apologize for her quick temper, or to pound him into the ground.

After all! Did she look so helpless that she would have to collaborate with a couple of old women to trap a man?

She shook her head again, remembering how she had thought the same thing of him at one point or another and she decided to be nice for a change. That attempted kiss was real and she held no doubt about that on either account.

"No. I suppose it doesn't." He let out a sigh of relief as he came from behind the table, scooping up the tea tray.

"Want to come with me? I really don't look forward to facing this alone you know." Lyssie chuckled but declined, saying that she had to get her housework finished.

Brent took the refreshments outside without apologies or excuses for what the two had seen. They were old enough that he wouldn't dare insult their intelligence with a lie and he wouldn't satisfy their curiosities with an explanation.

He excused himself, heading back indoors to help Alyssa with the dishes.

Raw energy fueled both of them and they managed to clean the kitchen in record time without much discussion.

Though confined to the exchange of fond glances for fear of being caught like a couple of unruly high school kids again, they each held the thought somewhere close to their hearts, that they could share that kind of moment again someday... in private.

End of Chapter Five

Chapter Six: The Waking Dream (PART I.)

Brent playfully ran upstairs to his bedroom and crashed onto his bed in a flurry of giggles. He hadn't been this excited since... hell, since never! If not for gravity, he'd have floated to his room. He wondered if she was thinking about him. If he'd a few years younger, he might have called her on the phone to ask her as much, but... he was grown. Funny, he kept having to remind himself of that.

Stripping down to his underwear, he melted onto the bed with an impish grin jumping around his sleeping features. The sandman embraced him almost the instant his head connected with the pillow. And Brent lost himself in the picture of her at church... yellow light glittering on her hair as she sucked at her finger.

****

The clock's eerie chime touched Brent's consciousness, as it erupted into the twelve gongs that signify the coming of midnight. He jumped awake, suddenly aware of the fact that he didn't own the kind of clock that chimed like that.

He sat up with the sheets pulled over his chest and then realized that he had clothes on. Gazing down at himself, he saw a pair of well-worn overalls with a red long john shirt underneath.

"A thousand great ideas and I had to dream I was Jed Clampett." He muttered, inspecting the old clothes.

Tossing it off that he must have held a larger impression of old Jack from the Biggmann Ranch than he had supposed, he decided to return to his slumber when something moved over in the corner. Fear gripped his heart as he became acutely aware of the fact that he was no longer alone in the room. From the shadows a form moved toward him, its shape passing through shades of night and moonlight. He looked up into the face of the creature and happiness spread through his whole being.

"Gram?" He whispered, tears forming in his eyes. He hadn't seen her, even in a ghost state, since the age of ten. The image of her hadn't changed in the least.

Without speaking, she put her hand on his shoulder and disappeared. When Brent once again opened his eyes, he found himself in an alley of the city, which rested at the foot of the mountain.

Rising, he made his way toward a street lamp that lit one end of the alley. Caution became the dictate of the moment as this dream mirrored reality. He had been here before… just not at night.

By the time he reached the brighter end of the alley, a dark, misty clump-of-a-thing lurked in the path ahead. It had no definite shape that he could distinguish, its guttural growl issuing fear that rampaged through Brent.

"I just want to get by, buddy." he said, hoping this to merely be some unfortunate homeless person, though his senses told him otherwise. The black thing began to grow. As it did, such hatred welled within him that it nearly drove him to the brink of insanity. Brent put his hands to his head, clutching to it in the hope that the pressure would relieve the thoughts clouding his mind. Finding himself enveloped in darkness, his fears pinned him to the spot he occupied.

Nothing could help him fight the horror he experienced except for his will to do something terrible. He had to kill, hate, hurt... destroy... anything to stop the burning sickness that invaded every facet of his soul. It was as if some twisted artist had taken a dive into that part of the spirit that man tries to keep down, and dumped every color of oil onto the vast canvas of Brent's life; leaving nothing behind but swirls of muddy blackness.

Somewhere in his mind, he heard the wild screams of a woman as she begged for help. At first a glint of thrill inhabited him. Then, silence. Faint remorse made its presence known before hope returned; the hope that he perhaps had saved the one who cried out for help.

Her hair cascaded over his hands, the sensation of tearing flesh filling him with utter glee. A brilliant light from above fawned over his quarry. As he reached a blood-soaked hand up into that light, he sat straight up in his bed drenched with sweat. Staggered by the realism of the dream, Brent wept deep cleansing sobs with a pillow pushed close to his chest.

(PART II)

52

The heat from the coffee burned the top of Brent's mouth, but he didn't mind. It reassured him that the dream had passed.

Leaning against the kitchen sink, the coffee maker still gurgled as he held the mug in one shaky hand, rubbing his forehead with the other. Suddenly realizing that the window was behind him, he hurried to the backside of his corner table.

He'd been rather pleased with himself when he finished putting that little breakfast nook in and found himself particularly happy to have it tonight. This put his back between two joining walls, as he tried to recount everything he had done that day.

A state of un-balance filled the air while his mind rocketed back to that dream and the events of the day past.

The flame of the candle he'd lit when he entered the kitchen made the busy wallpaper print of pink and yellow posies dance in a peculiar way. Brent always lit a candle if he planned to spend a little time in there. That particular room tended to smell a little damp so the pumpkin scented candle never failed to transport him back to autumn nights at Gram's, when she baked her home made "punkin" pies. It was perhaps his dedication to the memory of his grandmother and the time frame she'd come from that he'd chosen to decorate the kitchen in a "1950's" style diner look.

The red, chrome trimmed toaster, napkin dispensers and coffee maker added to the look but Brent was particularly proud of the small doo-dads he'd discovered at yard sales and antique shops that actually had come from that time period. These pieces made a discreet contribution to the room, due in part to their position on original cupboards hand crafted by his grandfather several years ago. He'd been obliged to keep those cabinets and shelves because of the fact that they were in themselves antiques belonging exclusively to that home, but most everything else had to go. He put in new red and chrome-trimmed appliances, old rusted pot racks and new hardwood floors.

One of the things he had not been willing to part with however, had been the fading wallpaper. Not only did it serve as a reminder of the original kitchen, there were crayon marks he'd made near the baseboard as a boy, and pen marks near the door facing to show how he'd grown.

Placing his cup on the red diner-styled table in front of him, he glanced at his watch while the circular neon Coke sign blinked over him from behind.

"After four in the morning." He muttered.

He should have been on his way back to bed, but there was no merit to the idea. He'd never get any sleep now. He put his head down on his arms, resting for a moment on the table. Blinking heavily with the weariness that drowned his mind from understanding what had transpired, a sigh escaped him.

His whole body hurt. His legs ached as if he had run fifty miles in three feet of mud. His shoulders stretched tight at his back and his breath remained ragged. His head and heart pounded furiously at their casings as he sat up once more. Even the coffee could do nothing to wet his dry mouth. His hands had become so tense from clenching them in fear as he slept, that they ached. A mental mess of repulsive images jumbled themselves around inside of him.

How could he possibly put his Gram into that kind of dream? Had he gone completely bonkers? Through it all though, he continued to think of his love for Gram, and it kept him sane.

Rising from the table with a sigh of exhaustion, Brent began the long journey to the attic… leaving a wake of lights as he went. He lugged down the antique trunk of pictures and sat at the table, preparing to go through it to find that photo.

"It's got to be the key to this mess somehow," he murmured, although he couldn't begin to explain how he knew that. Opening the creaky lid, he sneezed. Dust bounced into the air from the years of neglect and Brent started straight away to the task of picking through pictures and trinkets.

To save his life, he couldn't come up with the one that had hit him so hard outside the barn the other day. He had seen it before. He could be sure of that because its memory had been so singular, pronounced.

Gram had been in love with the person who took that picture. It oozed from every pore. He would not stop until he knew what day that was. Reaching the bottom of the trunk, he realized that he had run out of stuff to look through, when he found a secret compartment. It had become more apparent through the age of the facility to which it was bound.

Tugging at the frail fabric with as much care as he could, he winced as it tore a bit from the ages of dry rot. Beneath the torn and fading paisley print, a very small compartment appeared with the corner of a book just peeking out. Bringing out an old diary that had his grandmother's name inscribed in the front cover, he rubbed his finger lightly over the first page, and then closed the book. He couldn't violate her privacy even in death. It just seemed an undignified thing to do…even for a desperate man.

Brent paced the kitchen floor staring at the open trunk whose contents had been so carelessly strewn about. The item stood on the rustic–looking floor, its top open and the sides bubbled as though it had once been underwater. Brent mused how it resembled a pirate's treasure chest. Deciding at last that since his memory of that picture was so far back in his mind, he must have seen it as a child. He then deduced that the photo must have belonged to his mother!

The thought hadn't even fully developed as he called Janet and begged her to collect every single picture she owned of Gram because he was on his way over.

****

Although his mother had been half-asleep at five a.m. in the morning, she'd run the kitchen quite smoothly before he got to her. Brent eyeballed the breakfast casually, and then looked at her.

"What about the pictures mom?"

"You eat, hun. I'll go look for them pictures. I already hauled one box from the attic. You sounded so hysterical on the phone that I went to get them before I even realized what I was doin'. Now eat and as soon as you've finished, we can meet at the dining room table. We'll have room to look through them better in there."

Brent walked right past his breakfast as if he were going to the dining room at that precise moment, but his mother jumped in front of him, blocking the doorway.

"No!" She said, pointing to the bar that separated her kitchen from the breakfast nook, which Brent had built for her after he'd finished his own. "You *sit* yourself down on that stool and eat first... or no pictures at all."

Brent hadn't the strength to argue with his mother and relinquished command to her. She would never shut-up and let him look if he didn't satisfy her need to feed him. His fingers drummed at the sea green Formica surface as he gazed at the food. Cramming a flaky yellow biscuit into his mouth, he began to feel a sweat coming on. It had been a little nippy out earlier and he'd worn a jacket that would hide his Gram's diary.

Removing it, he hung it on the back of the chair as he hurried each bite into his mouth. Once he'd finished shoveling the breakfast, Brent scurried to the table. Instead of putting his jacket over the back of the chair as he had earlier, he thought it best to place it over his lap to keep his mother from trying to hang it up. He didn't want to let it out of his sight.

55

"I wish I knew what I was looking for." His mother grumbled trying to prod him for answers.

"Just a picture of Gram on the porch in a rocking chair, breast feeding a baby."

Janet's head jerked up at those words spoken with such a casual air and gaped at her son with her mouth open.

A moment of awkward silence lingered in the room before Brent realized that his mother had fallen quiet. He looked up to meet her gaze, chuckling out a few words as he went back to the pictures.

"Close your mouth mother. I'm not a pervert. I had a memory of it the day I fell and hurt my leg. It was about that particular photograph, something odd about it: something different from the others. Maybe it's because she was so much younger than I imagined her being when she had you. I don't know. Anyway…

"I didn't see it when I went through my old pictures, so I figured you might have it. She was wearing a pink dress with yellow roses scattered over it and her hair was piled up on top of her head, so that little shiny red ringlets stringed down onto her shoulders. You know."

There was such certainty in his voice that Janet caught herself nodding before she realized what had been said. Then she looked at him again in puzzlement.

"No. Actually, I don't know. I don't remember any pictures like that and even if I did, photographs taken back when my mama was bearing children were not in color yet."

Brent's face shot up as he glared at his mother.

"What?"

"You heard me." His mother could see the obvious concern furrowing his tired brow and, hating to see her only son in such a disheveled state, she decided to offer a solution.

"But honey. You know how different things seem to folks when they're young. Just like when you came home from college; you said your room looked like it shrunk, 'cause you remembered it bein' lots bigger. The room hadn't shrunk, you had grown and there wasn't as much space as before."

Brent rolled his hand at his mother signifying that he wanted her to just get on with it.

"And?"

"You could have seen a picture in a magazine that looked so much like mama that you thought it was her. Children have silly notions like that all of the time. Why, even Geraldine Grayson down the road from the church said that her three-year-old thinks she's Dolly

Parton. Every time that young'un sees Dolly on T.V. he stands up, no matter where he is, and shouts 'look ever'boddy... my mommy's on T.V!'

"Of course, Geraldine wouldn't dare shun such a compliment. The only thing that old gossip has in common with Dolly is those incredibly big wigs she wears!"

"Mother!" Brent exclaimed. "You're straying from the subject. Now quit gossiping and start looking."

"You mean you still insist on poking through this mess for a picture? Brent, it could have been anythin'..."

"But it wasn't just anything mama!" Raspiness had settled into his throat and he grew sick of the conversations with her.

"I know what I saw. I'm not crazy... despite what everybody around here thinks! I got some ideas in my head last night that cost me a great deal of sleep. So, if you don't mind, I'd like to get on with this because I swear, the only way to get it out of my head is to see it again. Somehow that picture is the key."

At this point his mother stared at him with a look of total exasperation. Brent had not often spoken that way to her before and he looked positively frightful. His eyes had brown circles under them from the lack of sleep and there was puffiness in his eyelids, making her quite sure he had been crying.

He didn't shave that morning before going out either, and he never did that. The biggest of her worries perhaps, was that after taking that horrible tone with her he seemed oblivious to her feelings... another first. He plucked the photographs up from the table one by one, examining them like some sort of mad scientist.

After a long silence, Janet decided to try to humor him at least and began going through her stacks, even though she knew the search was futile. She'd have remembered if such a picture existed, (and it didn't).

****

They had been at the table in the tumbled down mass of photographic debris for at least two hours when the doorbell rang. Janet glanced at her watch with both eyebrows up and murmured something about folks who bother to call so early in the morning. Brent's thin stretchy smile widened somewhat when he heard Doc Taylor's voice at the door.

"*Good old mother.*" He thought. She could always be counted upon for a conniption.

Morning light filtered through the dainty lace curtains as the house faced the rising sun, giving the room what seemed almost a holy glow. A soothing turquoise color fawned over the room due to the deep hues of the blue lace curtains in his mother's dining room. It made Brent feel cool and relaxed.

At least now with the sun up, he might rest without the threat of the dark dreams that had frightened him so badly the night before. Still lost in a daydream that reminded him of Alyssa's lovely smile, he nearly didn't hear his mother come in with the doctor. Brent got to his feet, spilling his jacket onto the floor and walked over, giving him a hardy handshake.

"Good morning Doctor Taylor!" He beamed. "I wondered when you might show up." He cast a smart aleck smile to his mother and walked Doctor Taylor over to the table, which remained littered with old pictures and dribbled coffee.

The therapist sat down and brushed some white donut powder from the table before retrieving a pen and paper from his bag.

"Sorry about that." Brent blushed. "But for some reason mother hasn't stopped cramming food in my mouth since I walked in the door."

"Yore mama tells me you were here rather early this mornin' too. Tell me. How are we feeling today?"

Brent's mother had made herself disappear or he would have loved to embarrass the living hell out of her just then; by letting some spittle run down his chin and barking like a dog. However, it wasn't likely he would see Alyssa again, or find the picture if he let on that there was anything amiss.

"I don't know about anybody else, but I'm on top of the world doc."

Doctor Taylor studied him curiously, making a notation in his book. As he did so, Brent couldn't help but actually absorb the sight of the old man.

All country Doctors were different from most, but Doc Taylor even more so; probably because he was a family shrink, a rarity in those parts to Brent's thinking. The doctor was an old man, not heavy like most of the doctors Brent had met, but more rigid and thin. His impending height belied a gentle demeanor, his scarce weight making him resemble a thin scanty beanstalk. He had a long-hooked nose with large nostrils that flared on command to give people the illusion that he maintained full control.

He had long, unkempt gray hair and a huge handlebar mustache that looked as if it hadn't been combed in ages. Brent mused that Rip Van Winkle himself couldn't have looked much different after his long sleep. Doctor Taylor always dressed in old-fashioned suits and though to a younger set he might appear strange, the elder women doted on him.

"Why are we on top of the world today young man?"

Brent hated the way he always spoke to him using the word "we", so he made it a point to use it against the conversation whenever possible.

"I don't know about you... but *I*..." Brent's mind reeled for an answer, when he heard his mother creeping up to the doorway to listen in. A clever grin touched his lips as the answer presented itself. "I was kissing a very pretty girl last night..." He could actually hear his mother's breath catch in her throat.

Doctor Taylor wrote things down and tried to look interested, but Brent could see that the man felt as though he had made a useless trip to satisfy a woman with an over active imagination. Still, ever the professional and never ready to dismiss a mother's concern entirely, he continued his inquiry.

"Then tell me why finding a particular picture is so important."

At first, Brent wasn't sure why it was so important, but he didn't have any trouble thinking up an answer without missing a beat. That at least would give him the time to work things out in his mind.

"Well. This girl I met... Alyssa. She's a gorgeous girl and I was telling her that something about her made me think of family and home, but I couldn't put a finger on what. Well I slept on it and this morning, it hit me like a ton of bricks.

"I was about to let out the cows and remembered a picture of Gram wearing a pink dress with yellow flowers on it and... I guess because of the color of Gram's hair and Alyssa's being so similar and all... that was probably it.

"Well I didn't want Alyssa to think I was weird or anything, so I decided to find the picture and show it to her.

"I think she would enjoy some of the family photos and I wanted to have it with me when I went back today to see her. I just wanted to see if I could find it. It's not that it's so all fired important or anything."

"I see." Doctor Taylor looked over his shoulder to the doorway where they knew Janet stood hiding. He then turned back to Brent, winking.

"Are you sure there isn't anything else you want to tell me this morning?" Brent grinned. There was no revenge like getting even with mother.

"Well..." he started a little slow, trying to come up with something, then decided to tell some of his dream.

"Go on my boy. I'll listen. I think you know by now that I won't tell your mother anything that would get you into trouble. I never told on you for stealing Ms. Grayson's rake. Now did I?"

"Guess not." Brent smiled, knowing that though he had been accused of it he didn't do it.

"And you didn't tell on me when I got that white trash McNeal girl pregnant either."

They could both hear Janet's gasp but Brent talked a little louder so that she wouldn't know she had been discovered.

"And since we're on the subject Doc, I wanted to tell you about this awfully cool dream I had last night."

"Please. Go on."

"Well." Brent's features darkened as he recalled his horror, but he had been trained by Doctor Taylor to talk about dreams. As long as he maintained control, he should be able to dispel his fears of them.

"I dreamed I was in this dark alley last night, about midnight... I know because I heard a clock chiming somewhere off in the fog." Brent's voice rose and fell in spooky octaves to set the "mood" and Doc Taylor chuckled silently as he pointed to the doorway. He walked over to the other side of the door so that he could jump out and scare Janet at the right time.

"I was going to walk home, but there was this tangible blackness blocking me from the path of the light..." Brent's heart quickened as he recounted his grizzly fears, but fortunately for him the doctor wasn't paying much attention. "I thought it might be a bum and told it I just wanted to get by, but it wasn't a person. It was an emotion or something. And as it grew, it tormented me with such anguish. The next thing I knew I wanted to taste blood... to kill for the love of killing, to control for the pure lust of power. I grabbed a girl and did unspeakable things to her right before I..." Brent paused to catch his breath, when he realized that the doctor was waiting for a grab line to scare his mother with. Brent pointed to him just as he screamed...

"CUT HER HEAD OFF!"

The doctor grabbed Janet just as Brent finished his grizzly account and Janet's scream seemingly sounded through at least half the county. Both men laughed hysterically at her expense. Though her face flushed red, she turned a knowing look to her son.

"That's okay Brent. I know when I been whipped." Then she turned on Doctor Taylor.

"As for you Doctor Taylor, he isn't your son. You wouldn't notice the changes in his appearance and behavior as I do, but there was something very serious in his tone just now. I don't think it's funny.

"He's pulling the wool over your eyes and yore allowin' it... as much as even *condonin'* it."

"Mrs. Price." Dr. Taylor smiled wiping a few happy tears from under his heavily lined eyes. "He is fine. He was just doing that to get to you because we knew you were listening. He didn't steal the rake, or impregnate the girl or even kill that young woman in an alley last night. Half the town knows about that. He probably heard it on the news this morning. Now will you calm down?"

What the doctor had just said mortified Brent. What could he mean? Did someone actually get their head ripped off last night? He couldn't even ask the doctor now because everyone assumed he knew.

"What?" Janet looked at the Doctor. "What did you just say?"

"You mean you hadn't heard?" Doctor Taylor cast a questioning glance over at Brent. "You didn't tell her?"

"Well I only got it in bits and pieces off the radio while I was brushing my teeth, so I wasn't really sure I heard it right. I can't go spilling a story like that to mama without correct facts... you know how nervous she can get."

Doctor Taylor chuckled a bit and then turned back to Janet with a little more professionalism in his tone.

"Well now Mrs. Price. You needn't worry about Brent. The young woman in question has not been identified yet, but her head wasn't taken completely off. It looked as if someone wanted to mug her and she protested so fiercely that they were forced to strangle her.

"Upon trying to do so, the wire cut so deep into her throat that it partially severed her head from her body."

Doc realized that Janet began to look ill and he caught her up in his arms just in time.

"I am sorry Mrs. Price." He murmured, helping her into a chair.

"See what I mean?" Brent chimed in. "You have to be careful how you deliver a story like that to mother. Should I go get the smelling salts?" The doctor shook his head waving at him to stay put.

"This is such a small, quiet community. Things like this just don't happen here. This just can't be happnin'." She replied.

"Mrs. Price, I assure you that these things can and do happen in small cities across the country. But it's probably an isolated incident. I wouldn't worry too much about it."

****

Doctor Taylor did eventually go home and Brent did manage to calm his mother down enough to go home as well, but Janet would not forget.

She would not forget the frightening drone of her son's semi-baritone voice as he described such a horrible thing without remorse. She would never forget the gleam in his eye when she came back into the room.

Something bad had happened to him and she made a pact with herself to find out what it was. He might fool the doctors, but he couldn't fool his own mother. She knew his very soul was off balance.

[PART III]

Brent hurried home and pushed the cows out to pasture. His Collie, Randy, kept a constant place at his feet and it had begun to annoy Brent in the oddest way. He loved old Randy though.

Falling into the rocker on his back porch with his paper and his faithful dog, he enjoyed the peace and tranquility of home. Rocking back in his chair, he let the warm sun heat his aching muscles as he sipped coffee from his cup and daydreamed about Alyssa.

He would need to go out there now that he told the doctor he was going. It shouldn't be difficult to use the bull as an excuse and he could make the statement about her striking something in his memory after that.

He knew he had convinced the doctor, but something in his mother's voice told a story altogether different.

Janet would call Mrs. Johnson to see that her son had told the truth. Her embrace seemed distant and fear had been heavy in her voice when they hugged and said good-by.

Maybe he could start spending some time with Alyssa and get Janet so involved with the idea of grand babies that she would forget his sudden neurosis for a picture that probably didn't exist anyway. Any excuse to see Lyssie was better than none. Brent sat up and put his coffee down on the little table, picking up his paper to read. The lady Doctor Taylor had spoken of was front-page news.

He read over the article with a feeling of distance that quite surprised him. He had anticipated that the account of her death would bring him to the stark realization that he was some blood-crazed fiend: that like Dr. Jekyll, he morphed at the stroke of twelve, killing this woman in his sleep.

Brent chuckled and then, he felt that breeze coming back again. It wasn't normal. He looked to the trees swaying in the wind off in the distance, and he realized that this wind was seeping toward him and around him. It bore a sickening smell... a smell... from his dream!

He sat back in his chair, surveying the world around him for any sign of a threat and began counting frantically to slow his heart.

Randy sat up, the scruff of his neck hairs rising up like a shark fin right down to the middle of his back and Brent gave up any idea of getting a grip on his nerves. Randy snarled, baring his teeth toward the edge of the porch into the yard. He barked loud and slapped at the floorboards with his paws. He hopped backwards, screaming almost in a childlike voice that sent an eerie wave of fear all over Brent's body.

He stood up patting his leg as he ran into the house and called out to the dog with a whistle.

"Come on Randy. Let's get the hell out of here!" They both ran straight to the old blue Ford truck and were off down the road in a clatter of wheels and a cloud of dust.

****

Brent decided that he must have transferred his fright onto the dog and Randy had just reacted to it the only way he knew how.

He still struggled into his denim shirt as the truck ambled up the dirt road and he breathed a sigh of relief. Pulling over at the watering hole when they reached their favorite fishing spot at the lake, he walked around to the back of the truck, lowering the tailgate.

Randy jumped out and ran through the tall grass barking playfully at the wild ducks that typically found their way here, when winter had fallen over the rest of the world. As the dog ran about, happy for the opportunity to chase his illusive quarry, Brent reached behind the seat and brought out a blanket, which he took down to a shady place beneath a withering Magnolia tree. Spreading the cover out onto the dewy grass, he lay on the banks of the lake to watch the clouds roll by.

Soon enough, Randy got tired of duck chasing and came to lie down next to him. The warm and breezy weather soothed him so that as he lie here quiet and tranquil with his silly dog, he eventually found himself fast asleep, lulled by the roll of the cloudy sky and the giggle of the lake as its water trickled over some rocks. ... and Brent did not dream.

End of Chapter Six

Chapter Seven: Lightning Passion

Alyssa practically glided down the stairs that morning. She hadn't had such a restful night's sleep in, well... forever.

Sailing into the kitchen, she poured her tea with a renewed steady grace that had almost been forgotten. No longer did she see herself as the "Little Orphan Annie" girl she'd been, but as a desirable woman.

The very thought tickled her pink and she laughed, in spite of the fact that her aunt Edna was coming up the back walk. She had just come from milking the cows. Ordinarily, Jack took care of this, but he had called in sick for the first time in fifteen years, so the sainted woman had no choice but to take matters into her own hands as it were.

Crossness invaded her mood since the stubborn beasts had given her such a hard time, but after seeing her niece positively radiant with happiness, she decided not to spoil it for her.

Removing her work gloves and letting them slap down onto the sink, she took a long sip of the cold two-liter bottle of Coke she had taken from the top shelf of the refrigerator. The bottle was quickly emptied, having been only partially full to begin with, and she chunked it across the room into the trash bin on her way to the table. Positioning herself across from Alyssa with an exasperated gasp for air, Edna removed the bandanna from her silvery hair.

"Hate those cows." The elder woman muttered, running fragile fingers through her sweaty hair. "Love the milk."

Lyssie giggled, yet found herself hoping that she could be as beautiful as Edna was at sixty some odd years old... and in half the physical condition. As her aunt's wise, pale eyes lifted to meet with hers they both smiled a knowing smile at one another.

"Do you think he'll come today?" Edna asked. Alyssa had been so busy reliving last night that she hadn't really thought much about today. She pondered the question in useless contemplation. Of course, she hoped that he would come and she knew her aunt would understand that.

"If we're lucky." She answered. Edna knew better than to beat a dead horse and went upstairs to get bathed and changed. Next would come the household duties that must be tended to after the long outside chores were finished.

Alyssa watched her aunt amble slowly up the stairs and decided that maybe it was time she started doing more around there to help out besides nursing a healthy, spoiled bull. She got up, bustling around the kitchen, making coffee and cooking breakfast.

To Edna's astonishment, by the time she returned from her hot bath, Lyssie had cooked, made coffee and had a lot of the huge house cleaned already.

"You didn't have to do all of that sweetie!" Alyssa hugged her aunt tightly, forgetting that she still held a bottle of glass cleaner and a rag in her hand.

"I think it's time I did my share around here instead of acting like a spoiled child. Come on and eat your breakfast."

"Who are you and what did you do with my niece?" Edna quipped.

"Ha-Ha! It is to laugh." Lyssie giggled. "Sit. Eat. I'll take care of the indoor chores for you."

Without much of a look back, the elder woman sat down to her breakfast with a satisfied, but confused smile.

****

Alyssa spent the rest of the day scouring, scrubbing and dusting her fingernails to the frazzle, but she didn't care.

Toward suppertime, she became acutely aware of her motive for staying so busy. She hadn't heard from Dr. Price. She supposed he wasn't coming.

Who could blame him? With all of the attractive women flitting about town she had a hard time believing that he had been interested in her in the first place.

Relieving herself of the tiresome duties of the afternoon, Alyssa made her way to the room to sulk. She sat long faced in front of her mirror wishing that she could be someone else.

'*Those great big eyeballs on that little bitty head; that long thin nose,*' she thought, turning her gaze then to a thin, more athletic figure.

Her cheeks faded warm as her mind relived that tender moment when he'd almost kissed her. More warmth began forming… in her eyes. Her mind seized for a moment.

'Oh Gawd! I can't be reduced to crying!'

Tossing her long hair back, she took a deep breath and a long look at herself. The more she looked, the more she understood his purpose for not calling or coming by.

In utter silence, she considered her appearance and whether she should try to change it, dress up more often. The line of thought was short-lived, however. She wouldn't stepdown to a man. He would love her for who she was, or she didn't need him.

Suddenly, a faint groan drifted through the open window from afar off.

"Carlos!" She gasped, running from the room and down the stairs in a mad rush.

Twilight had fallen, so she could hardly see to keep her step once she'd arrived in the yard, but she knew every step of the way to Carlos's stall by heart.

Once she got to the barn, she could see that her aunt, unpracticed at performing Jack's regimen, hadn't locked up when she left earlier. Edna rarely ever left anything unlocked or unfinished and it bothered Lyssie to be seeing it here, in the dark.

Faint moonlight peaking in and out from behind dark clouds shadowed the barn in blue and gray light. The white cross-members shone so stark against the darker walls, that Lyssie appreciated Jack's hard work all the more. It might have been difficult to tell that the door had been left unlocked and just barely ajar if the thing hadn't recently been painted.

Pulling at the big heavy door, Alyssa walked in. The extreme heat of this summer could easily unsettle the stead-fastest of field hands. Lyssie reasoned that her aunt was just as human as the next person and could just as easily have forgotten to lock up in her hurry to get indoors. For the moment, she was thankful that there would soon be illumination. She couldn't imagine having to go out to the barn in the dark without having some way to see. The spooky thought caused her to wonder how her ancestors managed before the creation of electricity.

Reaching out to turn on the lights, she found that instead of finding the switch, she grabbed someone's hand. Alyssa's scream erupted at such a high octave that the intruder backed up yelling at her to please stop it! Upon hearing that deep voice bellow over her screams, Lyssie calmed down almost immediately.

"Dr. Price?" She whispered, as if someone might be listening.

"Quit calling me that." He grimaced at the name in the dark, but her eyes had apparently not adjusted to the absence of light yet, because while she yet looked in his general direction, she didn't appear to be able to see him.

"What are you doing in here?" She asked.

"Sorry I scared you." He whispered back, taking her hand and leading her toward the door.

"You didn't answer my question." She said sternly in a slightly louder whisper.

Brent stopped, letting go of her hand since she didn't allow him to move her toward the barn door. An explanation of his presence there would be in order, despite the risk of sounding like an idiot.

"I can't sleep at the house tonight. It's not something I can talk about either. My mother thinks I'm nuts. If I go over to her place, I'm liable to wind up being committed or something, so I snuck in over here hoping to catch some shuteye in the shelter.

"I slept at the lake for a while today, but it looked like rain. I'll..." He realized how stupid this must sound. "I'll just go."

"No no no." She shushed him as she took his arm and walked him out into the yard. "You can stay."

They sat next to each other on the top railing of the log fence that lined the pasture for quite some time, neither of them knowing for sure where to begin. Tall, silvery blades of grass swayed in the wind from the coming storm as the clouds parted above. Alyssa looked up at the sky, kicking her feet back and forth up against the fence post and letting the gusts push at her hair.

Brent looked toward the ground with big gentle hands resting on his knees. They finally looked at each other and Brent was the first to speak.

"I just needed to get some sleep. I ... I haven't been feeling well lately. I think I must be allergic to something in the house, because I can't get any sleep at all.

"I'm really sorry for bothering you this way, but I was pretty sure no one would know I was here and, in that event, I wouldn't be hurting anything. If it hadn't been for Carlos noticing me, I might have kept things a little quieter at least. He saw me and started begging for attention, so I went over to him and then I heard the big door swing over.

"I had adjusted to the dark, so I knew it was you. I guess it just didn't dawn on me that you couldn't see me until you let out that God awful scream."

Alyssa laughed at herself nervously. Brent on the other hand, did not laugh.

"I'm really sorry." He muttered again as he got off of the fence and dusted at the seat of his jeans. "I'm gonna go before your aunt sends the militia looking for you."

"Don't go." She urged. "I could tell Aunt Edna that you dropped by, and couldn't get your car to start; that way you'd at least get some supper." Brent looked at her sideways. He had felt like an idiot only a moment ago, but she had just that easily removed his awkwardness.

"I should like something to eat. I haven't had a bite since I left my mother's this morning... hey."

"What?" She responded as she jumped down from the fence herself.

"You think you could smuggle me some left-overs later?" Alyssa stared at him with one eyebrow up. "It's for my dog Randy. He's probably still sleeping in the floorboard of the truck."

Alyssa looked all around, but she didn't see any truck.

"I thought you drove a Jeep."

"Usually, but I figured I'd need the flat bed to sleep in." He pointed to the ancient trees standing off at the edge of the property line. "It's hidden in there."

Alyssa seemed to be contemplating something.

"You're not some criminal running from Americas Most Wanted or something are you?"

Brent laughed as she led him toward the farmhouse.

"No. It's nothing as bad as all of that. There's just a pesky ghost bothering me."

****

Pleased to have an unexpected guest, Edna spoiled and pampered Brent with the finest southern meal he had ever eaten.

To repay the favor, and to spend time with Lyssie, he volunteered to help with the kitchen duty afterwards.

Alyssa hadn't gotten anything out of him since the crack he made about a ghost, but she could tell by his pallid complexion that something serious haunted him and that it was far greater than he liked to let on. She rushed around the kitchen with her usual competence, but with a speed unlike anything her aunt had witnessed before.

Edna made herself scarce after the cleaning was finished, saying that she was especially tired from all of the work that had been done that morning... to which Brent replied:

"I noticed that the house looked like it had been cleaned by the household staff of Buckingham Palace. I think I'd be a little tired myself after all of this work!"

Edna wanted to brag about her niece's housekeeping, but Alyssa's warning glance kept her from it.

"Thank you young man. It's nice to be appreciated for something you're good at. Good night y'all."

"Good night." They both answered at the same time.

Brent and Alyssa sat quietly for a little while, both trying to think of just the right thing to say.

The storm had made its impending visit known early in the evening, so Alyssa and Edna had brought out candles, lamp oil, matches and the like so that they would be prepared for a power outage. The room was decorated in antiquities dating back to the 1700's, and there was only the light of a couple of old kerosene lamps around them. Deep corners bore dark purple and lavender shadows jumping around the thick moist air, and a strong electrical force built between Brent and Alyssa as well as outdoors. Each lamp was positioned on an oak table behind the couches, so that the light shone from behind them.

Brent wanted to forget he had said anything about the ghost situation. Probably, there wasn't anything really crazy happening to him at all. He looked at Alyssa's silhouette on the other couch, and a little smile hit him.

Maybe he was just scared because of the strange feelings he wasn't ready to deal with, and that fear was manifesting itself into something twisted.

Brent chuckled softly at himself.

"What?" Alyssa asked, her voice quiet.

Brent had only then realized that he hadn't laughed silently, and looked up at her. He thought what a boon it was that she couldn't see his face and the surprise that must be on it.

"I'm sorry. Did I do that out loud?"

Alyssa chuckled a little.

"Fraid so."

"It was nothing."

"Must've been something. People don't just start laughing for no reason."

"Sometimes my mind wanders. It was nothing. Really."

Alyssa became agitated with Brent's reluctance to share his thoughts. She wanted to jump up and down on the couch and yell out how he made her feel in a voice that would encompass the globe... and he sat here laughing at her.

Why else would he just start chuckling like that? Did he think that she was just some lust struck little kid waiting for him to make the first move?

"I hate it when people do that." Her calm tone defied her inner turmoil, but Brent could sense that it had started stewing again, even if he didn't know why. He thought about what Dr. Taylor would have said to that.

"Why do you hate it when people do... *what*?"

"When people laugh at you, and then won't say why. I hate that because it's like they're hidin' somethin', and I shouldn't have to tell you what I think of liars."

Brent grinned in the dark. He couldn't believe that someone as pretty as Alyssa could be so self-conscious.

He didn't want to ruin what they had finally developed either, so he decided to feed her the line he had been needing to give her: if he would ever get his mother off of his back.

"I just didn't want you to take offense by what had struck me as funny."

"Great." She grumbled clinching her hands together tightly and staring down at her lap. "I guess this is where you tell me you'd rather be sitting here with a two-headed monster instead of me, right?"

Brent was taken back by the severity of negativity with which she perceived herself.

"I can't believe you would think something like that about yourself."

He started to get up, wanting to go and sit by her and perhaps take her in an embrace... hug her little problems away, but she put a stop to that.

"Don't patronize me Dr. Price..." The title cut him like a blow when it came from her. Why couldn't she just call him by his first name?

"Brent." He said forcefully as he sat back down.

Alyssa hadn't noticed him standing until he returned to his seat. She mentally cussed herself out for not keeping her mouth shut. Maybe then she would be in his arms instead of sitting across a dark cool room, wishing for something that could probably never be.

Brent refused to be defeated completely.

"I was only chuckling about the way my mind works. Sitting here in the dark, your shadow seemed to remind me of my Grandma some... when she was much, *much* younger of course." He added hastily remembering her self-consciousness.

Alyssa relaxed a little, feeling stupid. Relief... he didn't see her quite as poorly as she saw herself.

"Where does your grandmother live?" Alyssa was just trying to ease up the conversation so that maybe they could actually get a little closer to one another again. She liked that warm tingle she felt whenever their skin touched.

"She lives in a world of night shadows." Weariness traveled the soft drone of his voice, and his eyes had glazed over as he stared almost through Alyssa.

He had no idea where that answer had come from. It was as if someone had answered Alyssa for him. The shock of hearing his own answer unnerved him.

The answer had chilled Alyssa too, because the voice was almost too cold and uncaring to belong to Brent, but there was no mistaking the fact that it came from him.

"Are you okay?" She asked, her voice trembling.

He snapped out of it.

"I'm fine." The voice maintained a soft "gravelly" feel, as he got up and went over to sit next to her on the couch.

"I haven't really been myself lately."

Alyssa was at odds with herself now that she knew his grandma was dead…obviously the subject of his Grandmother did strange things to Brent, so she would not bring it up again.

"I can see that." She breathed nervously as his big strong arm stretched around the back of the couch to encircle her.

"I've been having some really bad dreams lately. I mean *really* bad ones too. I'm starting to think it's because I took up Gram's old farmhouse and I have a very overactive imagination. But the dreams I have seem so real. They consist of such unreal horrors, but they still seem… real."

Brent's body tensed and a tremor ran through him as he remembered the dream from the evening past. He could have dismissed that damning dream by now if that girl hadn't been murdered in town. But she *had*… and it was just too coincidental for his liking. And while he didn't dare wonder why, he was becoming more and more aroused by the second.

His trembling under any other circumstance might have made Lyssie move away from him but she scooted closer, as if to let him know that he was okay because of her nearness.

His arm came a little closer to her on the couch, so he could stroke her bare shoulder with his fingertips.

The strap to her shirt was obviously too long, as it had slipped off of her shoulder with his slightest touch. Excited chill bumps rose to greet his fingertips with each stroke as he talked softly.

"I have been a bachelor all of my life and until a few days ago, I couldn't imagine letting a woman get into my mind for an instant…

much *less* for a lifetime, but there's something wildly challenging and yet, accommodating at the same time when I'm with you. Those are inviting qualities to me, and you're so beautiful..."

Brent's voice was nearly a whisper now. He leaned his head closer to her face as if someone might hear him otherwise.

Alyssa's body shuddered with pleasurable excitement, his hot breath upon her cheek.

"I just want to hold you Alyssa, to be lost in you for a while. To know that I'm not crazy... that there is *some*one **real** in my world..."

Brent had no idea where he had gotten the courage to speak the truth, but her chill bumps reacted to his touch, and his body thrilled to a taut knot at the thought of it.

Alyssa brought out a side of him that no one else had even known about... not even Brent, and he didn't ever want to go back to the way he was in that dream. He wanted to feel the sweet promise of life when death had seemed his only escape for so long. He had been looking for Alyssa his whole life it seemed, and he never knew it.

He pecked a small kiss upon her cheek and a slight, barely audible sound of pleasure pushed past her lips. Brent was so breathless in knowing that he could please her with so little effort that he wanted her to know the passion he could truly give her.

He ran tender fingers over her sleeveless arm, evoking chills. Leaning over, he lightly kissed the slope of her neck where it met her milky shoulder.

Alyssa had hoped for this moment all of her life... for a man to caress her, to speak to her with a want in his voice, to kiss her in places that actually invoked a reaction from her. Her whole body tingled.

She had never wanted anyone this much before now and couldn't imagine ever wanting another man. She adored every little idiosyncrasy about him.

His inexplicable good looks only intensified her reaction to the warm caresses. Just the *thought* of seeing him... every *inch* of him naked and glistening by the light of the moon aroused something inside of her that she never would have dreamed she possessed.

Alyssa turned to face him. Staring into the dark slots that would normally be his dazzling, blue-sky-colored eyes, she prayed that he would kiss her first.

Uncertainty gripped her despite his obvious intent, but it was short-lived.

Brent's lips touched hers with such heat and intensity, that she found herself reacting to him with equal vigor.

Her tongue probed into his mouth begging for more, seeking, touching, feeling and exploring the passion she had always hoped for. Her closed eyes painted a picture of his beautiful face in the afternoon sun the first day she had seen him, and her whole body shuddered with sexual excitement.

As if by magic, the kerosene lamp went out and deep emotion swept through her. It obscured any word she could have invented to describe it.

Brent's hands slid down her shoulder, and he began caressing her back with his firm gentle hands as he kissed her. Fierce heat escalated between them and they had to break the kiss to catch a breath.

Brent didn't waste a second, though. He sensuously pressed his lips to her neck again, his tongue moving softly against her skin.

Alyssa groaned, her silhouette painting an erotic picture in his mind.

Pulling hungrily at her with tight grasps, he yanked her up onto his lap, never taking his mouth from her shoulder.

Somewhat startled by the action of being lifted onto his lap, Alyssa had to stifle a yelp, but when she felt the protrusion hard and strong against her jeans, she moaned heavily.

His firm hands raced over her lightly chilled skin as his fluttering fingers found the strap on the other shoulder. Slipping it off of her, the flimsy cotton shirt drifted just below her bra.

Her skin's opaqueness shimmered in the streaking lightning as he uncovered her ripe luminous breasts.

Brent groaned with Alyssa as he began licking at her nipples, biting tenderly once in a while to keep them erect. His fingertips caressed her skin appreciatively as he cupped them close to his lips.

He'd been afraid at first to move against her, but Alyssa started on her own... taking him quite by surprise.

The very first time his teeth grazed the hardening nipple, she adjusted herself so that she pressed hard against his lap. Pushing down on her hips with his hands, he began rhythmically moving himself against her.

She felt so good in that position. The way the moonlight parted the clouds from time to time so he could see the ecstasy on her face, filled him with a desire to please her that welled from unknown pools of determination within him.

He stood up, her legs still wrapped around him, and pressed her gently down onto the floor.

The weight of his heavy, well-muscled body made Alyssa so breathless she couldn't stand it. The best night of her life stood on the brink of tangibility, and the understanding of it was almost more than she could bear.

She had wondered her entire existence whether sex was over rated or not and clearly… it was *not*. She wanted nothing more at this moment than to feel him moving deep inside of her.

His kisses covered her as his erection fluxed against her, making her wish she was shed of those damned jeans. As if answering a sweet wish, Brent fumbled with the button, and then gracefully slid the zipper down.

He managed to slip her out of them without breaking too much stride and then readily began kissing her stomach in soft begging kisses. Thrilling at his touch, she shook to the very core.

Lithe fingers danced softly over her thigh leaving chills in their wake, and then found that private area, which had been so guarded by her in the past.

As his fingers gently pressed and moved against her, Alyssa found herself squirming! Despite the want to fall into a sexual whirlpool of emotionally founded feelings, she also feared allowing herself that pleasure.

She had been taking birth control for some time, but that didn't make sex a safe thing. Curse her good sensibility! She chastised herself mentally, but Brent sensed that something had gone wrong.

He produced a wallet from his back pocket, and a condom from his wallet. He quickly flashed it before her, lying it to one side as before flicking her nipples with his tongue, and probed into the inner part of her with sensuous fingers.

She flexed to move with his hand that so gracefully thrilled her. Clutching hungrily at his shoulders, she groaned softly as he kissed her bare skin and licked against each erogenous zone.

She pushed herself against his hand harder, moving faster, unable to manage the greed that enveloped her.

Pleasing pain stopped her for a second, but she refused to accept it.

Brent had seen her wince and whispered onto her skin.

"Slow down. It's okay. I'm not going anywhere. Just slow... slow... slow..."

His words held a hypnotic effect with their deep soft promises and Alyssa complied as if by magic, even though she wanted to engulf him whole.

Brent marveled at her beauty. The rain had begun falling and abundant electrical cloud surges streaked light onto them through the patio doors. In the white-blue flashes, he could see her. He never in his wildest dreams imagined such a woman being a virgin, but clearly, she was.

God! Had no one even *tried* to daunt that haughty air of hers? A sudden self-loathing invaded his thoughts. The question of worthiness entered his mind as he considered the prospect of removing her innocence, but then she didn't exactly seem reluctant once she had seen that condom. She was big enough to know how to stop this at any time, but she hadn't.

His whole body was erect with the thought of burying himself deep inside of her and thrashing away until they both had been pleased.

Breathing heavily upon her face, he kissed her; praying he wouldn't release before he had a chance to please her. She deserved her first time to be memorable.

"Do you want me to..." He broke off in mid-sentence afraid of her answer, his voice thick with wanting, which deceived his utter control to that point.

"Yes....yes...yes..." She whispered in the sweetest voice he had ever heard. His free hand reached to the condom, he didn't want to disturb the rhythm she had develop with his caress and opening one of those things with one hand was nearly impossible.

He shifted his weight off of her, lying on his side and with one hand and his teeth, he opened the package almost spilling the contents onto the floor.

Alyssa closed her eyes, allowing her hands to roam freely over her body. The sight of her writhing with pleasure made it necessary for him close his eyes and concentrate on keeping his stamina.

He opened them wide however, when he felt the warm rush over his hand and the contraction embraced his fingers.

Alyssa's body knotted and tensed as she slid onto her side removing his hand and grabbing his shirt.

She pulled him down toward her so that she could see his face. He got so close that he could have licked her without doing more than parting his lips.

"*You had better get that thing on... I want you now...*" She growled. She enclosed his mouth with a passionate kiss, and a surge of excitement ran like lightning through his veins.

She began undressing him as he fumbled with the object of necessity. He thought he'd never get it into place but once he had it, he didn't waste a moment sliding on top of Alyssa.

He wanted to make sure that she would be ready and toyed with her again, making her wet.

He rubbed her gently, licking her lower tummy area until he felt the warm rush again, and then, ever so slowly, he pushed himself inside of her.

Alyssa stifled a tiny yelp so as not to wake her aunt as fullness flowed through her so quickly that breathlessness overcame her.

Her body rose and fell to meet with his, begging him for more speed, more intensity, which he readily supplied. An urgency filled her, a want, an actual greed to consume him, to be part of him, to be the insider in his life.

She believed that they were built for one another, and now that she had tasted that pleasure of fullness, she would fight for it tooth and nail until she hadn't any fight left.

Brent thrust in and out of her with precise agility and at one beautiful moment, their bodies met, clinging and meshing together, until there was nothing left in either of them. They had emptied themselves into each other, and while that jumbled mass might be disorganized, it was part of them now, and they each greeted the challenge to be one with each other again... and again ... and again.

End of Chapter Seven

Chapter Eight: The Visit

Brent rolled over to take her into his arms and found that she had her back to him as she lay on her side. He didn't mind. He nestled up to her from behind, breathless and more comfortable than he had ever been in his life.

As she lay naked on the big-blue Persian rug that covered the hardwood floor, Alyssa sighed a happy sigh as he tucked himself against her. She delighted in his slightest touch. She had never been so whole, so complete, or so belonging to another.

"Are you all right?" Brent had succumbed to his fear of scaring her away. He couldn't afford to do that. Not now.

Nodding, she feared saying anything. She'd read a lot of horror stories about the "first time" in the in-vogue magazines, and she didn't want to say anything that would ruin this sacred moment. She hoped desperately to keep that particular instant of ecstasy suspended in time forever.

He caressed her arm lovingly, her bare skin invoking a spell of desire within him as it lit up in the flashes outside.

This night, this passion, had been a first in his life. Brent longed to tell her that she was the only woman he had ever done this with... but that would be a lie. She *was*, however, the only woman he had ever made love to in every sense of the words but saying so seemed repugnant somehow.

Marveling at the joy that something so small as a single touch could bring, Alyssa wondered what he might be thinking. Probably he was trying to think of a way to get out of staying the night so that he could ride away into the storm without having to cast a backward glance.

"Is it still okay for me to stay?"

He had instinctively asked her that question and Alyssa's heart gladdened to hear it. Her face almost radiated an inner light as she rolled over to embrace him.

"I'll take that as a yes." He said with quiet surprise as he tightened his arms around her and kissed her slowly, lingering on the contours of her lips.

■■■

Later, after dressing, they walked up the stairs hand in hand like a pair of youngsters in the throes of first love, then came to a stop in front of a bedroom door. As it opened, the ominous creaking noise made Brent cringe.

Alyssa could see the shadows changing on his face even in the dark corridor, and wondered what he was really thinking. She had wondered earlier in the evening as well but hadn't asked for fear of chasing him away.

Once inside, she tiptoed over to the nightstand next to the bed. Clicking on the antique brass lamp, she let her fingers linger in the gold fringe, which rimmed the ivory colored lampshade. She hardly noticed Brent as she turned down the covers on the old bed.

He surveyed the room from the doorway before entering. The furnishings reminded him of a nineteenth century bed chamber from some bad vampire picture, and a visible chill passed through his body.

The red velvet wall paper bore a paisley print, which was creepy enough all by itself, without the impending presence of the oversized, four poster bed. It's hand-carved, antique, mahogany posts reached almost to the high ceiling, and were clothed in red velvet drapes.

As Alyssa turned the covers back to reveal the soft peach hues of the flowery sheet underneath, Brent caught himself thinking how the bed looked like an open wound.

"What is it?" Alyssa asked, her voice teetering, as she stood back up next to the bed.

He shook his head softly as though convincing himself rather than her.

He absorbed the sight of her, standing there next to the huge, dark wood of that bed, and it was as if the light of the room came from her alone.

For however a brief a moment, he felt as if he were living another life, even while seeing what transpired in this one. He went to sit on a big cedar trunk at the foot of the bed.

Lyssie sat next to him, placing her hand gently on his knee. He had become somber, with an almost sick-looking pallor replacing his prior conviviality.

She knew that something greater than anything she'd ever expected must surely have been troubling him, but she would chance dancing with demons if it meant she could keep him next to her.

"I think I deserve to know what's bothering you, Brent."

Brent's eyes met hers, a temporary sparkle from having heard her speak his first name.

She was glad for the change in his appearance, if even for a second. She knew what she had pulled just now, about deserving something, was a cheap shot. She suspected that if she hadn't strategically used his first name, they might even now have been engaged in another shouting bout.

"I suppose I have been acting like an ass lately, and I can't tell you how much it means to me that you would still be with me in spite of it."

Alyssa shrugged sweetly with a smart smirk on her face.

"It's a dirty job, but someone's gotta be crazy enough to do it." She sighed theatrically. "It might as well be me."

Brent chuckled a little at her maintaining such candor even at this hour.

"I guess it could only have *been* you." He answered pecking her tenderly on the cheek.

"And don't you forget it doctor." She smiled giving him a big hug.

Brent had never been the type to enjoy physical contact, (outside of those necessary to enjoy carnal pleasure), but there was no turning back now. He embraced her as if his very life depended on knowing that she really existed, and that she was not just some figment of his warped imagination.

"Okay *okay* already!" She laughed mimicking Bugs Bunny. "You'll wrinkle the material!"

Brent was still chuckling as he released her, but there were tiny teardrops in his eyes that upset Alyssa.

"Come on Brent. Something's really wrong here. I may not have known you for a very long time or anything, but even *I* know there's something not right. Won't you *try* talking to me?"

He had to tell someone sooner or later, or he'd be forced to agree with his mother and go to an insane asylum. His eyes almost seemed to have a film over them as he began his story. By the time he'd finished, Alyssa had moved even closer to him, giving him subtle reassurance that she wouldn't bolt as soon as the story got messy.

"I can understand why you might think there is some connection between you and that girl, really I can; but Brent, even your therapist thought that was an isolated incident. It isn't likely that anything like that will happen again..."

"It *will* happen again. I know it! I don't know **how** I know... but I know!"

Alyssa looked piteously at him before she continued.

"I'm sure that the rest of it is all just something you're self-inflicting because you're so tired. Maybe some rest here at the Biggmann Ranch is just what the doctor ordered."

Brent's hands were clasped tightly in his lap, his eyes never leaving them when he spoke. He was reassured by the sight of them somehow.

"What if it *is* me Alyssa? What if there is something mentally wrong with me, and I do something..." He couldn't bring the thought of harming her into words. He felt that if he spoke them, they would become reality, and he would sooner die than do that.

"Oh, good grief!" She fussed getting up and staring down that dignified nose, wide eyes blazing with indignation.

"Get into that bed and stop raving about this crazy shit. I'll show *you*!" She sputtered pulling an old, well-worn wicker rocker over to his bedside. "You get into bed and go to sleep. Just to prove that you're overreacting to this whole coincidence, I'll sit right here until I have to go to bed or risk getting caught by Aunt Edna."

"You can't!" He nearly shouted getting up, then realizing that he was getting loud, he cleared his throat and tried to recompose himself. The grandfather clock against the wall bonged loudly once to let them know that they were fussing at each other at one in the morning.

Glancing from the clock to Alyssa, he let his hands drop at his side. She was relentless. He knew that. Even if he did make her leave the room for the time being, he would either find her camped outside the door come morning, or right there in that chair, having come in while he was sleeping.

"Okay." He said, barely above a whisper. Alyssa's eyes were alight with triumph.

"What did you say?" she asked rubbing it in.

"I said okay." He resigned as he walked over to where she stood. "But I'm begging you... please. Run if something seems to be happening. And I don't mean stand here trying to decide if it's normal or not. I mean don't wonder at all. Just run like hell!"

Alyssa stifled a laugh. She couldn't believe it. All of the men in the world to be with, and she had to fall for a weirdo. Despite the obvious hilarity of the idea that he was some ridiculous monster in his sleep, there was some very deep emotion in him that she didn't understand. It was as if some terrible vision even now haunted his mind to the point that if she tried hard enough, she might almost reach out and touch it. Shivering visibly with the thought, she rubbed at her chilled arms.

Seeing her indecision, he wrapped her in a big warm hug that put her immediately at ease... monster indeed!

Brent couldn't afford for her to feel that this was some joke, so with all that he had in his heart he would plead with his eyes to let her see the fear... the raw anguish that the killing vision had caused.

The moment he realized she had seen it, he was afraid he might lose her. That would be worse than any monster from the dream world. He took her in his arms, and she relaxed. Leaning back, he continued the embrace while looking into those brilliant green spheres.

"Promise me." He pleaded.

"And for the best actor in the role of the tormented lover..."

"I'm serious!" He shouted stepping away from her. "I can't believe this! Of all the stubborn, pigheaded things..."

"Okay! Okay!" She laughed. "Don't get your boxers in a bind. I promise. If you grow a sixth finger or sprout hair in the palms of your hands I'll start running. Okay?"

Brent exhaled in a heavy, exasperated breath, as he let his arms fall limply to his sides. He regarded her curiously for a second: her fair hair, emeralds too big for her head giving her a magnetic appeal. He was never more pleased to have the pleasure of a woman's company, and that bothered him. He couldn't allow anything to happen to her before he had a chance to find out if he really did the things he thought he did, or if he had only been tortured by some insane dream.

He didn't even try to argue. Spinning on his heel, he headed for the door.

He had to get out now, before the sight of her made him a complete idiot and he stayed. Alyssa realized he was leaving the very instant he tried to do so, and would not be beaten at her own game. He would *not* love and run on *her* and get away with it.

Catching both of his arms in her hands, she dug her heels into the carpet, making him sway and stagger to keep from falling back onto her.

"Wait." Her voice was softened, but firm as she trotted around to stand in between him and the door.

"I'm sorry. I didn't believe you. I thought you were trying to make me get away from you so that you could get out of here without having to feel committed to me... but you're serious! Aren't you?"

It deeply wounded him that she thought of herself as an emotional victim of some sort, but then he hadn't exactly acted "normal" since they'd met.

"It's okay." Alyssa didn't waste a second making up her mind about this. If this bothered him, then it bothered her too.

"I think this may be the best idea after all. You say you think this will happen again right?"

He nodded, wondering what her crazy mind was cooking up now.

"I don't think Alyssa... I *know*."

"Will you cut out the drama here? You're starting to scare the crap out of me. Anyway. If you sleep here the night and I watch over you without sleep..." She held up her hand to ward off his intended protest to her lack of sleep... "I might help you forget this. If it happens tonight, and I have seen you through the night without fail, then you'll have to know that there is some other explanation for all of this. You'll know you're not some estranged lunatic running around town stealing candy from babies, and tearing tags off of mattresses and stuff. Right?"

Her choice of words with this subject didn't please him in the least, but inwardly he welcomed her sane antics as a child welcomes a helping hand from an adult. Again, he nodded, frowning.

"Oh, for crying out loud! There's a gun in the top drawer of the night table because this was my Uncle's room before he died of cancer."

Brent looked at her as if to say '*What has cancer got to do with a gun?*'

"Oh *you* know..." she supplied. "he got a little paranoid toward the end. He wouldn't sleep in the same room with Aunt Edna because he thought she was out to get him, so we fixed up this room for him and gave him an unloaded gun for comfort. It's loaded now though, in case of prowlers or wolves getting in the chicken pen. So, if you like, I'll spray your brains on the wall at the first sign of possession. Okay? Just get some sleep. Please?"

At this point, weariness had him so disoriented that she could have been talking gibberish and it would have made enough sense for him to stay with her. He *wanted* to stay and besides, there weren't any more rational reasons to leave.

Sitting on the edge of the bed, he held his hands out to her. She took those hands as warmly as she could, then leaned over to hold him tightly.

It seemed to her that they had been cut from the same fabric; each fitting into a certain groove of the other, making it inevitable for them to be together.

"Okay now?" She asked politely brushing the hair back from his forehead.

Brent nodded. "Tired though."

"I know. Just lie back and relax for a while. I'm sure the sleep will come."

"What about you?"

"You're looking at the woman who pulled two triples at work in a row without sleep. This should be a cake walk." There was no explanation for the kind of comfort Brent found in being there with her, but unlike the other unexplained matters in his life, this particular part was welcome.

Not long after his head hit the pillow, he fell into a very deep, dreamless sleep.

Alyssa sat next to the bed without fail, watching over him. This wasn't as easy as her all-nighters at work because at work, she was busy working and getting things done; operating on sheer adrenaline, but now, she was just watching a man sleep. For a great deal of time, she sat wondering what kind of child he would have been. She spent the rest of the time remembering the night of warmth just past, and then thinking about his wild stories.

Those stories. How odd the way he described them... not as if he had dreamed them at all, but as if he were recounting an actual event in his life. That was too frightening to think about.

She shook her head of the weary fog, and walked around the room for a moment, stretching and groaning. She heard Brent murmur something into his pillow and went to see if he was all right.

Stroking softly at his hair, she waited until the murmuring ceased, then sat back down. This must be what it was like to care for a child afraid of the boogey man.

She chuckled a minute and then laid her head back against the chair, recalling the thin line of chills his fingertips raised across her arm. The hair on her arm stood in what she thought at first, might be the memory of that event.

Suddenly out of the corner of her eye, she could see someone standing at the foot of Brent's bed!

She didn't look all at once, because she knew that those kinds of visions were often the result of someone nodding off to sleep, and then back awake.

However, the longer she sat still like that, trying to see the figure at the foot of the bed without looking directly at it, the more she came to realize that she hadn't been nodding off to sleep again. She was wide-awake. Her adrenaline was pumping through her at a rate she was certain could pass a 747.

This personage seemed to float in the air, but more like an angel than a boogey-man looking for nightly quarry. It emanated a spectral light that actually drove the shadows into the farther reaches of the room. Lyssie was terrified beyond belief.

She thought about the gun in the nightstand and Brent's desperate plea for her to run but for some odd reason, the vision had her spellbound.

It didn't appear to be some menacing force, it almost seemed like a woman in a long white gown, hovering there as if guarding the bed and she hadn't noticed Alyssa was even there.

Finally, curiosity overcame Lyssie and she sat up in the chair to look right at the apparition. The second the thought even crossed her mind to sit up and ask it what the hell it wanted, it was gone.

She didn't dwell on the matter however. She knew the effects of sleep deprivation, and knew that what she had seen was probably a hallucination or a bad dream, or both.

All of Brent's talk had spooked her, even if she wouldn't openly admit that, and this was the result of it. She did, however turn on the lamp again before she nodded off to sleep.

II.

Curled against the floor of the cavern, his wrinkled skin shivered in the dank night air. He woke, no longer dreaming… yet still seeing the vision he had been watching in dream.

"It's *her*" he whispered, elation filling his evil heart as he touched her in the night, he could almost feel his own fingers stroking her skin. Oh, unbelievable ecstasy!

Closing his eyes against the outward world he just concentrated on her.

Her angel face glowed in the lightning as it streaked the sky with passionate fingernails, and the beauty of it wrought deep erotic shudders through the cold chasms of his soul.

His body twisted in nervous knots as he writhed on the floor of the cold cave. How unfair that he could see the beauty of touching her, and not actually be able to touch her or even share the same space with her! Oh, to feel his fingers tightening around her lily-white throat.

He growled, vile hatred welling within him. Who was this horrid vessel, which brought him visions of the woman he so desired to possess? Why had he not seen her before? Who *was* she?

"Is it you?" His gravelly voice erupted into the silence of the cave. He let out an inhuman wail and ran furiously into the wet of the storm, seeking instant gratification in some other vessel, which would have to satisfy his need for now. This other one, would be saved for another day… a midnight soon when the time and the setting would create perfection.

End of Chapter Eight

Chapter Nine: Linking the Chain

I.

When he went downstairs earlier that morning, Brent planned to sneak some food out to Randy, (who he prayed would still be sitting in the truck), but there wasn't time. Edna had come down the stairs humming and he didn't want to get caught.

He'd left both windows in the truck down the night before, but even a dog would most likely have run to seek cover from a storm like last night's.

When he opened the door to the old Ford truck, he could see that Randy had not left, he had just crawled farther under the seat to avoid the rain that managed to get in through the trees.

He smiled as the Collie wriggled from under the seat. Scuffing at his silky coat Brent nuzzled Randy, face to face.

"Good boy." He flattered his faithful canine. "Let's go get you some breakfast."

■■■

Brent drove quietly down the mountain toward town. He had been listening to the radio and watching Randy eat a couple of dog biscuits he'd picked up at the bait shop, when he heard the report.

Another girl was accosted last night, and authorities were beginning to think that this was not a random incident.

She had been badly beaten, her neck had been broken, but a bit of mottled hair and skin from the killer had matched some taken from the crime scene of the other girl.

Brent had *known* this was going to happen. He'd felt it in his bones.

He had to get a grip on his fear, and let his curiosity do the work for him or he would be a nut before long... stealing candy from babies, and tearing off mattress tags and stuff.

The thought of Alyssa lifted his spirits enough that he felt he could get past anything, no matter how macabre it might be. His truck flew as fast as its wheels would carry it down the side of the mountain. He didn't know what he would do, or how he would go about doing it, but he *had* to see the girl... or at least the crime scene. He had to feel it. *What* he had to feel; he did not know for sure, but he was sure that if he got there in time, he would have some feeling left over from the event itself.

Brent shook his head and let go of the gas pedal a bit as he rounded the last bend toward town. This seemed so crazy, even to him.

Alyssa had been with him all night long. He hadn't gone anywhere but, just as he promised her, it had happened again.

He seemed the only person with some sense about what had happened to those girls... and what would continue happen. He held himself responsible for getting to the bottom of it and putting a halt to it before this could go any further.

He had been trying to increase the volume when he heard the broadcast, but accidentally turned it off. After becoming agitated as he struggled with the knob, he finally got the radio to work. The news had gone off and some nose twanging country music came on, but he didn't mind. It was better than static and the singer had some inside track to the way he felt. Besides, this station was always the first to break a news story.

Pulling to a stop at the edge of town he closed his eyes, waiting for... he didn't know.

Nothing.

The foolishness of it all made him laugh. He'd run out on Alyssa, and she was probably feeling abandoned by now.

"Price." He smarted, looking in the rear-view mirror at the reflection of his eyes... eyes that belonged to him but that seemed to hold the forbidden horrors of another man. "Price, you're an idiot."

Brent shook his head sharply as if trying to wake himself from a stupor. Randy whined in the seat next to him, and Brent reached over to stroke his shiny fur.

"Yep Randy. Your master's a complete idiot." He decided not to dawdle. He would have some big explaining to do when he returned to Alyssa as it was, might as well not make it worse.

He drove up to the little diner on 7th that had been under the same management since the sixties and ran in to grab a cup of coffee and a few pastries.

A woman of color in a pink uniform dress stood behind the counter smiling and putting a coffee pot on the burner. She had a deep burgundy color to her hair and a white hair net which, to Brent, made her look like a human version of a mixed-berry tart.

Her obvious height made her appear larger than she actually was, but thickness still showed in her bone structure. Brent stopped at the doorway to look at her curiously before he entered.

"What'll ya have hon'?" She asked, ignoring the fact that he stared at her.

It surprised him momentarily, that she spoke to him. For that brief moment he seemed some sort of ghost just hanging on the outside of the world looking for a way in. Her recognition of him shocked him back into his body.

"Yes." He stammered. "I'd like a dozen donut holes, and a cup of coffee... please." He added as she flew around filling a small, clear plastic cup with donut holes the second the words leapt from his lips.

He noticed that a newspaper had been left on the counter, and that the front-page story was about the young ladies who had been killed.

Both of their pictures were on there, and he was drawn to them as if the universe were a magnet inside, hoping to envelope him whole.

"Be XXXiggingXXX else for ya sugar?" The woman asked sliding Brent's order in front of him.

"Yes, thank you. I *do* take sugar in my coffee." He was so far away reading the words on the page that the woman regarded him as if he were an unsightly wart.

Quickly handing over little white packages instead of the decanter, she hoped to get rid of him before anyone else came in. She cleared her throat.

"Now will that be all for you shug...?"

"Thanks." He hadn't even attempted to look up from his paper.

"That'll be two-fifty hunny."

"Hmm?" Brent looked up. Money had a way of getting his attention no matter the circumstance. "Oh. I'm sorry. I was just readin' bout these two women. I feel so sorry for them." He had reached into his front pocket and pulled out a few dollars, making sure to push the change back at her when she tried to give it to him.

"You keep it." He sighed again looking at the paper. The paper had at least given locations and he realized he probably wouldn't be going back to the Biggmann ranch today. He would just have to explain to Alyssa tomorrow.

"Yeah." She seemed to be talking to him, in answer to his previous comment.

"I feel sorry for 'em too. Darn shame 'bout that first one specially. They were both so young, but *this* poor girl he got last night" she said, tapping the woman's picture on the paper. "She didn't have no family. She was working over at the restaurant on Fifty First Street, and left a little later than usual. The county's holding a funeral service for her since no one else would be here to mourn her. That first girl though..." She rattled like an empty wagon as she marched around behind the counter grabbing this and cleaning that, and Brent instantly became a very ardent listener.

"That first girl was working to take care of her grandma ... her last living relative. That poor old woman's got to pay funeral costs all by herself, and no one around to help her now. Don't know *what's* going to happen to her without little Eloise around to take care of her. Yep. Darn shame 'fya-ask me. Folks just don't love one another like they used to."

"I gotta go. Nice talkin to you ma'am." He smiled at her politely as he grabbed his coffee and headed for the door.

She just waved politely as he left, and Brent decided that maybe he should start his work at the coroner's office. He had a friend who could get him in there and at the cemetery, and the time had certainly arrived to find out just what was going on in that town.

In such a small rural area, it surely wouldn't be so easy for the assailant to keep finding detached young women to attack. There had to be a catch, or a pattern somewhere and Brent considered it his duty to uncover it.

II.

Alyssa came downstairs in her white cotton shorts and a red T-shirt feeling unsure of herself as always, and worse because Brent had gone before she woke.

As she lighted at the foot of the stairs, voices floated through the living room from the patio. Her aunt Edna engaged in a social chatter, but Lyssie could not make out the voice of the visitor.

Wandering out to the kitchen, she ignored for the moment that she had heard anything and began searching for Brent.

Maybe he had seen that they had company and slipped out to his truck to keep her from looking like an easy woman.

She tiptoed out the back door, sneaking quietly to the barn, but only Carlos bade her welcome.

Sighing heavily, she patted the bull on the nose before heading out toward the woods to see if he was in the truck. She cursed the heavy mud from the rain the night before as it darkened the exterior of her favorite white canvas sneakers. She finally got to the general area that Brent had pointed to.

"Fresh track." She whispered sadly as she squatted down to place her finger in the muddy tire track. She sighed again, and headed back toward the farmhouse with her head down.

"Serves me right." She muttered. "my own fault for letting my guard down in the first place".

She'd known that man was trouble the first time she laid eyes on him, but if he was trouble... she must thrive on it. She refused to give up hope just yet.

He might have been feeling a bond with the boogey man again and in that event, she would just give him some room to breathe.

Moving through the kitchen, she heard the voices again, this time heightened from that of idle chatter to mild shouting. After washing her hands and scuffing her feet on the welcome mat, Lyssie slid silently up to the patio doors. As she passed the overstuffed white couch, she nearly grimaced at the blue rug. Making a mental note to have that thing cleaned as soon as possible, she peeked through the crack between the white embroidered lace curtains.

She could see her aunt crocheting some green and red yarn and nodding as she rocked in her big whicker rocker and to the left of her aunt, on the other side of the porch, she could see Janet Price wailing into a handkerchief.

Lyssie's breath caught in her throat. No wonder Brent had snuck out.

She wondered how long Mrs. Price had been there, when her aunt raised her head and caught sight of her standing in the shadows peeking through the curtains like some sort of sneak thief.

Alyssa didn't waste a moment throwing the doors open with a broad smile and shouting:

"Good Morning all!"

Evidently, Mrs. Price had not known of Alyssa's presence, because she nearly jumped out of her seat at the sight of her pouncing into the morning sunshine like that.

"I'm sorry Mrs. Price. Did I startle you?" she chirped, positioning herself in the patio chair next to a round glass table, and directly between the two women.

"No." Janet snipped, watching Alyssa closely.

Pouring herself a tiny glass of lemonade from the pitcher situated on the table, Lyssie leaned back in the chair trying to put on an aloof air. She crossed one leg over the other, smiling sweetly as she took a bite of the sugar cookies assembled strategically on a platter next to the lemonade.

Noting the fact that her aunt regarded the mud on her shoe with a smirk, Lyssie bore little doubt that her aunt knew more than she would have liked.

She sat up straight, pushing her feet under her chair and used her hands in a wide gesture to keep Janet Price from noticing.

"Isn't it a beautiful morning?" She asked stretching her arms wide.

"Yes. Isn't it?" Janet answered looking curiously at Alyssa.

Lyssie choked back the cookie and stared quietly at the two older women waiting for the questions to come, praying she would say the right thing.

Though still unsure what the shouting had been about, she could tell that it had something to do with her. The fact that Janet Price sat there eyeballing her like she had three heads, meant it also had something to do with Brent.

Alyssa pushed out her proud chin, tossed her head back, and prepared for the onslaught.

■■■

III.

Brent walked with his friend Bubba in the graveyard quietly for a time, letting this new sixth sense work for itself. In doing this, he missed some of the prattle about Bubba's mama and the son that his "ex-ole'-lady" never let him see.

A blanket of blackness consumed his mind, as he waited for the invisible force to scribble white chalk onto it, but all he found was emptiness.

"Are you alright man?" Bubba seemed perplexed by the idea that someone might get bored with a conversation that encompassed marital spats and monster truck races.

Brent looked up at his tall friend.

"I'm fine. Why?"

"You look like you just saw a ghost."

"No. That at least would be something. I didn't see anything or *feel* anything... just nothing."

"Man." Bubba looked at him funny. "What in the world is the matter with you?"

"Nuthin' alright?" Brent gave an exasperated grunt.

"Are we ever gonna get to the grave of the last victim, or are we just wandering aimlessly around the graveyard?"

Bubba stopped in his tracks, took a long hard look at his buddy and pointed to the hill where a tall white angel monument stood.

"She's up there, right next to the angel."

Brent nodded and started walking up toward the fresh upturned earth, when he discovered that Bubba did not follow.

"You comin?"

Bubba shook his head sadly.

"I can't. If you'd seen that one when they brought her in…" He shook his head incredulously, too wound up in the memory for the moment to even speak about it. "It's too hard for me. I've been here for lots of things, but nuthin' like *that* one."

Brent let an apologetic frown tilt the lines of his face downward.

"Gotcha. I'll be down in a minute."

The familiar smell of that wicked breeze moved over Brent as he topped the hill and stood perfectly still, trying to will it to stop... but he couldn't. The vile thing rushed around him, coursed right through him.

Something pushed itself into his mind, refusing to let him fight the darkness inside of him.

Falling helplessly to his knees, dirt crunched tightly in his fists.

He conceived that his hands clutched at the damp earth, but his brain could not refrain from the action. Brent... was blind. The smell of rich soil permeated his senses and, in this state, though his sight had been stolen by some unseen force, his other senses heightened.

Only darkness existed around him. Screams refused to come. He found himself running through a wood, familiar trees, familiar surroundings... something off balance in nature. Evil breathed foul breath into the very soil on which he ran.

Instantly, he stood in the alley from his first dream. A young woman sauntered down the street. A sense of idleness dictated her steps and she was not afraid. Passing beneath him, she whistled to herself... sounds like... "It's a Small World". Smiles moved through the hatred for a moment, then the scream, the blood.

Then, watching her float away on a river of blackness, a spiraling descent pulled him down and he found himself sitting in front of the grave of a stranger.

Brent rose to stand before the fresh upturned ground, wiping the tears from his face with the back of his hand. Having not let go of the mud in his grasp as yet, dirt smeared his cheek. He flung the earthy mass down onto the grave and retracted a sob as he thought of his Gram's grave looking just like this the day of her funeral.

Bubba's voice broke through his thoughts from the foot of the hill as he shouted something. Brent turned to face him.

"What?" He shouted down at Bubba.

"Not that one. The other side." He yelled pointing to the covered grave on the other side of the angel monument.

Turning to his left, Brent faced the direction Bubba had suggested, and saw that this resting place was also new... it just had fresh sod thrown over it. Cautiously, he made his way over to the other grave, thinking he would have another horrid experience, but he didn't.

The stench of the sickening breeze that usually accompanied these macabre images still lingered, but this time, no image invaded his mind: only the feeling that he had felt in his dream the other night.

Resentment festered inside of him to say the least, but at this point he'd begun to realize that these hateful notions and killing desires were not his. They had superimposed themselves upon him through the mind of a lunatic, and Brent decided that maybe he should get out of there before he had another vision.

As he passed the other grave, he looked at it curiously before walking down to Bubba. His friend waited, chewing at the nubby tip of a fingernail.

Walking up to him with tearstains streaked across his face in dirt, Brent asked what he knew he must.

"Is that the grave of the girl who was killed only last night?" He'd asked hoping that it was, but knowing somehow that it wasn't. People who were killed the way that young lady had been killed didn't get buried the next day.

"Nope. That one was a drowning victim they pulled out of the lake last week. She was so blue and puffy, they couldn't even identify the body."

"Call it what you will." Brent droned in a deep steady voice, "But the girl buried under that mound of dirt up there... did *not* drown."

Brent turned away from Bubba, walking toward the funeral home. His buddy kept a steady stride next to him.

As they went inside Bubba turned to him inquisitively. " There's a woman in your life, ain't there Brent?"

"What makes you say that?" he wondered if maybe he had the word "sucker" tattooed on his forehead or something.

"Because you're I' weird in your old age, man. That's a sure sign of a settled guy." They both laughed as they went inside.

IV.

"Lyssie." Edna smiled politely. "What time did Brent go home last night?"

Alyssa thought the question through carefully before answering.

"I don't know what time he left." She responded in truth. Janet raised a skeptical eyebrow at Alyssa, and she readily got defensive.

"Why?"

"Another girl was killed last night." Janet blurted out as her knuckles whitened over the book she held in her hand. "Brent's bed hasn't been slept in and your aunt tells me he was here rather late. Please." Janet begged with saddened eyes. "If he's here, let me know he's safe."

Alyssa felt cornered and her temperature began rising. It could be a dangerous thing to back down a wild cat and Lyssie was no exception to that rule.

"Oh calm down Janet." Edna snapped at the risk of sounding too firm. She had seen Alyssa in this sort of temper before, and it was never pretty for the other person. "What time was the girl murdered?"

"They're calling it between midnight and one in the morning" Janet sobbed again into her handkerchief leaving the old battered book exposed on her lap.

Alyssa's eyes flashed over the title of the book before Janet could cover it.

"Well then it couldn't possibly have been your son who did it, Janet. I distinctly heard Lyssie and Brent arguing at one o'clock this morning." Enda cast a smug smile at her niece, who returned it, gradually.

Janet looked at Alyssa as if to ask '*is it true?*'

"I'm afraid that's the truth." Lyssie supplied. "He wanted to leave, but I felt that it was too late for him to be out on the road. I think what my aunt heard, was our argument about whether or not he should go. I gave him the guest room and went to sleep."

Another truth. Alyssa was pleased with herself. She was getting good at this.

"Well. Just so that you're aware," Janet drawled in her thickest southern accent. "Brent has a series of problems stemming from his childhood, and we have to worry about him a lot. You just wouldn't believe what I went through with him the other day."

Alyssa wanted to slap the woman for insinuating there was anything the matter with her son, but controlled herself as Janet squeezed again at the book.

"Brent's not the stable doctor type dear. He's not at all what he seems. I mean I love him, he's my son, but he has problems and I don't expect you to understand but..."

Lyssie had heard enough.

"That's right." She snapped before regaining her social composure. "He's your son and you love him, and that's all I need to understand. That's *all*." She reiterated stamping her feet to the floor of the porch.

"Now Lyssie." Edna headed her off. "Give Janet a chance to explain why she worries. After all... he *is* her son."

Alyssa nodded and plumped back into her chair, waiting to listen to Janet's paranoid delusions about Brent. As Janet relived the experience with Doctor Taylor the other day, she listened only partially as she was too busy thinking about being in Brent's arms again.

When Mrs. Price finished, brief silence ensued.

Edna put down her knitting and looked right at Lyssie. She could see how this conversation might make her niece uncomfortable, but she didn't want her associating with a man who might have homicidal tendencies either.

"Lyssie. I think maybe you and Dr. Price should stay away from each other until he's been able to work out his problem a little better." She had been unprepared for her aunt's disapproval and sat gaping as Janet offered further explanation.

"Yes dear, it would be in the better interest of both of you if Brent checks in to the hospital for a few weeks to get well."

"Well?!" Alyssa glared as she stood up and began shouting.

Edna had seen this coming and had tried to prevent it, but seeing that there was nothing else she could do, she put her eyes back to her crocheting and let her niece speak her mind. No use trying to stop her now. That would only have made matters worse.

"The only *sick* people around here are the two of *you*!" Lyssie shouted slinging her arms around and pacing like a caged animal.

"Brent doesn't need to get well... he needs a vacation! From *you*!" She shouted glaring down her imperial nose at Janet Price. Alyssa knew the advantage of standing taller than your adversary and she used it to its full advantage standing as straight and as tall as she could.

"Brent is the most stable, most good-hearted person I have ever met and in *my* business, I meet a lot of people, Mrs. Price. Your son has so much love to give. If someone would just take the time to tap the well, they might have a lifetime of happiness with him." Alyssa's voice softened when she spoke of Brent, as if the very thought of him smoothed her rough edges and made all her dreams come true.

"He's not a killer. Killers don't have enough love and respect for life to become doctors."

"Doctor Kelvorkian..." Janet began.

"How can you put your own son in a category with someone like that?" Alyssa was kinder now taking Janet's hand in hers as she knelt in front of her.

"Listen to me. I know he may act a little funny from time to time, we all do... if you don't believe me ask my well-intended aunt over there. I'm sure she has a lot of strange stories about me too."

Janet seemed unconvinced, but Alyssa's reference to her aunt brought a brief smile to the older woman.

"You have to know what you're capable of in your own heart, before you can understand Brent's. I know you're a warm, caring, intelligent, understanding person, because I know your son... and he's just like *you*. So, take a little credit for the work you did in raising him right, and let him be whomever he has to be. He's not a killer. You *know* that. I know that, and one day Aunt Edna will know it." She added shooting a smart look in the general direction of her aunt. She got up, having seen what she wanted to see on the face of the book and went back to her chair.

"Mrs. Price. I hope this won't upset you, but I think I'm in love with Brent and I hope he feels the same way about me. If *I* trust him... why can't you?"

"I don't know." Janet blubbered as she laid the book in the chair and got up to go to the bathroom. Alyssa took a deep breath, having aired herself out, when Janet stopped short in the doorway.

"How long have you been standing there, young man?!" She shouted.

"Long enough mother." Came the deep reply.

Lyssie's heart pounded around her body so fast she felt faint!

'*Oh my God*!' she thought. '*What if he doesn't feel that way and he heard me making an ass of myself*?!'

Her aunt jerked her chin in the direction of the door, first seeing Brent push past his mother, and then she looked at Lyssie as the man stomped toward her.

Alyssa's face was almost purple as she held her breath and Edna took the opportunity to offer and help Janet.

"Go to the *bathroom*?" Janet blurted as Edna pushed her into the living room and slid the doors closed behind her.

"When you're finished, we can make some more lemonade." Edna added through gritted teeth.

Janet looked out at her son looming over Alyssa's chair.

"Oh. Sure. Acourse." She conceded.

The instant they were gone, Brent fell to his knees in front of Lyssie and put his head into her lap.

"It's not me." He wept, as she began stroking his shiny hair.

"Come on now." She soothed. "What are you talking about Brent? What's not you?"

"The killer. My own mother thought it was me... hell until this afternoon, even I thought it was me, but it's not."

"Of course it's not. I checked my mattress tags this morning and they're still there."

Brent broke into robust laughter and before Alyssa knew what hit her, she had him back from his "night world". She smiled as he told her of his trip to the graveyard, worried for him as he told her of the trip in his mind, then she laughed with him when he told her what Bubba had said about the woman in his life.

She only laughed for a moment, realizing that he had heard what she told his mother and while he seemed happy to be there with her, he had not as yet returned her confession.

"What is it?" Brent asked, rising to his knees at her feet. She'd stopped smiling and laughing. Sadness spilled over her features.

"Probably nothing." She forced a polite grin. "So, what do you want to do?"

He knew she was talking about his brush with the paranormal, but he couldn't keep his feelings bottled up any more. In the short time he had shared with her, he'd learned that life was a precious thing and that he had been wasting his.

He wanted to live, love and cherish every minute of the rest of his life and could think of no one else he would rather do that with.

The murderous peril in his life remained trivial compared to the way she made him feel, and his addiction to her drove madness to the farthest reaches of his mind. With her, life made sense at last.

He had lived his life hiding his feelings, rarely expressing them and *never* sharing them, but he had been born anew with her. He would keep it that way as long as she would have him.

Though still unsure if it was the rush of the new sensations he experienced, or if because he had already fallen to his knees in front of her, those scary words drifted past his lips without a thread of remorse to stop them.

"I love you... and I'm going to marry you."

"What?" Alyssa's excitement peaked so high, that she thought she heard the words because she had always hoped to hear them.

"I said I Love you Alyssa Johnson... and I am going to marry you. Or something to that effect." He added.

Under any other circumstance she would have merely arched an eyebrow and said something like '*Really?*' in her usual sarcastic tone, but *not* now... not with him. She would never dream of giving him the chance to change his mind. Throwing her arms around his neck with tears in her eyes, she whispered: "I love you too! And yes… you *are* going to marry me! Like it or not."

Their embrace only tightened as Edna and Janet came out into the sunlight with the lemonade. They stood frozen, staring at the young people.

They half thought Alyssa and Brent would jump away from one another when they saw them coming, but the fact that they continued hugging, prompted Edna to clear her throat.

"I know y'all are there." Brent smiled holding Lyssie closer than ever. "And you had better get used to these public displays of affection because it's commonplace for a man to hug his wife."

Janet dropped the pitcher of lemonade and the glass splintered across the white wooden planks of the porch.

Brent got up to help his mother clean up the mess, chastising her with his eyes from time to time, and Edna ran over to hug Alyssa and breathe words into her ear.

"I hope you know what you're doin' girl."

Alyssa smiled, batted back some happy tears, and snuffed back:

"I've never been surer of XXXnything' in my whole life."

This response was good enough for Edna, who was so busy wiping the tears from her eyes, that she didn't notice Alyssa hiding a book beneath her blouse… the very book that Janet had left behind.

V.

(One month, and two murders later.)

Lyssie stood on the front porch with her aunt, the two of them watching Brent pack the last of Alyssa's things into the bed of his truck. Edna's eyes were tearing up as she looked at her niece.

"How did your boss take the news of you quittin'?"

Alyssa chuckled.

"He didn't take it, I'm just doing the book work via internet." They both laugh to themselves.

Edna looked at Lyssie seriously nodding toward the truck where Brent now sat in the driver's seat listening to the radio.

"You know what they're saying about him don't ya?"

Lyssie nodded looking down at her feet as they nervously scuffed about in a small pile dirt that Atilla had left behind on the porch.

"And you know what will be said about you moving in before y'all are actually married."

Alyssa chuckled again as she slid her hands into her back pockets.

"Yeah. I know. The police were out there last weekend because that idiot friend of his told on him for snooping after the bodies. I believe him Aunt Edna. As crazy as it sounds, I believe him."

"He still dreamin'?" Edna asked, raising her hand against the glare of the morning sun, and squinting to see Lyssie's expression.

She nodded, stifling her tirade for the moment.

"He's known every time, Aunt Edna. Every time."

"Then why are you *doin'* this?" Her aunt protested in a gentle thin voice.

"Because when I rose from my bed this morning, the sky had darkened. I stood at the window leaving emptiness in the bed behind me. And suddenly, a sunbeam drove into my heart, and he was the handsomest thing I'd ever seen. I knew I had to love him, Aunt Edna... like I have never loved before.

"Ever since I was a little girl, I wanted one thing, and that was to keep my mama's love alive, but I couldn't. There was nothing in me that understood that sort of love... and now, now that I know what it is, I don't ever want to part with it.

"I have never been more comfortable in my own skin than I am right now. All I know is that we belong together, and I'll do whatever I have to do to see that it stays that way."

"No matter the price?"

"No matter the cost." She replied with deliberateness.

Edna smiled warmly as a trickle ran down her face, and she hugged her niece tightly.

"I love you, kiddo." She whispered with a sob. "Don't be a fool in love Lyssie, love a man for love's sake, not for the sake of company... and if you know what you have is right, then God be with ya hunny."

"Thank you, Aunt Edna." She replied, pecking her aunt's cheek with a sad kiss. "I love you too."

Alyssa drifted slowly toward the truck, wrapped in her insecurity and guilt for questioning Brent. But then, he looked up from his reading in the front seat and smiled at her, the sun glinting off his sunglasses as he took them off, and every worry, doubt or fear she had ever had about anything, disappeared like a child's nightmare. Lyssie was finally alive.

End of Chapter Nine

Chapter Ten: The Chase Begins

I.

Alyssa stood on the back porch staring out at the pasture where the cows had been earlier. Brent had gone inside to clean up before they left for town. They had decided to eat out, so that she could turn in the report her boss needed.

Sighing a bit, she sipped hot tea and thought about the little book she'd confiscated from Janet.

She read it from cover to cover. She'd laughed, she'd cried... and *now*, she needed to tell Brent about it.

She didn't *mean* to pry, but he had been so secretive about his grandmother that when she saw the title "My Diary" on the little book, she somehow knew in an instant who it had once belonged to. She *had* to get to know her better if she ever hoped to understand Brent. One thing was for sure... his grandmother's acorn not only fell a long way from Janet's tree, it down right skipped his mother's generation altogether and Brent was nothing like her.

Gazing after the sinking sun, her heart went with it. She dreaded telling him that she'd done something behind his back so early in their relationship, but secrets of any kind only stood to complicate matters. And Brent had chosen to keep that chapter of his life closed to her.

It was his fault, really.

She didn't have a choice if she wanted to learn anything about him, because he would never tell anything on his own. Moving in hadn't provided any great revelation. He had a Ham Radio set up in the basement and a CB station in the front room that he loved tinkering with, but other than that... he was just Brent.

She'd heard his stories about childhood. They weren't much. Most of them were from the time he was ten on up... from the time that his mother began ushering him off to shrinks and specialists of all kinds. Brent would tell her one of his childhood experiences, then silence would follow. If he did wish to tell her more, he hid it from her.

Maybe she could find some other way to bring that part of his life out. Maybe if she found something from her own childhood that was similar to something he did with his grandmother, he would be inclined to share his memories. Maybe once he had opened up that part of his heart to her, he wouldn't care so much that she had read the book.

Her head was so muddled she could hardly get her ideas straight, and it started pounding.

Maybe time would present a better moment to tell him. She'd wait. The opportunity was bound to present itself, and that way she didn't have to feel like a back stabber about it. Lyssie took another sip of her drink then, with her eyes lifting from the teacup, she thought she could just make out a forest-darkened shadow that almost resembled a man running from behind one tree to the other on the edge of the woods.

Her eyes followed the darting figure for a moment and just as she thought it would bolt again, Brent came up behind her and asked if she was ready to go.

Alyssa jumped half off the back porch at the sound of his thunderous voice, and Brent nearly fell over trying to catch her so that she didn't tumble over the edge of the railing.

"Oh my Gawd!" She drawled in an accent so southern that he almost didn't recognize it.

"Don't *do* that to me!" She slapped at him as she jumped off of the porch to pick up the teacup that so carelessly sprang out of her hand.

Brent grinned as she turned around with the cup in her possession.

"You don't really hear that accent until you're upset. Do ya?"

"Ha ha ha." She mouthed as she came up the steps into his embrace. "Yore a fine one to talk. You sound like a damn yankee."

"Sorry." He grinned kissing her on top of her head. "Big city college can take the country right out of ya. I didn't mean to spook you. You looked like you were daydreaming or something and I didn't want to break in, but it is getting late and you know how far it is to town."

Alyssa took a deep breath after he kissed her and she looked up into his beautiful eyes, smiling.

"Yore forgiven... just don't do that anymore. I don't care if you have to stomp everywhere you walk and wear a cow bell to let me know yore coming, just make sure I know it."

Brent chuckled and made a cross over his heart with his finger. "Promise."

II.

Gnarled red tufts of hair caught in the branch of a small whispering tree as he gazed at his "lovely" from the distant security of the forest. He almost wished he hadn't moved because the instant that he did so, his hair had been caught and he had to struggle to free it. His movement had gotten the immediate attention of the "lovely" standing on her porch like he had seen her do so often before.

He had to get away! He couldn't let her see him.

Not until he was ready to be seen; ready to bare himself in all his freakish size and splendor beneath the light of a pale moon.

He would make her beg him to take her. He would please her so much she would want to fuck him like no one else had...then he could kill her for doing this to him. He snarled through a scraggly grin as he made his way through the trees, making it impossible for lovely's eyes to keep up with him. Suddenly, he stopped, ducking behind a tree. As he peeked from behind the trunk of oak, he could see a man! How dare that man touch his lovely! He would make him pay for touching her. She was *his* now. No one had a right to go anywhere near her!

He would get young buck, but in his time. He wanted "*lovely*" first... then to make right with the young bastard for getting in the way.

He smiled, gazing down at the green canvas duffle bag dangling from his grasp behind him. It kicked and pushed, but it couldn't get out.

He smiled a devilish smile thinking what he would do to her...but first to go where he knew his "lovely" would be... and he would take the canvas bag's car.

Yes.

That was the way.

He wanted *Lovely* to see what painful pleasures he could give her. This would be the way!

III.

Brent and Alyssa headed down the old mountain road in Brent's truck. As they quietly listened to some soft rock music, neither of them spoke for a long while. Finally, as they neared town Brent broke the monotony of the silence. His voice tinkled softly in Lyssie's ears, but she didn't hear him. Her mind was with the shape in the forest.

"*So.*" He said louder, clearing his throat. He grinned, when she jumped. "What was it about?"

"What was *what* about?"

"Your daydream. *Hello.*" He giggled reminding her. "The one... you know on the back porch earlier when I scared you."

"I don't know." She replied monotone. "Did you lock the house up?" She asked earnestly dismissing his charm.

"Yes. What's with the sudden change of subject? You don't know something I *don't*... do ya?"

"No." She lied, not wanting to upset him over what may have been her imagination in the first place. "It's just that most folks up our way don't bother to batten down, and that's how bad guys get in."

"Expecting company?" He questioned cutely.

"No." She replied. "I've just had a lot on my mind lately, and wondered. That's all."

Brent knew when a line like that was really meant to say '*Mind your own business*', so he didn't pry. He had been crazy to assume that she hadn't other things to do and think about in the first place.

"Sorry. I guess I just wasn't thinking. Anyway. What kind of food would you like to eat?"

"Oh. Uh... I don't know. I know I have never tried a food I didn't like so I'll just follow you."

Brent smiled comfortably as they headed into the last corner into town.

■■■

Alyssa's boss was genuinely glad to see her. Not only because she had his books done and he was two weeks late getting them to the accountant, (Frawley despised computers or *any* technology and refused to do his bookkeeping online), but also because he knew she had moved in with a man who had been the only possible suspect in the recent murders.

Though a short, fat, bald-headed man, Frank Frawley had always treated her more like a daughter than an employee, and he worried.

When Brent walked by them on his way to the bathroom, Frawley snuffed his nose at Brent and went on hugging Alyssa.

"So?" He began once Brent was out of ear-shot.

"How *is* old Blue Beard?"

"Not funny, Frawley. He's wonderful. He'd *have* to be to put up with me, wouldn't he?"

Frawley had to concur on that account, but gave her a stiff warning to behave herself and to be careful.

Taking up her arm, Frawley began walking her through the kitchen, introducing her to a few new employees as they passed, then he took her to the office to get some of his computer disks and bookkeeping paraphernalia.

■■

Brent had finished using the bathroom.

He stood at the sink washing his hands and face. It had gotten awfully warm over the last couple of minutes, and the heat pricked at his skin.

Splashing cool water onto his face, he lifted his head to look in the mirror.

Autumn was coming.

The weather looked nice out as he tip-toed to peer from the roll out window above the sink, and there seemed no reason for the sudden heat flash. In the back of his mind, he knew what pressed at his consciousness but refused to admit it right away.

"No point in leaping to conclusions." He muttered.

The air conditioning vent appeared to be working as Brent fluxed his fingers in the draft coming from the ceiling. He closed his eyes tightly against an impending headache, and began to smell that thick sickening scent.

He opened his eyes, thinking to look into the mirror, but found himself staring at Alyssa from behind a man's back!

Brent dashed blindly out into the restaurant shouting:

"*Lyssie! Lyssie!*"

The people dining turned a curious eye at him. He stood there with water splashed on his face and shirt, which was only half tucked in, and a bewildered look on his face. His horrible cry, so filled with anguish, terrified the patrons.

Scanning the room in desperation for the person he sought, Brent's fear seized his heart.

He turned his gaze from this face to that hoping at any minute one of them would belong to Alyssa. Finally, she came running from the kitchen with the books and things in her hands, and stopped short at the sight and sound of him screaming for her.

"*What* already?!" She shouted, embarrassed nearly to tears. "What's wrong?"

Brent's facial expression changed immediately from fear and desolation to complete happiness and awe. He ran to her and wrapped her in his arms whispering over and over again:

"Oh thank God you're all right. Oh thank God!"

"Brent." She answered into his shirt. "If I don't get some air I'll smother, and then I *won't* be okay." He turned her loose for a second, then realizing that the danger might not be gone, he started pulling her toward the door.

"We have to go." He blurted suddenly.

"But I haven't said goodbye to Frawley yet..."

"Text him later. I haven't got time for that now, let's go." He answered through gritted teeth as he pulled her along.

Alyssa dug her heels into the floor and pulled him back.

"*Brent*!" She shouted. Half the customers in the restaurant were standing at this point watching the spectacle.

"What's *wrong* with you?!"

"I don't have time to explain, Lyssie. He's here!"

Alyssa didn't have to ask who, because she could think of nothing else that Brent would be this upset about.

"See ya Frawley!" She shouted as she jetted past Brent and out the front door to the truck. Brent fumbled with his keys and Alyssa did a little dance next to the driver's side door.

No way would she chance going to the passenger side where somebody might jump out of the shadows and grab her.

"Come on Brent let's go!" She yelled. "Jesus this is like one of those crazy teenage horror movies!"

He finally got the right key, unlocked the door to his truck and they hopped in, him nearly knocking her into the other seat trying to hurry and get in. He didn't waste a moment stepping on the gas and getting them out of there.

■■

Shortly thereafter, having obtained KFC drive through food to eat on the way home, Brent began to explain what had happened at the restaurant, and Alyssa's skin was immediately covered in goose flesh.

"You know what makes the whole thing so scary?" Alyssa asked.

"What?" He asked taking a big bite from a drumstick.

"While my boss was XXXigging' through the drawers of his desk, I thought I saw a rustle in the curtains behind him."

"Curtains?" Brent asked trying to remember something as he placed the drumstick back in the box and wiped his hands on his jeans.

"Black curtains?" He remembered peering from darkness.

"Yes." Alyssa was really afraid now. "How did you know that, Brent?"

"There was someone in there with him." Brent slammed on the breaks and spun the truck around to head back into town.

"Brent!" Alyssa shouted nearly spilling her drink into the floor, being held in herself only by the safety belt. "What are you doing?"

"He wasn't after *you*!" He shouted back at her, causing a tiny vein to pop up on his forehead. "There was someone with him. I could feel the terror!"

"Brent. If *one* Boogeyman is bad enough how are we to handle more than one of them!"

"Weren't you listening?!" He screamed at her, scarcely capable of breathing as he could visualize the killer pinching this woman until she bruised.

Alyssa shrunk back into the farther corner of the seat. She had never seen him like this, and she didn't know if she could stand it.

"There was a woman in there with him. He has already done some things to her, because I could feel *his* pleasure and *her* anguish. If we hurry, we might keep her alive. It's highly unlikely he would kill her in the back of the office like that with all of that commotion I made."

Alyssa sat up, finally understanding him. She reached into the glove box, pulled out Brent's pistol and began loading it.

She cast only a single nervous glance over at him before putting the gun into her lap and lifting the speaking portion of the C.B.

She radioed police and the two of them, being closer to the restaurant, knew they had to take it upon themselves to put a stop to this heinous murderer.

Brent squawled tires as the truck slid sideways into the parking lot of the restaurant. The customers who had been there when he came the first time stood up and asked for their checks, while the others just sat and stared with distant curiosity.

Frawley ran to the entrance with both arms out trying to keep them from passing, but Brent cast him aside like a rag doll as he made his way back toward the office.

Alyssa was close behind, stopping only to show Frawley the gun she had hidden beneath her jean jacket before continuing to follow Brent to the back office.

Frawley ran after them clamoring like a clumsy child and when they reached the office, everything fell silent.

Alyssa stood with the gun poised at the curtain, and Brent snatched it open to find that there was nothing in there but a small pool of blood.

"Oh my Gawd!" Alyssa screamed. "Frawley call for an ambulance. Brent and I will split up and see what we can find."

She was cut short by a scream, immediately interrupted by a loud thud.

"He's out back!" Brent shouted.

"Frawley!" He nodded to the elder man. "*Keep her here!*"

Brent pushed Lyssie onto him as he snatched the gun from her. Frawley immediately grabbed her up into his massive arms.

Brent ran from the office as fast as his feet could carry him, while Lyssie struggled to break free of Frawley's grip. She *had* to go with Brent.

What if something happened to him?

She finally managed to kick her boss heavily on the shin, (her trademark death move), and ran for the back door.

As the door flung open to reveal the night-darkened street, Alyssa had to force herself not to vomit with the rancid smell of blood that permeated the alleyway. She covered her mouth and nose with her hand, and stepped into the darkness in time to hear two shots.

Her eyes jerked to where the shots came from and she saw Brent running with the gun drawn after some monstrously huge man, now no more than a silhouette against the dark. This hulking figure dropped what might have been a child's plaything, (had it been any smaller), then he rounded the corner and slunk away into the night.

Lyssie could barely see Brent as he ran, but she could see him lose all of his fervor as he slid to his knees in front of the body that the thing had dropped.

Brent screamed.

"*No!*" he cried, clinching his fists to his chest, and then let his head droop in defeat as he began sobbing.

Alyssa started toward him, but his head snapped back up before she could get to him. He shook a bit at the figure on the ground. Brent's shadowed head turned toward Lyssie in the dark, and she heard him shout.

"*Hurry and help me... she's still alive!*"

Her heart soared as she ran to kneel beside her future husband. She looked at the streetlight just barely reaching far enough to light his face, and then back to his gently shaded features. No doubt existed in her at that moment. Brent not only *wasn't* the killer, having a love of all life and being *incapable* of doing it, but more importantly... this was the man that destiny ordained her to marry.

Everything Brent told her to do, she did diligently and without question.

She lifted the poor girl's blood-soaked head, trying to be extra careful when removing the ball gag from her mouth.

"Can you help me get her inside?" he asked softly as he lifted the woman's limp body from the ground.

Lyssie dropped the ball to the ground, wincing at the loud crack it made hitting the pavement.

"What should I do?" She questioned, realizing then that he had the lady in his arms already.

"Just get the doors for me and make sure Frawley clears his desk to make room. It's the only place I can think of to put her down without risking injury to either one of us."

"Okay." Alyssa replied. She took great strides to the door and made haste getting to the other doors ahead of him.

For all the woman's obvious size, (she looked fairly heavy to Lyssie), the adrenaline coursing through her fiancé helped him moved without missing a step.

As they entered the office, her boss was just hanging up the phone when he saw them coming.

"Ambulance is on the way." He blurted, shocked by what he saw.

Raking the clutter from the desk, Lyssie and the old man just managed to get out of the way as Brent gingerly placed the girl's body on top of it.

▪▪

The hospital was in the next county, so it would be at least an hour before a rescue team would arrive, but Bubba was a certified paramedic and, hearing Frawley on the CB… he'd come almost immediately. As a skilled veterinarian, Brent had dressed many of the wounds before he arrived.

They had already radioed the Sheriff so after a while, Brent and Alyssa gave statements and were allowed to leave.

The woman never regained consciousness while they were there and Brent doubted that she ever would. The possibility of a brain hemorrhage was the likeliest diagnosis and he'd be pleasantly surprised if she even made it through the night.

Struggling with the mental pressure of his thoughts and adrenalin, Brent squeezed his temples and took a deep breath. The girl he had tried to save tonight had been someone who had worked with his wife to be. This *must* be harder for Alyssa than for him, even if she did take it well. She'd offered to drive home because the event had taken so much out of him, but he wouldn't let her.

Though adrenaline still sped through him, she seemed peaceful enough to go to sleep... and she did so on the way home.

End of Chapter Ten

Chapter Eleven: Curiosity and Doubt

"Sure thing boss. Keep me posted." Alyssa said, glancing at the clock on the wall. "Me too. Bye."

As she clicked the "close" button on her cell, she sat down at the kitchen table, picked up the new spreadsheet for the restaurant and took a sip from her ceramic mug.

Alyssa smiled as she swallowed her hot chocolate. Randy's shrill bark could be heard from outside and she knew the two of them would soon be playing together. Tiptoeing to the back door, she peeked out and watched them. When they'd first gone out it had still been dark, but the sun now kissed the dew-covered grass and she could finally watch him on one of his morning details.

Brent stood next to a large stack of freshly split firewood neatly rowed and about 4 feet high. He placed a log onto a large tree stump and let the ax drop onto it with a loud "CRACK"!

Randy barked, hopping playfully and Brent stood up, stretching the kinks out of his back. He was wearing his white undershirt, his blue-checkered button-down hanging from his back pocket. Brent slipped the undershirt off over his head and wiped his brow on it. Alyssa was reminded of one of her favorite movies from her teenaged geekdom and started giggling.

"This is too good to pass up." She said out loud.

Knocking on the window to get his attention, she put on her best Alan Rickman swagger and mimicked the line that had come to mind when he took that top off.

"I see you managed to get your shirt off!"

Not missing a beat, Brent mimicked a line from one his favorite childhood movies right back at her. He stood up and pointed his finger at her like a little boy and said; "And you *LIKED* it!"

He did that so well, Lyssie immediately shot back with another quote from the same film.

"You're *killing* me Smalls!"

Brent busted out laughing and that got Randy worked up. The collie started bounding around and the two of them were off on one of their morning adventures.

Lyssie sighed dreamily. "Some job." She giggled watching him jump into a pile of freshly raked leaves with the dog following after him. Brent would run one way and the minute Randy caught up to him, he'd jump around and run the opposite way. The dog barked, the leaves trickled down from the trees in burnished orange and gold, Brent giggled like a child and a warm maternal feeling swept over Alyssa.

"I bet this is how you were as a boy." She grinned, knowing full well that she had brought some happiness into his life that he had never experienced. Warm satisfaction wafted over her again, as she wandered back to the kitchen table and sat down. Pulling the tablet to her and opening the ledger, she daydreamed over her work... thinking.

Brent would make a wonderful father someday. She couldn't have prayed to be any luckier than she had been in finding him.

He had wanted to marry her the very day he asked her to, but Alyssa had always wanted a December wedding: to be married in white and silver while the new snow was falling outside. That would be perfect. They had set the date for the first day of winter. Being that they lived in Georgia the odds of it snowing that early in the winter were pretty slim, but the wedding was in the mountains so she could hope.

"We'll just have to make do." She murmured glancing briefly over the names on the company employee list. Lyssie shivered happily thinking about it. They were to be married in the church where they had argued for the second time.

She chuckled quietly to herself. They hadn't done a whole lot of arguing since then. They had been so busy loving each other that there hadn't been time to disagree about much.

Her face fell a little. Her mother had been the most loving person in the whole wide world, but it didn't save her from the car accident that claimed both of Alyssa's parents when she was very young.

She'd recently found herself keeping her mother's memory vivid by wishing she could have been alive to help her plan her wedding... to accept Brent as a son she never got to have.

Alyssa tried very hard not to cry. A tight knot formed in her throat. Her eyes burned with the need to weep and her head throbbed from the exertion of restraint. She had been so involved in thought that she didn't really hear Brent come in.

Randy sped past the table to his dog bowl, always placed neatly in front of the pantry. Brent dropped the ax by the door and hung his overshirt on the small coca cola rack by the back door.

"Hey!" He chirped as he pecked her on the cheek and went straight to the refrigerator. He took out the half-gallon jug of milk and spun the lid off as he was about to drink some straight from the container.

Then he noticed Alyssa appeared to be unhappy. He promptly reached into the old cherry wood cabinet to take down a tall glass. Pouring out his milk, Brent replaced the jug and took a deep, long drink. He then looked at Alyssa half expecting praise for doing as he should have done anyhow, but he found that she still looked as she had before. Realizing that this wasn't about him drinking from the carton of milk, he looked at her cautiously. There was definitely something wrong.

"Did you call Frawley this morning?" He asked trying to stay safe instead of drawing out an argument.

Alyssa nodded, keeping her eyes on her work as he came and sat down in a chair at the table.

"What did he say?"

"Not much." Alyssa kept looking downward. "He wanted to see that I didn't forget I have to keep these books."

"I meant..." Brent sighed. "Did he say anything about last night?" Alyssa looked up now that she had her tear ducts under control.

"He said that the girl you rescued last night is stabilizing in ICU at the county hospital. They expect her to get her own room today."

"We ought to go down there." Brent said with growing excitement. "She may lead us to the killer!"

Alyssa shook her head sadly.

"If she comes out of this alive, she isn't likely to function as a normal person. She's gonna be quite some time recovering and it won't even do the police any good to try to talk to her for few months. She might not ever recover."

"It may not help the police, but it might help me just to be around her. You know, because of this link I have with the guy..."

"Please don't start that again Brent!" She snapped.

He sighed.

"Always the skeptic. How do you explain last night then?"

"I don't." She answered. "I consider it a boon that we saved Betty Jean from possible death, but I don't call it a cosmic link, or some psychic good fortune."

"Certain death, Alyssa. Make no mistake about that... and I don't care *what* you call it, it's there and I consider it my responsibility to stop it from happening again."

Alyssa sprang from her chair to begin pacing.

"You don't know that he wasn't trying to take her wallet ...or..."

"Alyssa, he had already been torturing that woman for at least an hour, and he hoped to kill her." Brent looked at her as she paced and fidgeted. This went deeper than his inside glance of a mindless killer; there was something else. Brent thought for a moment.

'*Of course!*' he thought. He had read about people who seemed calm in a crisis and then lose it a day or two afterward because they had not exerted a healthy reaction to what had happened. Alyssa had known that girl.

Maybe she was trying to rationalize this so much because she couldn't dare to think of the possibilities involved. Maybe she felt like it had been her fault in some silly way.

"I'm sorry if I seem insensitive, Lyssie." He soothed, using her pet name. He used that when he needed her to cooperate, or to relax. Sometimes, he just used the name "Lyssie" because it suited her sweet childlike nature so well.

"If you don't want to go visit the woman, we don't have to. I keep forgetting that you knew her."

Alyssa turned a glare on Brent. How dare he blame their discussion on her feelings for a woman that she hardly knew!

"I knew her *name*, Brent... and her face. I know she's single and has no dependents or relatives because she is on my employee list. I helped her with her taxes last year... but personally knowing her, no. That's not what this is about!" By this time, she was almost shouting.

Brent's mind reeled from the effects of the new information she spat out like venom. Maybe there was a pattern after all. These women didn't have children. The third or fourth one had a husband, but no children. Brent refused to let his curiosity get the better of him and run the risk of fueling her fire even more. He looked at her squarely and asked what he knew he must.

"Then what *is* this all about?"

Alyssa let out an exasperated sigh. She didn't remember what she was mad about right off hand. She thought for a moment, and her chin quivered.

"This is about losing you. You know how badly it could cost you if the police misinterpret your intentions like they did after that third girl got killed. I've never seen so many police cars in my whole life!" She was sniffling back a few tears. "I've lost everyone I ever loved but Aunt Edna and I don't want to lose you too! Why can't you let the police just handle this thing?!" Brent got directly out of his chair and held her close to him.

"It's okay, Lyssie." He soothed. He hated to see her like this even if it *was* nice to know she wasn't made of iron after all. "I'm sorry. It's gonna take me a little time to get used to considering anyone other than myself. I promise to try harder. Now." He smiled taking her little chin between his thumb and forefinger while kissing her on the nose. "For one thing; you know you haven't lost everyone but Edna. You have your Carlos..."

Brent started thinking. He hugged her again and then asked her:

"Hey? Why don't we bring Carlos out here? I mean he'd have *you*, and he'd have companionship. There's an awful lot of lady cows out there that ain't seen a man in I don't *know* how long."

Alyssa laughed a little.

"Would you like that?" he asked.

She nodded and then, as Brent started for the phone to call Aunt Edna, Alyssa asked:

"That's the for one thing ... what's the for *two* thing?"

Brent turned a sweet casual smile to her.

"*I'm* not going anywhere. You could bet your last penny on that."

****

Edna had been truly glad to see them, and Lyssie agreed to spend the night with her aunt, to visit. Brent secretly suspected that Edna didn't trust him and wanted to prod her niece in privacy, so he was more than gracious about their request.

Besides, he had every intention of making a trip to the hospital in the next county. Stopping off at the house, he fed Randy, locked up and headed off for the long ride.

The sun cast its perishing pleas at the sky by the time he reached the hospital, and visiting hours were nearly over. A mild sense of hunger pulled at his stomach, but he had to ignore it. He'd eat at a restaurant on the way home. Pushing through the emergency room doors, Brent rushed to the counter, quickly asking the surprised clerk for directions to Betty Jean Jones's room.

The door of the elevator opened and he stepped inside. Pressing his finger on the appropriate button, he began trying to clear his mind.

He'd found over the past months that when he did this, he could usually pick up on the killer. Of course, this did not always work, as he could rarely pick up on anything unless there was some emotion involved, strong ones… like when he was thinking about killing, and especially when he *was* killing. They'd never lasted long enough, however to get a fix on who the killer was or what he intended to do next. Relaxing music piped into the carriage, but his mind never truly left Alyssa. Unrest began to settle over him.

She seemed as if she had been hiding something from him since the very day he asked her to be his wife. He refused to question her about it though, because he feared she might leave him.

This was particularly true if it turned out that she had only been experiencing cold feet or pre-wedding jitters. Then she'd be angry enough with his assumption that there'd be no controlling her.

Brent chuckled to himself with that thought. Lyssie was not to be controlled anyway. It just wasn't in her. In his heart, he could see her as some sort of wild thing, too beautiful to be tamed, and only truly gorgeous in her own habitat… bossing everyone else around.

Maybe it was his imagination too. After the crazy things that had been happening to him, he couldn't dare rule that out.

The elevator jostled him a bit as it came to a halt. The entry doors once again parted and he stepped into the hall on the fifth floor.

Reading the sign that greeted each passenger as they stepped onto the floor, shock ran through his body. Had he pushed the right button in choosing this level of the hospital?

Turning to peek inside the elevator door, his hand caught it trying to close on him. Fifth floor. Yes. He was supposed to be on this floor. Shrugging, he walked down the hall. Disney Baby wallpaper and soft pastel colors greeted him from every direction as he made his way toward Ms. Jones's room and away from the sign that read: "*Maternity.*"

****

Alyssa sat on Edna's elegant couch, sipping warm tea and listening to her aunt give quilting instructions to one of her friends on the phone in the kitchen. Lyssie chuckled to herself. She couldn't understand why Edna never got a cell phone. She persisted in remaining a relic of the "pre-technological era".

The elder woman quickly finished the conversation and came back to sit on the couch next to Lyssie.

"How's livin' in sin treatin' ya?"

115

Alyssa grimaced at the sound of those words.

"Oh Aunt Edna. Don't start. Please? I know I'm doing the right thing. I love him and I want to be with him the rest of my life. Why can't everyone understand that?"

"What do you mean "everyone"? I thought I was the only thorn in your side." Lyssie stood up and straightened out her cream-colored slacks, and stretched until her back popped.

"No." She groaned. "Brent's mother has become a bit prickly since I moved in. She is always looking at me funny and catching me when Brent's out on a call somewhere, telling me to get out now while there's still time."

Alyssa motioned her pointer finger around in a circle while making a goofy face as if to say that Janet Price was completely insane.

Edna didn't smile.

"You know what everyone thinks about him. They think he's the one. You know that don't you?"

"Not anymore!" Lyssie snapped at her aunt. "He rescued Betty Jean Jones last night from certain death." Alyssa thought how Brent had used those same words on her that morning, and had to refrain from smiling.

"And the word in town, is that he has to have an accomplice." Edna interrupted before she could sing his praises any further.

"What?" Alyssa asked, facing her aunt.

"If you think about it. It makes perfect sense. The manner of brutality in the short length of time, would certainly be more probable if there were two of them, or a group of them doing this for ritualistic reasons."

Alyssa sucked in a gasp. How could Aunt Edna buy into all that?

"That's not possible Aunt Edna. I was with him last night. He *couldn't* have been in on that!"

"Oh NO? And it doesn't strike you as unusual that this incident occurred at the *one* place among many that you just happened to be going last night?"

Alyssa started to object, but Edna held up a hand.

"I'm not trying to hurt you. I want him to be as innocent as a newborn babe because I happen to like him, but I want you to be on your guard if you insist in this." Edna sighed. "You know, smarter women than you have wound up dead because the person they chose in life was only a little smarter than they were.

"*Think* Lyssie." She urged. "What better way to win your confidence than a show of gallantry like last night?"

Alyssa did not attempt an answer. She didn't dare to think of Brent as some sort of sick, twisted person who committed such unspeakable things.

"You said yourself that he goes out on call from time to time. You don't really know he's going out to take care of animals."

"Yes I do." She retorted before thinking.

"No, you don't." Edna replied. "Have you ever gone along?"

"No." Lyssie answered. "But he always asks me if I'd like to go."

"Unless you've gone, then you don't know."

"Aunt Edna. This is getting... almost silly. How could Brent pay the bills if he wasn't making any money? He has to go on calls to make money."

"You don't know that he has any bills, Lyssie. A lot of your older farms like the Price Old Southern run on generators, have cellar furnaces, and wells. His grandmother left him quite a lot of money too. It wouldn't be difficult to pull this off."

Alyssa had been standing as she listened to this, and found herself a little light headed. She had to sit back down, but she sat across from her aunt instead of sharing the same space with her.

"I won't even consider this Aunt Edna."

"Fine. But I should remind you that the Bible says to be sure of all things. So, see that you *do*. That's good advice in any century." Edna still longed to give Lyssie some sort of saving grace.

"Okay. So have you ever seen his pay stubs... or maybe a bank statement?"

Alyssa shook her head, stunned.

"Brent said he doesn't believe in banks. He claims that he likes to know where his money is all of the time."

Edna tried to be understanding and patted her niece on the knee, but ultimately couldn't let it go.

"What about *your* pay?" Edna asked with one eyebrow up. "Has he been getting that too?"

"Oh that's right. Let's just crucify his ass why we're at it!"

"Lyssie! You watch your mouth young lady!"

"I will not!" She shouted back at her aunt. "Ass *ass* **ASS**!" She yelled at the top of her lungs, while springing from the couch and jumping up and down like a four-year-old.

"I still manage my own bank account, *and* my own money. We aren't married yet Aunt Edna, and I wouldn't dream of handing my hard-earned finances over to any man I haven't known more than a few months! I am not a child!" She added stamping her right foot.

"Ok." Edna answered in calm even tones. "Then where does he keep his money at?"

"What?" The calm question threw her completely for a loop.

"You said he likes to know where his money is ... do *you* know where it is?"

"No. And I don't care where it is either. I've learned what it is to love a person for all or nuthin, and I refuse to let it go over money, or bad gossip. This gossip isn't even entertainin' any more for Gawd sake."

"Lyssie." Her aunt interjected quietly. "Calm down. I just want to make sure that you understand what everyone else sees. Sometimes, when we love someone, we're just too close to the trees to see the forest. I don't want it to burn down, because you didn't see the flames. I love you."

"I love you too." She sniffed. "But I like being closer to the trees. I enjoy experiencing each new aspect of the whole as it arrives. Studying it, learning it and loving it. I'll brave the darkest regions of it, knowing in my heart, that I can conquer any dangers as they arise. Now if you'll excuse me, Aunt Edna." She bowed sarcastically. "And if you don't *mind*, I'm going to the bathroom, and when I get back I'd like you to take me home."

Enda looked tired and disillusioned, and seemed diminished in some way to Alyssa.

"No need of me goin' out this time of night. You can take the wagon. I've recently had it serviced, and it has a full tank of gas. Good night. The keys are hanging by the back door."

Alyssa felt as if a part of her died forever as she watched her aging aunt ascend the stairs, but she had to remind herself that she had promised all or nothing and she was going to stick to it ... forever.

End of Chapter Eleven

Chapter Twelve: Goldilocks and Bubba Bear

Disinfectants and astringents permeated the air as Brent entered the woman's room. Wiping tiny vaporous tears on the sleeve of his brown suede jacket before approaching the bedside, he looked down at her face.

Youth and innocence showed in her rounded features.

"Early twenties at best." He murmured to himself.

Obviously, she'd been pregnant before falling prey to the attack, or she wouldn't be in the maternity ward. He wondered if she had been looking forward to having her baby and then had lost that hope, or if she was just in a bad situation to start with.

His features softened as he looked down at her. She looked more to be sleeping than in any sort of coma. Though her face was bruised and cut in some places, the wounds would heal with minimal scarring if any at all. It was a shame that the inner wounds would never heal.

He thought about her hair. Obviously, hair color hadn't been a factor. There had been a red-head, a couple of blonds and a few brunettes.

Using his first two fingers, he smoothed some of the blond hair back from her brow, saying how pretty she was. As his tender touch swept across her brow, a faint smile tickled Betty Jean's lips, followed by a dreaming sigh. A slight grin touched him as well.

Closing his eyes, he hoped he might learn something of her attack that he had missed... something that only she could know. No matter how much he wanted to get a vision of a killer however, he only got sweet images of this woman holding an unseen child and cooing softly to it. Apparently, Brent couldn't draw visions from the living and he was glad of it.

He had subconsciously picked up her hand seeking some unseen horror, and still squeezed it snugly when a nurse came into the room. She stopped at the door and caught her breath as she approached the bedside.

"Are you the father?" The nurse asked the question in a pleasing enough way, but he could tell by the tone of her voice that she masked something awful with her professionalism.

"No." He answered frankly turning to face the woman who now stood beside him. "Just a concerned friend. Why? She lose the baby, did she?" He hoped that by adding his concern he could flush some information out of the nurse, and he got lucky.

"No." She answered happily as she bustled to the other side of the bed. Here, she began adjusting the wrap on the girl's upper arm and then started moving a tray around with clear, liqiud goodies to put into the IV. "The baby is doing just fine."

Brent watched this busy little woman with growing interest, as she seemed more than happy to chatter now that she established him as a friend of Betty Jean's.

"I only hope that this sweet child lives to see her beautiful baby grow up."

"Is it a boy or a girl?" He asked casually trying to flash a big white boyish grin.

The nurse smiled so bright at his interest, that her face made the hair line on her wealth of tightly curled, gray tresses scoot back a touch.

"It's a fine baby boy Mr... Mr..."

"Price." He grinned at her.

She was well into her fifties, but soft laugh lines that creased the pretty caramel color of her skin, and sparkling brown eyes disguised much of her age.

"Well Mr. Price, you'll be glad to know that your friend has stabilized nicely, and should be up and around in a few weeks."

"Weeks?" Brent repeated to be sure he heard her correctly.

"That's right." She cast a motherly smile down at Ms. Jones. "She regained consciousness last night for just a few moments, and she knows she has a brand-new baby. The baby is a preemie, but as a relatively large seven-monther, he's gonna be just fine."

"Well if she's all right, why did you say you only hoped she would live to see the baby grow up?"

"Because." She replied in a hushed tone, coming closer to Brent and checking to make sure they were alone.

"I believe that the man who did this was that monster who's been torturing and killing young women around here lately."

"Is that right?" he pretended surprise. Evidently there was some kind of cover up going on and the police had not told anyone that

Betty Jean survived. That would explain why there hadn't been any mention of the event in the paper.

'*Still*', he thought... 'it wouldn't be so hard to keep a secret from a neighboring county. Most likely the police didn't want the neighbors involved just yet.'

"Yes." She continued lowering her voice as a patient walked by with her family.

"The police say it was a jealous boyfriend incident or something, but this girl talks in her sleep, and you wouldn't believe the horrors she talks about. I keep looking over my shoulder thinking he might come back for her.

"I've decided to put in a little over time looking in on her until we can find some sort of family. Say!" She smiled up at Brent. "You're her friend. Could you contact her family?"

"I just met her a couple of weeks ago, so I don't know much about her... or her family, I'm afraid. I just heard about her incident today when I went to her table at the restaurant for lunch."

Frowning, he released the girl's hand and continued his conversation.

"One of her friends told me she was here, and I came as soon as I could. So, you think this has something to do with those women they found who had been attacked?" He was fishing. He wondered how much this girl knew.

"Shhh!" She whispered putting a finger to her lips.

"You didn't get that from me. It's bad enough I have to worry that there's some sort of Boogey man hunting this woman, but I don't need you telling people I told you so. They're liable to fire me for something like that."

Brent nodded politely and pretended to be zipping his lip.

The nurse smiled and took up his arm...

"Would you like to see the baby?" He didn't dare refuse as she began chattering, and leading him from the room.

"I sure would!" he chuckled.

"You know what?" She started as they left the room and headed for the baby window.

"What?"

"I wish I could shake the hand of the man who saved that woman and this baby, and tell him how special I think he is… what a wonderful thing he did."

"I'm sure he knows somehow." Brent's smile was such that the woman soon forgot what she had been talking about. She chattered with him about babies and families and so forth, and pretty soon, he forgot why he had come in the first place. He was just glad he had decided to come at all.

****

Aunt Edna's wagon screeched to a halt in the front yard of the old house and Alyssa got out, slamming the car door behind her with both hands.

"Ridiculous Bullshit!" She yelled as the door slammed.

Stomping all the way to the front door, she stopped to dig in her front pocket for the keys. Then the thought occurred to her that Brent wasn't home, and the door was locked.

"Brent's not home?" she mumbled.

The thought banged at her skull, crashing her thoughts to a thunderous stop.

She had stormed out on her aunt with the hope of coming home to get some hugs and reassurances that everything would be okay, and clearly, it wasn't.

"Where the hell *are* you Brent Price?" She muttered, stepping from under the porch to look up at the windows of the house. All of the lights were out except one... the attic.

"Great" She complained. "He's been playing in the attic."

Stamping back up the stairs, her Aunt Edna's advice pounded her brain...

'Be sure of all things.'

She grumbled, again cursing her own sensibilities. For the first time, she seriously contemplated his motives in wooing her, in hunting the boogey man, and it scared her to death.

In the dark of the house, her fingers flailed sightlessly for a moment, then flicked on the light switch before she entered. With a sigh of relief, she walked into the front room to find it unoccupied.

"*Whew.*" She whispered collecting a deep breath as she dropped the car keys onto the table next to the CB base station. Randy wagged his tail at her from beneath the table, but seemed too busy sleeping to do more than that. Alyssa sat down for a moment to shake the cobwebs from her head. Maybe seeing *wasn't* believing. Maybe half the battle was being able to see only because she believed in Brent.

'But then would I only be seeing what he wants me to see?' She wondered silently.

Clearing her tired mind, she thought for a moment... about everything.

122

He had asked her to be his wife, his partner in life, and she had accepted.

That meant they would be honest with each other, tell each other as much as memory would permit, or they didn't really know each other at all. She tried to think what she knew, what she *really* knew about Brent. After a few moments, she deduced that she didn't know anything... except that she loved him.

She thought about all of the stupid young girls who worked with her at the Restaurant. She considered how she constantly found herself marveling at why it was, that every single one but them could see their boyfriend was a loser.

"Too close to the trees to see the forest." She uttered under her breath.

Maybe Aunt Edna had been right.

Lyssie wasn't about to take any chances at being an idiot. She wouldn't stoop to doing anything behind Brent's back any more either. It seemed that there had been a lot of that going around lately between them... like tonight for instance. She didn't like it.

Alyssa got up from the recliner and started up the stairs to bed. She would talk to Brent in the morning if he decided to come home. Reaching the top of the stairs, she turned in the direction of the bedroom, when she thought about that attic light being on.

'*What if he has dead bodies hanging in there?*' she thought to herself.

Then sucking at her teeth in disgust with her own childishness...

'*Then I would have smelled something by now. Good Grief.*'

She made a mental note to really get even with Aunt Edna for this before it was over with; poisoning her mind with crazy talk.

She pulled the chain and let down the attic stairs, being careful to step back as the ladder came down to hang in front of her.

She tugged at it, but it stuck and she had to hang on it in order for it to even budge. When it did, she nearly fell backwards. Taking off her jean jacket, she wiped the dust off the ladder with it before starting into the attic. Arriving at the top of the stair, she found the lack of dust surprising for a place that was supposedly uninhabited.

Before she actually surveyed the surroundings, she patted her hands on her jeans and tugged some spider webs out of her hair.

"Gross." She complained, pulling an ugly face. The attic might have been clean, but it had obviously been a while since Brent visited.

'*How long has this light been on?*' she pondered.

The window was open too, and cold air was coming in.

Lyssie carefully picked her way around the old furniture and closed the window to the autumn night. Patting at her arms to ease the chill, she looked around at the attic, and found herself in a place that had a time and space all of its own. Its old-fashioned, "sitting room" furniture, with antique do-dads placed here and there gave it an almost "*lived-in*" look. If it weren't for the coat of dust on the less used items, she might have wondered who Brent was keeping up there.

Off to one corner, pictures hung on the wall and she proceeded toward them, checking the boards before she went. The instant her eyes beheld Brent's grandmother she knew her.

It didn't have any dust on it though, which meant that Brent had been coming up there to dust it... probably why the light was on. He must have forgotten to cut it off.

Looking back toward the table where the old-fashioned lamp cast eerie light, which danced on the windowpane, she shuddered.

Thinking again of her mother, she looked back at the picture of Brent's grandmother.

His grandmother had been a very pretty older woman. Her hair had been white in this picture, but Alyssa knew beyond doubt, that it had been red in her younger days. In fact, if her eyes had been a little larger, (and her nose a little longer), she could have been Lyssie twenty years from now. She stepped back with the very thought touching her mind.

Did Brent only love her because she reminded him if his grandma?

"Oh pish-posh!" She scolded herself with one of her aunt's favorite expressions.

She flattered herself. To her mind, she and this woman hadn't been cut from the same fabric. Lyssie thought herself no beauty queen, but Grandma Price obviously *had* been at one time. She glanced off to one corner, and saw a trunk lying open on the floor. Slowly she made her way to it and bent down to have a better look. Sitting on her knees with her back to the exit, Alyssa found some old photographs of Brent and his grandmother, when he was still a baby.

She knew those pictures were of Brent, because the shape of his face, the twinkle in his eyes, and the curve of his smile hadn't changed in all of those years. Lyssie decided to make herself comfortable. She liked looking at old pictures and besides, Brent was obviously off ... stealing candy from babies and stuff... she grinned.

She couldn't believe she had let her aunt's crazy talk scared her like that.

Sitting Indian style in front of the trunk, she began pulling out the old pictures and small trinkets so that she could examine the contents of the trunk a little closer. She'd lain the jewelry and what-nots aside so that she could see inside it a little better.

"Nothing." She mumbled as if she had been digging for buried treasure.

She flipped through the old photos, never having felt more like an outsider than she did just now, and she decided to put everything back. Brent would bring her here and show her these things, when he was prepared to do so. She had been wrong not to believe in him, and even more wrong to rifle through his personal things.

Standing up to stretch, she accidentally pushed the trunk forward a bit with her foot and beneath it, she noticed that the floorboards squeaked loose.

She kneeled, pushing the trunk off of the boards and the farther the trunk scooted, the more she came to realize that this compartment had been hidden for some time.

Alyssa lifted a couple of the floorboards, wondering if Brent even knew about them being loose or not, and she found beneath them, a tall, round hatbox.

She shook the box by the ribbon that bound it before moving it, just in case some sort of crawling creature were living in it.

"Probably some moth-eaten old hat." She whispered to reassure herself. The truth was, the first sight of it made her innards squirm for no good reason. It was just a hat box. She loosened the bow and snatched the lid off.

Papers. It was filled with paper. She picked up the yellowed pages that looked, judging from the brown edges and the smoky smell, like they had been rescued from a fire. The handwriting was exquisite, and each letter had been signed... "*Always with love, Hans*".

These weren't addressed to Brent's grand-mother, but as Alyssa took the love letters out, reading them and placing them to one side, she began to realize by the descriptions of each sentiment that they were in fact for her. As the box slowly emptied, she began to see another photograph at the bottom of the box.

This photograph appeared to be different from the others there in the attic. It looked as if it had been taken by a professional photographer, and Brent's grandmother looked like she had posed for it.

Alyssa removed the papers, gently set them aside, and took the old picture from the box. She held it up so that the light would touch it, and she could see it better.

Brent's Grandmother sat on the back porch of Brent's house in that old rocking chair, with a baby in her arms. She had her head held high, and smiled in an odd sort of way... as if she was so lit up with love that she glowed from within. Alyssa traced around Grandma Price's face with her forefinger.

"*Exquisite.*" She whispered in awe.

The picture had been badly colored at a later date, but the true beauty of its subject was not likely to be changed even by poor photography.

Alyssa sat looking at that picture as if spellbound by its oddity, and then whispered...

"*Wow.*"

****

Brent stood looking at the baby whose life he had a part in saving, and was very satisfied with himself at the moment. Maybe they were going to stop the killing soon after all. For now, though, he had to get back.

He didn't want Alyssa to call and not be able to reach him. If she tried the cell phone, she wouldn't be able to get him. It had stopped working the minute he stepped through the hospital doors earlier, and though he had composed a text to see how she was doing, it was still queued, waiting for signal.

He had sent her to her aunt's house hoping to steal this opportunity to see the woman they had teamed up to rescue and in his heart, he wished that she had come with him. It might have cheered her up, as she had been acting quite different lately. He wouldn't have left her at home to come this far away, as he had worried about the killer.

That fiend still lurked in the shadows of their world, and he didn't dare leave Lyssie alone. It had given him a piece of mind indeed, that she had wanted to be with her aunt for a while. With Atilla the wolf around, there was little chance of that monster getting anywhere *near* the Biggmann Ranch.

Passing by the nurse's station on his way to the elevators, he gave his contact information to the friendly nurse. He also left instructions to call him if Betty Jean came to, or if anything out of the ordinary went wrong.

****

He had gone quite a way when he started having those scary visions again. They were brief little blue and green flashes this time, nothing concrete yet.

Brent worried that they would come some time while he drove and he might wreck, but he didn't want to pull over just yet, either. He didn't exactly embrace the idea of sitting in the dark, on the side of the road while he was having a terrible flash like the ones he got when the killing machine was loose again. He had found recently, that the flashes he got when he was actually awake were brief, and rarely involving enough to make heads or tails of... it was the sleeping visions that disturbed him, and yet showed him the most. Memories of those dreams racked his body with shudders, just thinking of them.

He often doubted that this man was even human because of the twisted things he was doing to these poor innocent women.

Soon, anxiety rose within him that he couldn't explain: something warm and safe, begging him not to do what he had to do. The monster was worried about treading on these grounds, and something in him was off.

Brent got flashes of a hardwood floor: something warm and fuzzy tickled his tummy. Were these *his* feelings... or the monster's?

Usually the killer's feelings were so clear and concise... must kill woman to kill all. Those were his usual feelings. The delight usually came during, or after the killing.

This was something else... something that felt like inviting sunshine in a world of shadows: something soft, and gentle. It was pleasing to touch... to see... to feel... to feel dying...

This was more like it.

Brent pulled off onto the side of the road, removing the seat belt just long enough to lock the doors. He had to concentrate on clearing his mind in order to get any sort of bearing on where the killer was, and what he was doing.

The flashers blinked against the night, and he closed his eyes hoping to control the vision, as if by controlling the vision he could somehow control the killer.

He knew it wasn't likely, but he *had* to try.

Ten minutes stood between him and a telephone and this thing could very well be over in five. He'd have to try to do something right then and there, from where he was.

Closing his eyes, the killer's odor permeated Brent's senses as he began honing in on where it was.

Usually the murderer only let him see through his eyes, which meant that somehow Brent was in this man's mind.

Maybe, in theory, he could make this person look around him, make him curious about his surroundings.

Once Brent honed in, he found himself crouching in a shadow, watching a glowing yellow light in a confined place.

Slowly, he concentrated on making the man show where he was. His host was suddenly standing, looking around a small, unusually shaped room. Familiarity echoed in every item of the room but in another way, he recognized nothing.

Someone was coming: invading his sanctuary. They would die for this.

He had been happy.

Someone was breaking the solace of his secret wishes.

Brent suddenly scurried back into the shadows like a rat afraid of being squashed under foot, and as soon as he had gotten settled, a woman stood right in front of him.

Brent stared emptily at the backs of her legs, jeans. He wanted to scream at her to run but he had no voice in this state. Being awake this time, he might not have the opportunity to get any more involved than this.

He sat quietly, hoping he could somehow keep control of the monster. The creature began reaching out with an almost inhuman, mangled looking hand, as if he would grab the woman but she walked over to the far corner of the room and he missed the opportunity.

Her back was to them, but Brent thought she looked familiar. This whole thing was so familiar it scared him.

The woman walked along the wall as if trying to keep from falling into a deep cavern, her arms behind her for balance, her eyes upon the wall. It was odd.

Somehow, in his own mind he knew what the woman was doing, but in the mind of the killer, couldn't seem to understand. Then, as quickly as she had walked over to the wall, he blinked, and she disappeared. He found himself feeling along the floorboards with hardened warped fingers, trying to get to his bare feet.

He rose, freakishly tall and extremely cumbersome at first; as if he were taking a moment to make his body obey.

Slowly, quietly, he walked nearer to the back of a couch. Soon he peered soundlessly over it, at the top of the woman's head.

The creeping, evil longing swept over the monster so fast, that Brent was afraid something terrible would happen before he could interfere.

Remembering that he wanted to help and not be a victim, he forced himself to think of the person who was being stalked, the consequences of hurting them... and the killer paused in a temporary stupor, to shake his head softly.

So quiet was this killing menace to stand right behind the woman, and her not to hear it. Maybe she just wasn't paying any attention. Yes, that was it.

Brent forced curiosity into the mind of the madman. What was the woman doing? He wondered in the hope that the creature would become preoccupied with the curiosity enough to realize that this was a human life he prepared to take.

Brent found the eyes of the murderer averted for a moment over the shoulder of the girl he was stalking. She held a picture between her thumb and forefinger, delicately tracing something with her finger.

The abominable personage went soft and fuzzy again, warm and tingly, and for a brief second, Brent could see clearly without the fuzzy haze around his vision. That was the picture of his Grandmother that he had been looking for!

"Oh - my - God!" Brent screamed sitting upright.

"He's in the house! *Lyssie!*" he screamed fumbling for his cell phone. He speed dialed her but the phone sat quietly with the little wheel of destiny spinning and no connection flashing into view. Apparently, whatever had messed his phone up at the hospital hadn't let go yet. He quickly grabbed the handle of the C.B.

Brent cranked the jeep, and struggled with the C.B in the other hand while he ripped out into the road in a flurry of squalling tires, and flying gravel.

"Breaker Breaker 1 - 4. This is the Doctor is Goldilocks at home?"

No answer.

Brent's jeep tore down the highway at a dangerous speed. He had a lot of time to make up and he didn't expect Lyssie to be alive when he got home. God if he could just get her to hear the C.B. from up there... impossible.

"Come *on*." He urged through gritted teeth.

"Breaker Breaker 1-4 this is the Doctor... Got your ears on Goldilocks?"

Brent's mind raced at the speed of light. For ten minutes he pondered:

'what in the hell was she doing at the house in the first place? She was supposed to be at her Aunt Edna's for the night.'

Maybe she didn't trust him and was looking for an excuse to go through his things. Either way, he couldn't let that stop him now. He hoped like hell that he wouldn't be stopped for speeding. Every second counted just now.

He knew! He would take the old bridge road. Sure, the bridge was old, but he could go that way and cut out the speed deterrent in town as well as cut his thirty-minute trip in half.

He would only have to slow down for the bridge over Toad Bottom Creek, and then he would be free to drive like crazy.

"Breaker Breaker 1-4!" Brent screamed. "Come on Goldilocks ...got your ears on?"

"Breaker Breaker 1-4." Came a reply.

"What's your handle friend?" Brent asked hurriedly.

"It's me... Bubba Bear." Came the reply.

Brent was so happy to hear Bubba's handle that he thought he would split wide open.

"Yeah. Breaker Breaker what's your 20?"

"I'm on my way home. What's up Doc?" His friend chuckled.

"I got a problem. I think Goldilocks is being jumped by the bears over at Doctorville, and I need someone closer than me to get over there to her. Over."

"Bubba Bear is on the way. I been kind of hungry for some huntin', and I got my gun. What's your 20 Doctor? Over."

"Highway 27 turning left toward the old bridge road. How much closer are you than I am? Over."

"I'm in the driveway Doc. Keep your ears on. Copy?"

"That's a copy Bubba Bear. I'm on my way with my ears on."

Brent relaxed for a second, taking a deep breath. Maybe there was some hope now. Maybe Bubba would get there before... before... he didn't dare think about that now. He had to concentrate on getting to Lyssie. His foot went to the floor as he ignored the cramps in his calf, and barreled down the highway toward home.

****

Lyssie looked at that old portrait, smiling. Such a lovely picture: lovely girl. She hugged the thing close to her chest sighing as a chill spread through her. Oh, to be that beautiful ... just *once*.

****

Downstairs, Randy lie in his soft wool lined bed under the C.B. Home Base Station.

He whined in the quiet house and raised his ears to better hear the noise.

Barely audible was the transmission, but to a dog... well, he stood up, his brown eyes peering over the tabletop at the black and silver mechanism. Still whining, he placed his wet nose upon the table knowing he was not allowed to put his face on any surface.

He perked his ears toward the radio. Lyssie's phone was on vibrate and rattled against the desk, Brent's picture showing in the window.

Darting back and forth, his eyes seemed checking to see if anyone had noticed him doing something that he shouldn't. Then he heard a noise from upstairs.

Randy started trotting up there. He stopped at the top of the stairs where he could see the attic door had been lowered. He tipped his nose to the floor for a scent. Lifting his soft Collie ears, he caught the woman's scent. He licked nervously at his chops peering up the ladder into the yellow glow of the attic. Suddenly, another scent caught his nose.

The smell of death.

Randy began to bark as loud as his tonsils would allow. He slapped at the floorboards with his feet. The upper part of his mouth raised so that it looked as if his teeth had grown three inches.

He barked loudly, and the hair on his back stood up like an Arkansas Razorback. He tried to get up the ladder, but the steps were so far apart that his clumsiness caused him to fall several times. He would not give up. Something evil lurked in their home, and Randy would not permit it.

****

Lyssie heard the dog barking, as did the unseen. He heard that foul creature ruining his nightly kill, and darted across the room at the sound of the first whimper.

Alyssa however, not having heard Randy until he barked, saw nothing and knew nothing.

She dropped the portrait, breaking the glass onto the floorboards.

"Darn loud mouth dog." She muttered. "It's okay Randy. It's just me." She called, hoping to calm him down.

The dog stopped barking for a moment, and then resumed the annoying sound to call her out.

"Oh, for crying out loud." She griped sweeping everything back into the hole. She replaced the board as Randy finally got up to her. He licked his lips and stopped barking. His nose dropped down to the floor as Alyssa scooted the trunk over the hidden place she'd found. She looked down at Randy who seemed to be tracking something.

"I'm right here Randy. What's the matter with you?"

The dog completely ignored her, and this frightened her.

"Randy?" She whispered in a wavy voice. "What is it boy?"

The dog looked back at her for a second, and when the killer shifted from one foot to another in the corner, barely audible to Alyssa, but to Randy... he began barking and slobbering on the floor.

Lyssie remained in the dark about the things happening around her, but was too scared of Randy's behavior to try and find out why.

'*Probably just a rat.*' She thought as she made her way to the entrance. She had decided that since Brent left the light on, maybe she'd better do the same.

Slapping playfully at her leg, she called the protective canine.

"Come on Randy. Let's go downstairs and eat something."

Randy still slapped at the floorboards with his feet and bounced backwards, while barking like a wild animal.

His teeth glinted in the yellow light and Alyssa's fear reached heights she never dreamed possible.

'*What does Randy like best?*' she wondered.

At that moment, she heard the sound of a vehicle coming into the driveway.

"Randy." She smiled cunningly, knowing she had to be out of the attic before Brent came in and caught her.

"Daddy's home!"

Randy turned his head toward the window with his ears up like antennae. Darting for the exit, he went sliding down the ladder, spilling himself onto the floor.

Alyssa looked down the ladder at him curiously before following. Randy hit the ground running and headed right down the stairs for the front door.

She looked up the ladder into the attic ruminatively, and then shook her head.

"Crazy dog." She complained as she let the attic door spring closed. Just then, the doorbell rang.

"Oh *now* what?" She fussed, starting down the steps to answer the door.

Randy already stood at the entry with both ears up, and looked to be waiting anxiously for her to come and answer the door. Alyssa nudged the dog away from the door as she looked out the lace curtains. Finding Bubba there was nothing short of shocking, but she was glad just the same after what had just happened upstairs.

She threw the door open with a wide welcoming smile, but Bubba didn't seem interested in small talk.

He reached next to the door, and swiped up Brent's big double barrel shot gun. Alyssa's eyes widened as Bubba put a finger to his lips.

"SHhhhh. Are you in any trouble ma'am?" He whispered.

Alyssa shook her head 'no'. She knew Bubba, but he was acting strange, even for him.

"Anybody been here tonight?"

Alyssa shook her head again.

"What's wrong?" She whispered back.

"Nothing I don't guess. Probably just Brent's over active imagination again." He said reclaiming the right to use his voice.

"Where's yore base station ma'am?"

" My... *what?*"

"Yore C.B?" He added shortly in a sarcastic tone of voice.

Alyssa stepped aside so that he could see it sitting on the table next to her cell, still lit-up from Brent trying to call.

Bubba went straight to the table and checked out the C.B. Adjusting a knob, he picked up the handle to speak into it.

"Breaker breaker 1-4 this is Bubba Bear come on. Got your ears on there doc?"

"Breaker breaker 1-4 this is the doctor. How's nurse Goldilocks holding up?"

Bubba looked curiously over at Alyssa, and then smiled.

"Pretty as a picture doc. Them bears must have bugged out. You want I should have a look? Over."

Brent pondered the question for a second, then decided that he didn't want his friend in any more life-threatening danger than necessary.

"No. That's all right Bubba Bear. Just baby-sit for me till I can get that way."

"Okay. How long you gonna be? Over."

"I'm coming up on Toad Bottom creek now. I reckon I got about ten more minutes. Can you wait that long?"

"10 - 4 Doc. See ya in a few." Bubba put the handle down, and then looked over at Alyssa who nervously tapped her toe on the floor with her arms crossed over her abdomen.

"Got any coffee?" He asked.

"I sure do!" she answered. "I'll trade you some coffee for an explanation of that conversation." She giggled walking past him toward the kitchen.

Bubba walked behind her shaking his head.

"You know ma'am, I don't mean to tell ya yore business, but if yore goin' to be home alone at night, it's not a bad idea to have the volume on the C.B. turned up."

"Hmm?" She asked only half listening as she walked into the kitchen.

She looked immediately to the floor where Randy's dog bowl usually was, and realized that it had been moved about two feet from its regular position. That wouldn't have been quite so unusual under the circumstances, except that the back door was wide open, and the cold air rushed in.

"Not a good idea to leave the doors unlocked neither." He added, closing the door and locking it.

Alyssa couldn't say anything about the door, because she had been in such a foul temper that morning when she left for her aunt Edna's, that she couldn't remember if she locked it or not. She couldn't say anything about the dog bowl either after the way Randy had been acting, but she had an answer about the C.B.

"Brent usually sets the C.B. I haven't messed with it, but I'll be sure to check it from now on. Thank you for the advice."

She had changed her tune with Mr. Bubba. In fact, she so welcomed company right now that he could have been an angry skunk, and she would have detained him.

"Do you take anything in your coffee suh?" She smiled putting on the southern social banter that served her so well in times of trouble. Bubba was taken back by her beauty and kindness, but it didn't take him a second to recover and answer.

"No ma'am. Just plain old instant black coffee if ya don't mind. And please..." He blushed to say it: "Call me Bubba, miss."

"Certainly." She smiled fondly as she patted him on the shoulder. "Have a seat... Bubba, and maybe while I'm making our coffee, you could explain what all of that technical jargon you and Brent were using really meant. I do like a C.B." She rambled politely putting the kettle on the stove, "But I declare! All of those codes, and interesting words are a little much for me."

Bubba liked the idea of something he did being educated and, not noticing that she played him like a stringed instrument, began to unfold all of the technical details involved in using the C.B. radio.

Alyssa had quite a time trying to look interested with the obvious questions plaguing her thoughts, but assumed that Bubba was dim witted enough not to notice that she patronized him.

She knew about C.B.'s.

After a few minutes of C.B. jargon and colorful stories about 18-wheelers, Alyssa's heart lit up at the sound of Brent calling from the front door.

Trying not to appear too anxious, but certain that she did, she got up from her chair and beat a path into the front room. Here, she promptly threw her arms around Brent's neck with an embrace that lingered, and longed for acceptance... where there wasn't any.

Brent pushed her back a little too quickly after hugging her, and went to the doorway where Bubba leaned staring at them.

"Got your gun?" Brent asked hurriedly.

"Got *yore* gun." He quipped showing the weapon. "What the devil for?"

"You'll need it." Bubba turned on his heel and went back into the kitchen and paused a moment to knock back the rest of his coffee and to pet the dog.

Alyssa knew that something was wrong, but not just wrong in the present danger sense, but wrong as in... emotionally off balance all of a sudden.

A cold shiver rushed up her spine as he turned his cold stare to her from the doorway of the kitchen. The light filtered around him like a ghostly glow.

"What is it?"

"Back door locked?" His voice drilled the room like a blank order rather than a loving worry. Alyssa nodded, feeling the guilt of her actions, but not understanding Brent's behavior.

"Stay here." He told her, pointing to the floor in front of him. "We'll be right back." He said as he stood with one foot on the bottom step looking up toward the attic with a hand on the banister.

Bubba rounded the corner from the kitchen and stopped short behind Brent long enough to get a good long look at Alyssa.

He thought what a lovely creature she was, and how he pitied her. He had known Brent most of his life and, while he didn't know what she had done to make Brent mad, he worried for her. No one had a temper like his buddy's, and the coldness in his voice said that she was in way deeper than she knew... or than Brent knew for that matter.

Bubba let his head droop down a bit, and shook it sadly.

"What are you shaking your head about Bubba? If you don't want to go up with me dammit just say so but don't stand there shaking your head at me like an idiot!"

Bubba looked up at Brent, wonder clouding his mind, and then looked back to the lovely woman who stood alone, tearful and shivering in the threshold of the kitchen. He lifted his eyes to meet Brent's, and for the first time in his life, he wasn't afraid.

"I'm goin. I'm *goin*." He griped as he pushed past Brent.

If they had been boys, that might have sparked an argument, but they were grown now, and there wasn't any more fear between them... they had each come to know their limits with one another, and they each respected the other for them.

As they went, Lyssie could tell that there was some sort of knowing disappearing up those stairs with that cumbersome red-neck, and at the moment would have given her eye teeth to find out what it was that caused him to stare at her like that.

****

Brent glared over at her as Bubba pushed past him.

"Not a *sound*." He grumbled as he went up the stairs.

Once they got into the attic, Brent went straight to the corner where the thing had crouched, waiting to catch Alyssa. He shivered with the thought only for a moment before he remembered how mad he was with her.

She had no business snooping through his things like that and... why would that thing be in here anyway... *in* his attic for God's sake?

It just raised too many questions.

Had he led the thing to Alyssa?

No.

Surely not! He would have felt it, or known it somehow.

Alyssa had taken that creature quite by surprise, just as she had Brent for that matter.

He chuckled a little thinking how guilty she had just looked when he snapped at her. He hadn't treated his friend very well either.

"Window's open man." Bubba said leaning his two hundred and fifty pounds out the open window.

"Careful there!" Brent shouted before he realized he was shouting. He didn't dare tell Bubba why he was really worried about the window being open. What if the monster was still there?

"Those old boards aren't too sturdy," He regained his composure "and I'd sure hate for you to fall from there."

"Tell me about it." Bubba breathed as he brought his body back in the window. "Break every bone in the old body falling from up here."

Brent turned toward that obscure corner and looked down into the darkness that had once hidden him inside the mind of a madman. A shiver passed through him as Bubba's hand pressed against his shoulder.

"Take it easy on yourself man. You got one fine lady downstairs. She likes to let on that she don't know nuthin to make folks feel smarter, but she's got to be one of the nicest and *smartest* people I ever met. Don't hurt much that she's purdy neither."

Brent chuckled as he shook his head and turned around to look at his well-intended friend.

He started to tell him everything, but then he changed his mind.

"Thanks for coming Bubba. I'm really glad you were out there for me."

"Anytime." Bubba answered politely knowing his speech hadn't done anybody any good. He started down the steps, and Brent caught his arm up.

"Wait."

"Yeah?" Bubba waited for a confession, or an apology, but it didn't come.

Brent let his mouth drop open as if he wanted to say something important... something necessary and valuable, but all he could think of was...

"Drive careful."

Bubba's brow furrowed as he shook his shoulder away from Brent's grasp.

"Yeah sure, man." He started to turn and go down the stairs but decided to speak his peace. Brent had been living in a quiet sort of secret all of his life, just on the border of telling Bubba all about it, but never actually imparting anything to him. Bubba had been holding on to a boyhood hope that his friend could be brought back after the death if his grandmother... but clearly, he couldn't.

"You know. I thought you changed. I guess maybe you didn't." Bubba skulked out with nothing more than a tip of his cap to Alyssa as he disappeared into the night.

****

Alyssa stood holding the door open, staring after that old beat up Ford truck as it creaked and groaned down the red dirt driveway. She just knew that her life would never be the same after that night.

Fighting back the tears she couldn't understand, she turned around just in time to see Brent stomping off into the kitchen where he would no doubt put his gun back on the rack.

He kept them above the window over the sink, so he could easily shoot anything that threatened to enter the barn. In truth, the only reason it had been at the front door for Bubba to find in the first place, was because Brent thought he'd heard something a few nights before and forgot to put it up.

Listening to Brent slamming things around in the kitchen, Lyssie looked at Randy who now cowered on the other side of the couch and she was sort of afraid to talk to Brent about what had just happened.

But, being the fighter that she was, there was never a better time than the present to meet up with a challenge, no matter how grim.

"What's wrong?" She asked clearly before even entering the kitchen.

"Nothing." Brent answered shortly reaching into the door of the refrigerator and pulling out a beer.

Alyssa couldn't stand the thought of living with her guilt about that diary any more, and refused to let him hide anything else from her either. It was time for them to tighten their relationship up, or why be together at all?

"That's a boldfaced lie."

"I thought there was someone in the house so I did what I hadda do." He answered, slipping out of his jacket and hanging it in the Coke peg on the wall, just over the old ax.

Alyssa studied his features, knowing all along that something else troubled him and that by admitting the truth, he couldn't be accused of lying. He hid something from her just now, and she determined to get it out of him.

"Oh, you're not foolin' anybody."

Brent turned on her immediately upon hearing the words his mother had so often used against him.

"I don't have to fool *any*body. I'm a grown man!"

His rage mounted as he threw the beer in the sink and started toward her.

Alyssa didn't know why she had no fear of Brent, she just didn't know how to be afraid of him. She defiantly upturned her nose as she tossed that soft strawberry-colored hair over one shoulder and waited for the onslaught.

Brent had been taking life way too seriously for way too long, and everyone needed the opportunity to explode once in a while. His time had come.

"I'm not trying to *fool* anyone either. I'm just trying to understand what *you're* hiding from *me*." Brent retaliated.

Alyssa's breath caught in her throat for a second, but she dared not let the guilt keep her from pulling the skeleton's out of their closets forever. They were going to either be starting with a clean slate before dawn, or ending it all right now.

Brent caught the hint of recognition in her eyes, but he didn't act on it. She had done it to him again... making him so mad he couldn't think straight, and he had to get control of his temper.

"Alyssa." He grumbled, his tone somewhat diminished. "I just don't think this is going to work anymore. You're trying too hard to keep some secret from me, and this relationship can't bear it. Your whole character changed when you moved in here.

"There just doesn't seem to be any common ground between us like before. Something had to give sooner or later, and I'm afraid it's going to be me."

He gazed softly at her, and then tried to clarify his meaning.

"I've never been the strongest person in the world. I guess that's what it is that attracted me to you from the start: your strength, determination and devotion to the creature you loved. Those are stronger qualities than I have ever possessed and I confess, I had hoped they would rub off on me. But a zebra can't change its stripes, and I can't deny what I am."

"You mean you won't deny bein' a damn chicken-shit." She smarted.

Brent chuckled a little though his heart shattered inside him. He didn't know what he'd been thinking when he asked her to marry him so soon. It would only bring him grief in the long run and he knew it, because he was too secretive and insecure, himself.

It shouldn't have bothered him that Alyssa had some secrets of her own, but it did.

Dammit... it *did* bother him!

He had no right to be placing the blame on her and he knew it, but it was the only way out.

Maybe by running her off he could get his life back in order... just him and his cows.

That encounter tonight confirmed his feeling that Alyssa was too close to his heart. He would never stop this maniac if he continually baby-sat her.

He regretted ever having that thought the moment he looked up at her big green eyes watering with tears. His heart knotted at the sign of her pain, but he couldn't cope with a relationship any more. Not now... not with this menace on the loose.

Then Brent realized something.

Pain was not all he saw in Lyssie's eyes... she was pissed, and he was in trouble!

"I can't believe that I have been listening to this bullshit! The only secret I have from you is that I'm tired of you yanking my chain!"

Alyssa was so mad she couldn't back up now if she tried. The tirade had begun and stopping was not an option.

"How *dare* you accuse me of changing my attitude once I moved in! You want to talk about a change in character? I'll give you a change in character.

"I sit up in the middle of the night to find you in a rocking chair at the window staring out at the damn graveyard!" She began pacing. "Then call you to supper, which gets cold because you're poking around in that infernal attic looking for something you can't tell me about because it doesn't concern me! Doesn't *concern* me?" She raised her voice even higher, rattling the pictures on the wall as she approached Brent where he had sat down at the table backing away from her.

"I'll tell you what *does* concern me mister... this little episode tonight. Bad enough that your flights of fancy aren't supposed to concern *me*, but I guess I'm not supposed to know what you were trying to pull tonight! Putting your friend in the middle of all of this craziness! I suppose that doesn't concern me either! I think that if anyone around here is keeping secrets and going through a change of character... it's *you* Doctor Price! You who don't think your personal life is any of my concern! That is just some bullshit excuse not to tell me what's *really* on your mind. If the truth of it was known, you're probably just getting' cold feet about the whole marriage thing, and I was willing to forget all of this with that in mind, but now I'm not so sure."

She virtually seethed with anger, plopping down at the table across from Brent, her breaths heaving and madder than a wet hornet.

He hadn't looked her in the eye since the first utterance of the argument, because he couldn't stand the truth of it.

Looking down toward the floor at his feet, he shook his head, searching for the right fords... for *any*thing to say to put this whole thing back to rights.

Weariness robbed him of his ability to think clearly now that the adrenaline rush had passed, and he feared her wrath if he did say something.

"Don't you have anything to say for yourself?" She asked.

He looked at her misty eyed and let his mouth drop open as if he to say something, but didn't. He couldn't know what to say to make it all go away now. The chance to take it all back had passed.

He wished this damn mad man had never entered his mind, never invaded his neat little space. He wished he hadn't seen her poking around in his personal things. He wished he had never yelled at her, and never had this stupid fight because then, they might be in each other's arms, not staring across a table like some Mexican standoff.

So, he said the only thing he knew how to say.

"Sorry. I didn't know it was so bad for you here."

"Oh no ya don't." She sneered shaking a finger at him. "Don't you *dare* turn this around on me now. You're only sorry I called you on it. And besides, if it had been that bad on me, I wouldn't have been here..." Brent didn't let her finish. It was time to end the frustration once and for all.

"Yes, you would."

"What?" Alyssa asked in shock that he had interrupted her.

The sudden interruption surprised her so much she almost forgot what she had just said.

"Even if being here with me was as bad as death itself, you would be here. Because you love me, and you know the extent of that love... I don't have that benefit." Brent sighed heavily. "I love you with everything that I own and with everything that I am... and it will still never match the love you have for me. You could love me only as much as a pretty outdoor scene, and it would be more love than every fraction of my soul could offer you; because your love exudes so much passion, so much... *every*thing. I wanted that and for a while, I had it... you could do no wrong. Tonight, when you looked through my things; as much as I hate to admit it, you took that away from this relationship... the trust is gone."

Alyssa stared blankly at Brent.

'*How did he know that?*' she wondered.

Brent saw the wonderment and answered the silent thought.

"I *saw* you. I know you went through my things and in all honesty, I have to thank you. You found a picture that I wanted to find so bad that it's tormented my every waking hour for over a couple of months now. But that doesn't excuse the fact that you went through my things without regard to my privacy, or without even asking me about it. If you are so willing to go behind my back and look for my past, how can you honestly embrace a future with me?"

Alyssa didn't answer.

Brent watched her, actual tears coming to her now, and he knew she understood what he meant. He knew also that she could not answer him.

"That's what I thought. You know what you have to do Lyssie. There's no turning back from this point. We both know it."

Brent stood up and turned to leave the room. As he left, Alyssa called out to him.

"How else was I supposed to find out about your past? You didn't want to tell me anything. You never *once* offered a single shred of information about your childhood that amounted to anything. What was I supposed to do?"

Brent looked over his shoulder, stopping only for a moment.

"And you never once asked me about it either Lyssie. Not once. Besides, it was the past, and I thought it didn't matter... it doesn't look as if much of anything matters any more. I'm going to bed. I'll see you when you're ready to come up."

Alyssa laid her head on the table and sobbed deeply as he ascended the stairs.

Brent stopped on the other side of the corridor to wipe a tear on his sleeve. Her sobbing dug into his conscience and though his heart went out to her, he couldn't bring himself to go in there.

He went up the stairs quickly and quietly, with the secret hope that she would come to bed. They could always work things out in the morning. After all, he had been awfully hard on her. Only time would tell.

End of Chapter Twelve

Chapter Thirteen: Old Trouble in the New Digs

Brent rose with the morning sun streaking across his room, and stretched dreamily before remembering what an ass he'd made of himself the night before. Falling back onto his pillow in exasperation, he groaned, noticing that Alyssa's side of the bed had not been slept in.

"Jesus. Was that me?" He muttered to himself.

Rubbing sleepily at his night-strained eyelids, he sat up on his elbows with the resolution that he would never yell at her again. He determined to find some way to make this work if it killed him. Which, considering the events of the night past, was probably the most likely scenario knowing Alyssa's temper.

Randy, who had been lying sleepily in the bed hoping not to be discovered so that he could sleep a little longer, raised his head up and licked Brent straight in the mouth.

"Thank you." He laughed, pushing the fur-baby away. "Now get down. Your breath reeks!"

Randy hopped down and padded out into the hall and down the steps toward breakfast.

Upon sitting up the rest of the way, Brent noticed something falling to the floor that had been lying in the bed with him.

Turning his head to one side to see what it was, he saw the book that had been long forgotten once Alyssa had come into his life... Gram's diary. There, floating down onto the floor beside it, was a letter in Lyssie's handwriting. He dreaded reading it.

He bent down, looking at the letter, which had fallen upside down onto the floor.

The decision to touch it was long in coming. He sat for a few moments in the silent stillness of the big, drafty room, his arms resting on his knees and his head hanging over the cursed letter.

Now, the silence bore upon its breath the reality that she'd left him... for good.

Finally, he stretched out his hand and picked it up, pushing the fire back that raged behind his eyes. The letter read thus:

"Brent. I realize that maybe I inadvertently obligated you to me from the beginning, and that this is why you felt responsible for my falling so hard for you. That I can forgive, but your inability to open up to me and tell me the truth about the past that *runs* your tomorrow, made it so that I couldn't function.

I wanted you to be happy again. I did what I had to do to understand, and to make a better wife for you. I realize now that you didn't want it in the first place and whatever it was that I thought you were, was just my hopeful imaginings, as usual. I won't trouble you any further. I promise.

I suppose that you're angry with me for having your Grandmother's diary but, judging by the way you've have behaved in life, I assume that you haven't read it. It *should* be read, and often. She was one miraculous human being.

I'm sorry for everything I ever did that hurt you, but you should know that whatever my actions, I thought I was helping, because I love you. Note that this was not written in the past tense. I will *always* love you. That love has become something that is so a part of me now, I will never part with what we had in the beginning.

Your mother had the diary and I took it from her the day you proposed to me so that she couldn't use it to hurt you... I just couldn't resist the urge to know more about your Grandmother once I had read that diary. I wanted to know how her outer beauty reflected her inner beauty, and I was not disappointed. You look remarkably like your grandmother... pity you didn't take more after her in spirit.

Love Always, Lyssie."

Letting the letter drift slowly to the floor, he wiped his nose with the back of his hand as it fell. The tiny, fine little letters on the page had been written by the hand of the last person who could have loved him just as he is. Even his mother hadn't been capable of that under the present circumstances. It looked as if he had gotten his wish after all, he had his life back... and hated every quiet, boring minute of it.

****

Alyssa pushed the last of her belongings into the back of her Jeep Cherokee and swallowed against doubt as she looked at the house one last time.

Brent had been asleep the entire time she packed, and she couldn't stand the thought of waking him. For the first time in her life, all desire for debate or argument had left her. She didn't have the drive to stand up for herself another moment.

Stepping into the jeep, she let it roll a respectable distance down the driveway so that Brent wouldn't hear her crank it before she had a chance to disappear into the light of a new day.

As she jumped into the driver's seat, slamming the door, she let the ringing in her head continue to resound without resistance. The slamming of that door meant the beginning of the end for her.

The dependency that had formed during her time with Brent would be no more. Henceforth, it would take more than a charming personality and debonair smile to win her heart. Wiping the tears onto her sleeve, Lyssie snuffled a little.

She didn't go to the Biggmann ranch this time. She hated to admit that Aunt Edna had been right about her ill-fated love affair, and she hadn't listened. Apologies would be in order, and she just couldn't bear the thought of it for the moment. She'd just have to call her aunt once she got into town.

This time, she would be on her own, without letting Edna pay the rent. The time had come that she act her age and take care of herself. Upon calling Frawley earlier, she had been offered an advance on her next check, and managed to get into a little duplex apartment he owned rather quickly.

A frown tipped her lips when she thought of leaving without saying good bye to anyone... even her beloved Carlos, but she wouldn't get to do that and she couldn't go back. Every minuscule grit of dirt around that place in the hills made her think of Brent, and she had to try and forget if she were to maintain any kind of sanity through this.

He'd been right about one thing... her strength, and though it was taking every bit that she had not to turn and run back, begging for forgiveness, she would not give in to her longing.

He as much as said that he had not loved her anyway.

Thinking of herself begging that insufferable lout, fueled her anger to the point that she was ready to go back and torch his house instead.

Alyssa laughed at herself. One minute she thought about running back to the ranch and jumping into the bed with him to "*persuade*" him into taking her back, and the next minute she considered burning his place to the ground.

"There are a lot of reality shows out there making boatloads of cash off of stuff like this... not to mention country singers." She smarted, listening to the lyrics of the song on the radio.

"If it had been me..." She retorted, turning off the noise and looking at herself in the rearview mirror. "It wouldn't have been '*who's bed have your boots been under*', but how are you going to get my boot surgically removed from you're as... whoa." She interrupted herself.

A small brown Pacer pulled very quickly out into the road behind her from an obscure driveway, and stayed with her at about the same speed. She slowed down hoping it would pass, but the car remained behind her, far enough back that she couldn't see the face of the driver.

"What if it's the killer?" she murmured, "but then it might just be a tourist trying to have a better look at the mountain."

That sort of thing happened every once in great a while.

Clicking the radio back on, she heard the voice of one of her favorite country sirens and made sure the tone and bass were just right, cranking the volume louder.

She rode along a minute or two singing with the music, barely able to make out the shape of the head of the person behind her, as she surveyed them in the rear-view mirror.

"Must be wearing a hat." She mumbled, noting the big odd shape of the person's head that was driving. "A really *weird* hat." She added straining to see them better.

Suddenly, out of nowhere Brent's truck appeared on the wrong side of the road, passing the Pacer, and he banged on the horn like a crazed lunatic.

The driver in the Pacer slowed down almost to a crawl having been frightened out of their wits.

Alyssa was near paranoia with his behavior. Evidently, he had lost his marbles!

"Good!" She barked shutting off the radio and mashing the accelerator to the floorboard.

"If he can catch me, he can have me!" She giggled, barreling down the mountain at a staggering speed.

He continuously blew the horn, waved and shouted something at her, but she rolled her window up and kept going.

She lost sight of him for a moment, and her heart sank. For the moment, she enjoyed having the space to collect her sanity.

"I'm *not* listening to him anymore!" she complained as the jeep slammed to a halt at the stop sign on the outskirts of town. She didn't see him coming, and so proceeded to the stop light at the next intersection. She breathed a sigh of relief as she came to a stop with no sign of him.

Just then, Brent's sky-blue truck sped through the stop sign and screeched to a halt behind her. He was out and running toward her before his truck had quite come to a complete stop; and the light didn't change. Apparently, she had missed trip switch, but she didn't see how.

Nervousness overcame her, and she fidgeted furiously.

Brent banged on her window and gradually she let it down, biting her bottom lip.

"What?" She pouted.

"You could have told me... talked to me or something Lyssie. Don't let it end... not like this."

"*Yore* the one who chose to end it, remember? *I just did what I hadda do.*" She mimicked him from the night before. "Besides... how did you know you were going to catch me on the road? You were sound asleep when I left."

"You were being followed and I was trying to protect you."

"Oh, here we go with the "crazy" routine again..."

"This isn't some routine!" He shouted before he remembered his vow not to yell any more. Lowering his voice, he growled through gritted teeth.

"It's the truth. He's after you. He wanted to kill you last night, but I managed to get to you before he had the chance. He's still after you, because he knows how much you mean to me, and he's going to kill you if he can. Please come home."

She shook her head sadly, gazing piteously at him.

"I can't take this anymore, Brent. I don't believe a word of it. I can't go on trying to convince everyone else that you're sane, if I can't even convince myself half the time."

The light changed to green, but Brent would not let go of the door he leaned on.

"Brent. Turn loose of the car. This is the only way..."

"I can't let go." his eyes pleaded with desperation. "You can't leave me. Not *now*. I'm sorry.

"I wish I could take back every stupid thing I may have ever said or did, but I can't. I don't blame you for not believing me, but you just *have* to. At least *this* time you have to, because he's after you Alyssa."

147

She listened, silently praying that the words "I love you" would fall from his lips, but they never did. He just continued to prattle on and on about saving her from the unseen, which, as far as she could tell, existed only in Brent's wild imagination. Her Aunt Edna had been right about him. She had just been too blinded by her love to see it.

"Brent this whole thing is ridiculous and you know it. I believe that you're sorry for everything, because it's in your nature to punish yourself for your emotions, but this constant ploy to keep me around by talking about this dangerous apparition… is just getting tired. I'm sick of it."

"It's the truth!" He pleaded. "Please *listen* to me. Look. We don't have to be…" Brent looked at her breasts and then down toward the ground "… Intimate or anything. Just come back until this nut is caught, and then I promise, if you still want to go, you can."

"I can any way, Brent. You know why I don't buy this? Because you keep saying that this monster wants to hurt you. *Not* me. Maybe once I get the hell away from you for a while, catching and killing me won't be such a big deal to him.

"I can take care of myself. I don't need you for anything. The fact that I wanted you was more than any need was worth to me. Now that I have accepted your decision to end this, it's kind of funny that you're the one hanging on. I don't want to talk to you anymore. Just leave me alone!" She shouted, revving the motor a little as a threat.

He leaned in the window, and kissed her on the cheek. Before he let go of the door he had something to say.

"I know this is all my fault, and I'm willing to accept that but if anything happens to you, it won't be my fault. I wanted to help you, and you wouldn't let me."

"It wasn't your *help*, I wanted." She belted out in a flurry of tears as she lunged the jeep forward and sped through the light into town.

****

The motion of the jeep caused Brent to stagger into the middle of the road. Defeated, his arms dropped to his side, and he wept. It was really over in her mind and if it killed him, he would have to find a way to get her back.

He didn't want to live without her, and vowed not to let that evil creature hurt her.

The time had come to win Aunt Edna if he hoped to keep tabs on Lyssie. At least he had one thing to his advantage… he knew where she worked and whether she went back to work there or not, he knew it would only be a matter of time before she went around there to see her friends.

Loneliness could be a terrible thing, and if she felt anything like she looked when she drove off, it wouldn't be long before she hungered for companionship.

****

Alyssa walked around the cute little duplex apartment, the phone pressed between her ear and shoulder, waiting for Edna to answer. She watered the plants Mrs. Frawley had been good enough to bring over for "*atmosphere*".

"Come on." Alyssa grumbled taking the watering cup to the tiny little sink. "Pick up. I know you're home."

"Hello?" Her aunt breathed heavily into the phone as if she had been running to answer it.

"Aunt Edna?" Alyssa began, but Edna cut her off.

"Where the devil *are* you yungun? I've been out of my mind over you, and that boy's been out here all morning fussing about not knowing where you are to keep you out of danger and all kinds of other crazy nonsense."

"I know. I know." Alyssa answered trying to calm her aunt with her tone of voice.

"Brent and I had an argument yesterday that set me to thinking that you were probably right about him. So, as per his request, I cleared my things. I would have come by, but it was awful early and in order to secure an apartment, I had to leave A.S.A.P. I rented a new place with a private land-line and had my cell number changed."

"Where are you and what's wrong with the apartment I had set up for you to start with? Couldn't you have gone back there?"

"I could have if I wanted anyone to find me. I need some time alone and with the raise Frawley is going to give me, I can afford my own place. Now if I tell you where I am... do you *swear* not to tell Brent?"

Edna was silent for a moment, then answered.

"I promise to try my hardest to keep it from him."

"What kind of promise is that?" Alyssa demanded.

"Well..." Edna added defensively. "He seemed so sincere this morning, and he looked like he had been crying. Janet used to tell me all of the time that she wished he would cry cause then she'd know at least that he was human. He didn't even cry as a kid... but he was crying when he got here. I wondered if maybe you hadn't rushed your decision to move out. This is kind of sudden you know."

Alyssa sucked at her teeth in frustration. It had been Edna's idea for her to get out while she could, to start with.

"What am I supposed to do? You told me yourself that I needed to get away from him at least until I was certain of his sanity and all. Remember the forest and trees thing? I did what you told me... and now *yore* having second thoughts? For heaven's sake Aunt Edna!"

"I know." Edna chuckled at her failings. "I never can make up my mind about anything. You know that. Anyhow. At least I'll be able to sleep at night knowing you're all tucked away safe and sound somewhere. Hold on and I'll go get a pen."

Holding the house phone's receiver between her shoulder and neck, she poured herself a drink of water and smiled, listening to her Aunt Edna puttering around the kitchen looking for a pen and something to write on. She had just tipped the glass to her mouth when she heard something moving around at the back door.

Carefully placing the drink and the phone on the counter, she went to the back door.

Stopping abruptly, she stood next to it and reached under the counter to grab a hammer she had noticed there earlier. If Brent had followed her he would regret it, and if it wasn't him, she would make whoever lurked there even sorrier.

She crouched down next to the door, so that if she flung it open and someone tried to rush through, she could trip them. They wouldn't expect her to be two or three feet tall.

Edna's voice touched her ears from the phone as she screamed for her niece to answer or she would immediately phone the sheriff. She could not bother with the phone now, however. Alyssa could still hear the faint whisper of movement outside the back door, and didn't dare walk away from it. Brent had turned her into a paranoid lunatic with all of his dribble and ghost stories. She would just have to put an end to it somehow.

Cautiously reaching to the knob, she turned it and flung the door open, holding the hammer ready.

Nothing happened at first. She sat holding the hammer for a moment, then heard a faint "*Mew*" coming from the back patio.

She stood up, looking out the back door at the garbage bin area and saw a tiny, wild kitten. It tugged a chicken bone across the patio as it had gotten stuck in its teeth. Lyssie breathed a sigh of relief and yelled toward the phone.

"Aunt Edna I'm okay. Hang on a minute!"

She picked up a piece of her cheese sandwich from the counter and walked out onto the patio with it.

"Here kitty, kitty." She cooed gently, reaching for the kitten.

The little black and gray tabby spit and sputtered at her in stark refusal of her help.

Finally, she tossed a dishtowel over its head and snatched it up quickly by the scruff of the neck. Once she had it in a trance, she turned it over and gently pulled the bone out of the cat's mouth.

Then, she replaced it with the piece of cheese sandwich, put the cat down and went back to the phone.

Here, she rendered an apology and explained what had happened, while pouring a small dish of half-and-half for the kitten.

Edna fussed about Lyssie being so far away, but took down the phone number and address and placed it in her purse for safe keeping.

****

Brent sat among dark, hidden branches in one of the trees bordering the Biggmann Ranch, and took up his night binoculars that he used for hunting.

Seeing Edna run for the back door like a locomotive on a tight schedule, he adjusted the binoculars so that he could see every line in her face as if he were standing right beside her.

Then, he readied his pen and paper.

He could tell by the look on her face that she spoke to Lyssie and he had intentions of getting that number if she wrote it down. When he saw Edna writing on the note paper that hung on the refrigerator facing him, he said a small prayer of thanks as he wrote it all down, and descended the branches.

Quickly, he headed home to tend to his farm and get some important reading done. With the picture and the diary, he hoped to unravel some of this mystery once and for all.

****

Lyssie wandered around the apartment waiting for time to go to work, and wished she had never argued with Brent. Still, every time she thought about the things he said to her, she just got madder at him, and madder at herself for giving up so fast. Nobody said it was going to be easy, so why did she give up?

She threw her arms up into the air as if to say… *"I give up even trying to think about it,"* when the phone began ringing.

151

She stared at it for a moment, and then decided to let her new answering machine pick up.

If it was Aunt Edna she would pick up, but some guy had been calling all day saying: "Sorry... wrong number." and Alyssa didn't want to encourage him to keep calling.

She figured he must have liked the sound of her voicemail message or something to keep irritating her like that. She stood across the room regarding the machine lightly until she heard the sound of Brent's sigh, followed by his voice. She found herself running for the phone, and then stopped short of picking up the receiver.

"What am I *doing*?!" She yelled at herself.

How could he have gotten her phone number... and why should she be the one in such a hurry to patch things up?

She had been gone two whole weeks now and Brent hadn't even bothered to look for her. Then she thought about that. Yes, he had tried to find her. He *was* talking to her answering machine.

Her hand hovered over the receiver, as if attempting to sneak up on an ugly bug or something, and she contemplated picking it up as she bit her lip thoughtfully.

She could hear him saying: "I guess you're not home. Sorry if I bothered you Lyssie, but I still would like for you to come home... I know you don't think of this as home yet, but it's not home to me without you.

"I hope that if you're home you'll pick up. I went through a great deal of trouble to sneak this number away from your aunt when she wasn't paying attention, and the least you could do is talk to me.

"Well. Anyway. I'm really sorry Lyssie. I'll do anything to work this out. All you have to do... (all you've ever had to do)" he muttered under his breath "is *talk* to me."

Lyssie stopped biting her lip and picked up the phone, answering: "Hello?" But he had given up, and there was nothing but blank air, followed immediately by a dial tone. Alyssa swallowed hard and went to the bathroom to talk herself out of crying as she wiped the tears from her eyes.

She would return to him when she knew for sure he had suffered enough. She just could not be sure that she could take it herself... not when it seemed that she was the one really suffering. No one had ever talked to her the way he did that night, and it had gotten the best of her that *he* was even capable of it.

'*Best to wait a while.*' She thought.

She cleaned up, and made her way into the tiny kitchen to fix herself a glass of ice water. As she stood at the kitchen sink drinking the water, something landed on the windowsill right in front of her.

She jumped, throwing her glass into the floor where it splintered into tiny pieces.

Glancing up warily, she could see the would-be assailant.

The kitten perched there, staring at her and mewing loudly. Its little pink maw stretched wide open, tiny red tongue slightly out, and its white teeth glinted in the window light.

"Oh, for crying out loud!" She grumbled as she picked up the pieces of glass.

After sweeping the mess away, she went out the back door to see if she could locate that naughty little rag a muffin that had long since disappeared from her windowsill.

Alyssa stepped out the back door into the darkness that wrapped itself around her like a big warm blanket.

The air was thick and wet from the last rain, but it wasn't as cold as it had been earlier in the autumn season. Alyssa stood peering into the black void of night calling: "Here kitty kitty?"

No noise disturbed the shadows... not the first semblance of sound. A cold chill crept up Lyssie's spine as the breeze raced over her. She feigned a mew of her own hoping the cat would come.

She only barely heard its answer, but could tell which direction it had come from. She sighed. She'd always been a sucker for a hard luck story, which, in retrospect was probably why she still considered going back to Brent.

Meandering off the edge of the flat concrete patio, she bumped carefully up against the dumpster that bordered the property line in the back yard.

Lyssie looked over the cyclone fence, and could just see the dark outline of Frawley's house in the distance. She grinned. Wouldn't he be mad when she came in late and had no better excuse than: "I was trying to rescue a stray kitten;" in the dark; without a flashlight; having been warned that a murderous maniac was supposedly stalking her.

"You really are losing it." She muttered to herself. Alyssa listened to the sounds of the night for a second. No crickets, katydids, or whippoorwills.

Odd, for a girl who had just spent the last two months out in the country. '*Two months*' she thought in wonderment. '*Two wonderful months.*' there was that sigh again.

Deciding that the kitten obviously didn't want to be found, and that she didn't have time to find it anyway, she started once again toward the back door.

A dank mist had set in and she had only walked a few feet, but had it not been for the yellowed light of the back porch, it seemed she would never have found her way.

As she arrived at the patio, she heard rustling in the bushes behind her. Turning quickly, she found herself being lunged at by a creature who seemed all claws and fangs.

She screamed, but no one could hear her. A moment later, her heart rate slowed as she pulled the tiny kitten from her sweater. Apparently, she had scared *it* worse than it had scared her, and she had to calm it down. Her quick movement must have spooked it into jumping on her.

Alyssa cooed softly to the kitten, and then realized that her radio had come on inside the apartment. It played softly, but loud enough that she could hear it.

Making her way inside, she kept the kitten close to her heart as she peered around the corner of the living room to investigate. The stereo wasn't on. The music was coming from the bedroom.

Creeping back into the kitchen, she shut and locked the back door, and placed the kitten on the floor. Quickly, she poured it a bowl of the canned milk she'd opened for her coffee. Bending and petting it, she put a finger to her mouth. "SHHHH." She whispered.

Alyssa grabbed the umbrella she kept next to the back door and tip toed through the living room, carefully looking into every orifice for some monster.

Nothing.

Seeing her old baseball bat leaning next to the front door, she exchanged the umbrella for it.

Lyssie took a right turn into her hallway just on the other side of the kitchen, and started down it toward the bedroom.

Fortunately, the bathroom was all the way at the other end of the hall so no one was going to jump out from a doorway and grab her. She stopped in front of the bedroom door, and placed her left hand on the knob, holding the bat upright in case she had to deck someone before she actually got into the room. Her heart pounded rampantly in her chest. Why couldn't she have just listened to Brent... stuck it out and waited for this whole thing to blow over?

She attempted to regulate her breathing. Finally, tired of waiting, she flung the door open, pouncing into the room with the bat askew.

She didn't see anything. Jumping into the center of her bed, she ran up to the headboard so that her back could stay against the wall. She perched for a moment wild eyed, and breathing heavy. The door to the closet had been left standing open, but fear kept her from stepping off the bed to look into the closet.

'What if he's under the bed waiting for me to make that mistake?' She thought.

She couldn't lean off of the side of the bed and peer under the edge, because that would leave her vulnerable. She put her free hand to her head for a moment trying to sort out what to do. Then, as if hit by lightning, she jumped off the other side of the bed, and crouched so that she was still facing the closet.

If she glanced briefly under the bed, she would see his feet as he emerged the closet, in which case she'd cap both his knees with that bat. Alyssa's crouching body bent closer to the floor than she ever thought possible before she actually took her eyes off the closet door. She glanced under the bed, long enough to find that there wasn't anything there, and nothing coming out of the closet.

Gradually, her legs straightened so that she rose to her full height, and she began to approach the closet.

Tip-toeing to the closet door, she threw it open, thrusting the bat into her gowns and dresses repeatedly.

She looked down into the bottom of the closet. Nothing presented itself, except for some shoes and a couple of books she hadn't found room for yet. She breathed a sigh of relief.

"Thank Gawd!" She gasped, leaning against the closet door and saying a silent prayer of thanks, for not having been in that apartment long enough to leave clutter under the bed.

The doorbell sounded loudly from the living room and Alyssa nearly wet her pants.

She walked over to the clock radio and realized that she had accidentally set the alarm for 8:00p.m. instead of a.m., and the clock had just been doing its job. When it went off, the radio had begun to play.

She took a deep cleansing breath, swearing she would never listen to "Stairway to Heaven" again as long as she lived.

****

"*What?*" She shouted through the lacey front curtain.
A deliveryman shouted back.

155

"All Bright's Florist! I have a delivery from the offices of Dr. Price! Where do you want it?"

"Wait just a minute." She grumbled back as low as her temper would allow at the moment. Alyssa went down the hall into the bathroom, and grabbed a rubber band. She had seen her hair in the mirror on her dresser when she leapt about on the bed during batting practice. The mist outside had taken all of the body out of her tresses. She stuck the rubber band into the pocket of her slacks, and started back toward the front door.

She let the door fly open and stood with the bat in hand waiting for the delivery guy to bring whatever he had from his truck.

The man came in wearing a badge that bore the name 'Mark', and he plumped some flowers down on the doorstep.

He regarded Alyssa's bat curiously at first, and then shrugged as he went back out the door. She was about the close the door behind him when another deliveryman named Jack, came in with another bundle.

"Where you want 'em?"

She shrugged as she looked around her at the last two boxes she hadn't even unpacked yet.

"At this point it doesn't really matter." He put them on top of a box and passed Mark on his way back to the truck.

Alyssa watched this for quite some time, and finally realized that she was going to have to French braid her hair, because at the rate these men were moving, she might not make her shift as it was.

She didn't want to leave them in the living room though, especially after the shocks she had taken earlier this evening. She sat down on the couch and began to braid. She was just a token manager on the 3rd shift until they finished training the new guy, but she hated being late.

The men glanced at her for a moment, then went straight back to their work. Her living room began to look like a jungle. She finished her hair, got her pocket book and stood next to the door with her keys in hand waiting for them to finish. Mark slid through the door with about a dozen white roses and a dashing smile.

"Your dog die while this guy was taking care of it or something?"

Alyssa laughed.

"Nothing so severe. My patient is fine." She nodded toward the kitchen where the man could see the kitten asleep on a dishtowel in the floor.

"Nice doctor. I'll have to bring my pig up that way. We fed it a peach last week, and his gut ain't settled to yet."

Alyssa laughed an answer at him.

"Yore right lucky he isn't dead. Peaches can be lethal to a hawg. Give it lots of bread and milk, and a couple of aspirins... and call me in the morning."

"You a vet too?" He asked.

"No. Just an observant country girl. Here." She smiled pressing two fives into his hand. "I wish I had more... but at least that's something for both of you."

He shook his head with a grin as he pushed her money back into her hand.

"Doctor Price took care of that already. But thanks... and for what it's worth, that's the first time anybody ever called up and asked for one of everthin'. He said he'd worry 'bout you might have allergies to some of these things, 'cept he felt like a rattle snake had a better chance of being allergic to you than you to flowers."

Alyssa's laughter lit up the whole room when it erupted. That sounded more like her Brent.

Relief had already lightened her spirits when the men had come to provide her with some company, but to know that there had never been any real danger, made it possible for her to laugh.

"Well. G'devenin." He smiled as he tipped his hat and headed for the van.

Alyssa smiled too, until she realized that he would be gone before she could get to her vehicle.

Slamming the front door, she checked to see if it was locked, then ran to her jeep and cranked it right up.

She stayed behind the delivery van, taking only small notice of the rounded lights of the car behind her.

****

Pulling up at the restaurant, she ran from her jeep to the front door. Once inside, Lyssie took a deep breath before noticing that everyone in the restaurant had seen her running from her jeep. They all gaped at her as though she were insane.

Grinning nervously, she waved.

"Running late." She supplied, tapping her watch.

Then, just as she thought she would sneak to the back of the restaurant, she came face to face with Frawley who appeared to be so angry, he practically stewed in it.

"Hi!" She chirped.

Frawley shook his head slowly and pointed in the direction of his office without answering her cheerful greeting.

Lyssie's cheeks grew hot, and she forced herself to maintain calm as she walked toward the office.

If the boogey man couldn't get to her, she'd not let Frawley get to her either.

Sauntering into the office, she sat down at the desk, fidgeting with a pen. She was a big girl. Very little existed that she couldn't handle.

She tapped the pen repeatedly against the desk, wishing Frawley would just come on and get this over with. She had quite a lot of bookwork to keep up with and a new night manager to help train.

This wouldn't be the first time she saw him upset over something, this had just been the first time that she became the object of it. She did not pretend to guess what this could be about, but she would be prepared, nonetheless.

The door slowly opened, and Frawley stepped inside, his oversized belly preceding his entry. He didn't look like himself just now. He looked like a man old beyond his years, with a lot on his mind.

Staring earnestly at Alyssa before taking his seat behind the desk, he pushed some of his paperwork to one side and rested his elbows on the desktop.

"So. You feel like telling me what's going on?"

"What?" She asked playfully, deliberately trying to keep things light.

"Don't even try that Lyssie." He grinned sweetly. "I have always thought of you as my own daughter, and I know you better than I know myself because of it. I think it's time you spill it. There's something wrong with you."

"What do you mean something's wrong with me?" She asked, mimicking his tonality.

"Lyssie, please don't be curt with me." He pleaded. "We have a real problem here in the restaurant and you have been so preoccupied with your personal life, you haven't even noticed. I remember a time not so long ago that if the books were just a fraction of a decimal off, you knew before I did, and could usually predict it before you even looked at the paperwork."

Alyssa sat up in her chair.

"What's wrong with the books?"

Frawley put his hands up to calm her down.

"It could be that you're just out of practice, because you have been tryin' to run the restaurant and manage the books all at the same

158

time, and you've been two months away from work. I think things might iron themselves out, but I need you to do me a favor."

"No favors till you tell me what's wrong with the books. I just went over them last night, and didn't see anything wrong with them."

"It's not any one, isolated thing Lyssie. Mostly, it's little things, like something in the wrong column, or something off by a decimal, or usually just something coded wrong. As a matter of fact, this is the slow season, but the way it's been lately, you'd think there was some sort of big tourist attraction in town or something.

"Heck. We're so busy, I can't keep my head on straight, and whether you know it or not... Becky has been running the restaurant for you in your absence. Any other time, you'd be pointing these things out to me... not the other way around."

Her anger simmered. She went flush red. Rejection of any kind, self-inflicted or not, never sat well with her.

Frawley was like her father. For him to say that she hadn't been doing her job, was more like punishment than anything. Even worse... that he'd said someone had been doing it *for* her.

She contemplated the situation closely. Everything she remembered doing since she came back to work flashed across her mind. She had to admit that Becky had been doing a pretty stand up job of upholding her usual duties.

Thinking of Becky, no matter how mad she wanted to be, she only found herself grinning. Kindness was the word that came to mind when she thought of her. She had always been there to lend an ear when Alyssa had something to gripe about, too.

As a matter of fact, she had listened to everybody's gripes while Alyssa doodled her name with Brent's last name on the back of a napkin two days ago at the company meeting.

"What are you grinning about?" Frawley questioned.

"Is this the part where you give me the speech about... *'you're a nice kid, but I think it's time you handed your work to someone else? You're the only one who knows the job like you do, so I want you to train them, and, I'll give you a raise to do something else'*?"

"Lyssie. This is *you*, I'm talking about... not just some employee."

"Funny" She retorted "That's exactly how this feels, and I've made the speech enough times myself that I should've seen it coming a mile away."

"The point is... that you *didn't*."

She stood up, leaning over Frawley's desk so she could glare into his eyes.

"You tell Becky, I'll be in town two days if she needs any help with anything, and then I'm off to live my life."

She turned to leave, and Frawley added: "I'll still need you to do the accounting."

"I don't want your accounting Frawley. I wanted your friendship and I can see that friendship and work no longer mix for me. I'll see ya 'round."

She stomped out, slamming the door behind her and left Frawley wide eyed, his mouth hanging open.

Alyssa passed Becky on the way out and stopped only long enough to congratulate her on the new job, and give her the phone number in case she needed any information, computer codes, or advice.

Lyssie decided that she had lived for the happiness of others long enough... Dr. Brent Price included.

She would only do what *she* wanted to from now on.

She thought about Brent, a frown creasing her mouth as she pushed open the double doors. Though yet unsure, she began to think that maybe she had just been attracted to him for the stability marriage would have given her.

Still, considering the more tender moments, she second guessed herself.

Brent's reflection appeared behind her in the window of her jeep. Gasping, she turned around and slapped his shoulder for startling her that way.

"Don't walk up behind me like that! Are you crazy?!"

Brent managed to control his laughter.

It seemed that he did more scaring than the boogey man where she was concerned.

"Sorry." He breathed, handing her a bankbook. "You left this. And I thought, since you might need it, I'd bring it. It takes two days for the mail to travel from up there to down here."

"Thanks." She smiled as she nervously took the booklet trying not to touch Brent's hand. She knew if she did, her charade would come crashing to an abrupt halt. Just the touch of his skin on hers stripped her of all logic.

"You getting off all ready?" He asked.

She looked through the windows at Becky cleaning a few of the waitresses' stations for them, and fought back bitter tears.

"Actually yes. I'm thinking about moving away." She lied.

She had to come up with some reason for leaving so early in the evening.

"*Away?*" Brent's voice cracked with desperation. "Away where?"

"I haven't made up my mind yet." She smirked, hoping to torture him a little more for his poor behavior with her. "I think I just need a change of pace. All of my friends act like they don't know me... Frawley included. I think if I'm going to start over, it might as well be somewhere... I don't know, where I don't already have a past. Ya know?"

Brent nodded, as if the action would release the pressure behind his eyes, but it didn't help much.

"I wouldn't want to tell you what to do. I'm sure you'll do well anywhere you choose to make a life for yourself. I wish I could be more like you, but you know me. I'm more comfortable with the tried and tested, in most areas anyway.

"With you... I don't know. It's different. I don't care how often I try and fail, something keeps me coming back. I want to work this out. Won't you give me a chance to make this up to you? Please?"

"What do you want from me Brent? A month ago, I would have given you my life... now, I don't know what to say. You *told* me to leave. Remember?" He nodded, looking toward the ground.

"If you weren't sure about telling me to leave, how do I know you're sure you want me to come home? For all I know, you really wanted me to leave all along and then later started feeling guilty, so you decided to invite me back to make yourself feel better."

As if saying those words sobered her, she realized then that he was not ready. He still had not said he loved her and from the looks of things, he wasn't going to.

"I need to be going." She finally declared as she started to open the door to the jeep.

"Wait." Brent held her by the elbow and looked deep into her eyes. "I can't live without you Lyssie. *Please* come home."

Her knees grew weak as she looked into those enchanting blue eyes, but she maintained her composure.

"That's not what I hoped you'd say Brent. Good night."

****

He watched her ride away with a smile on his lips. She had flinched. It wasn't a lost cause yet. He would just have to keep right on going until he convinced her to come home.

Chuckling as he got in the truck, he hoped she would come before the killer outsmarted him.

161

"Love you girl." He murmured as he cranked his vehicle, and took the long road back up the mountain.

****

Alyssa stormed in the front door grumbling to herself about Brent's audacity. How dare he ask her to come back when he couldn't even say he loved her? Stomping into the kitchen, she threw her keys onto the counter and slung her jacket over the back of a chair.

She had just begun pouring herself a glass of tea, when she realized she didn't see the cat. She looked at the dishtowel she had left in the floor for it, but it had disappeared. She called out for it.

"Kitty?"

No reply.

Lyssie decided that she didn't feel up to looking for that insane animal again. She sat in the chair staring out the window of her back door. There was such a lack of light out there tonight, that black sack cloth might as well have been thrown over the window. She wondered what she wanted for herself in this life.

Looking around the tidy little apartment, she sighed. So hollow was this new place. Every nook and cranny had been freshly painted, tiled, carpeted, polished, or wallpapered. She thought of Brent's house without him in it, and it remained a house, not a home, just like her apartment did.

When she thought of the two of them together in that house, a happy shudder passed through her. Every imperfection of the big home held someone's memory.

The ringing of the phone invaded her thoughts.

Diving to answer it, she hoped it was Brent. If he asked her to come home just one more time, she was going.

"Brent?" She asked hurriedly.

Silence at first, and then... a slight chuckle, a deep, throaty voice, and the unknown person hung up on her. She dropped the receiver onto its base, at first cursing the creep that kept calling, and then, remembering Brent's words of caution; she locked all of the doors and windows tight.

She hadn't even retreated to the kitchen yet, when the phone started ringing again. She'd had enough! "Listen here you piece of shit..." She growled into the phone.

"Oh... I'm sorry." Becky's voice was indifferent "I must have dialed the wrong number..."

"Becky?" Alyssa felt better all ready. She wasn't alone, threatened.

162

"My God Lyssie! Is that you?"

"Yeah. It's me." Alyssa giggled. "Sorry. I thought you were a prank caller. What do you need?"

"I just called to say that if you have some plans you want to go ahead with, you can. I've been secretly working on the books the whole time you were gone.

"Frawley didn't know it. I didn't mean to pry, I just figured that if you were going to get married, you would eventually want to quit altogether, so I was trying to be ready... you taught me that."

"Yeah." Lyssie confessed. "I guess I did."

She swallowed a lump in her throat. She could tell that Becky hadn't wanted to call her. Her voice wavered with fear. However badly Becky hadn't wanted to call, she managed somehow to muster the courage to do it anyway, and Alyssa respected that.

"I can't thank you enough Beck... let me know if there's ever anythin' I can do for you as well. Okay? I may even head home tonight if I'm up to it. Thanks."

Becky sounded as if she was still afraid, but she said Alyssa was welcome and they both hung up.

She had no sooner sat down with her drink, when the phone rang. Lyssie looked from the kitchen doorway into the living room. It seemed a long way to walk just then so she decided to let the answering machine get it. She heard the long steady beep, and had nearly fallen asleep in her chair when Brent's voice boomed over the answering machine. She jogged over to it and she stood looking at it fondly.

"Lyssie." He sighed. "Look. I know you've had time to get home, because I'm home. Won't you please pick up?"

She would not pick up... she was afraid. She found that when things felt good, they usually weren't good for you.

"All right. Don't pick up. I had hoped to be saying this to your face, but I guess you leave me no choice." A brief silence lingered before he finally said what he had wanted to say. He had hoped that if he held his silence long enough, curiosity would make her pick up the receiver. She wouldn't... and he took a deep breath.

"I love you, Lyssie. I can't live without you. Everything I think or do reminds me of you. I can't sleep. I can't eat... and I guess I don't want to. I want to hold you in my arms when I go to sleep at night, and know that we're there for each other. I want to know that when I put a morsel of food into my mouth, it will again offer flavor to my senses. I am senseless without you. Please... marry me."

Alyssa wiped a tear on her sleeve as she picked up the phone... but he'd hung up after he said what wanted to.

Glancing around the room at the flowers he'd sent her, she smiled.

She was going home.

As she began packing her things, the kitten emerged from under the bed, loving all over her legs the whole time, as if offering a plea not to be left behind. Having finished the packing, Alyssa stopped and scooped up the feline.

"Hope you packed your bags little kitty... we're going to have a real family for a change."

End of Chapter Thirteen

Chapter Fourteen: Always and Never Too Close to Home

Rocking in his chair, Brent gazed out the window at the graveyard.

Alyssa hadn't picked up the phone. She may not have been home yet. She might have stopped for gas, or got some groceries or something.

He sat watching, waiting for... anything.

The wind played on the tall grass, as the full moon drifted behind a cloud. Soon, all semblance of light dissipated into the darkness.

His mind wandered back to his link with the killer. Often his nights had been filled with thoughts about how to make some sense of the whole thing. He had noticed many things but so far, nothing helped. He began to see, for instance, that this thing hunted better now that he had become involved. It seemed to hunger for an audience that could experience remorse for him... and Brent did just that.

He shuddered with the memory of the creature's last conquest; an attractive, chubby woman with hazel eyes. She had pleaded for reprieve, and found none. She stood out the most in his memory, because she did not fit in with the others in any way. As he thought about it, up until this last quarry, there had been something familiar about all of the women. They shared similar physical characteristics. All were fairly well put together, thin, but agile... firm. All had similarly shaped eyes and lips, but beyond that, even their personalities were no match for one another. The last one, the heavy-set woman, did not fit the killer's typical choice pattern, whatsoever. He tried many times putting this last lady in some kind of category with the others, but failed. She was an enigma at best.

He supposed the killer took her merely to hurt Brent for watching. Nothing else made any sense. He hid no single desire or intent to hunt and kill Alyssa. Not only would this hurt Brent, but she had the "look" this killer sought most.

The notion of her looks filled his mind the entire time he found himself in the throes of murder. On that point, his mind was ever clear. He had been rather busy, in fact.

On the evening when the beast had hidden itself at her new place, Brent had seen a stray cat that almost got the beast caught. Then later, against the efforts of the little cat to frighten Alyssa, the beast stalked her again and Brent's flowers managed to intercept him.

If she didn't come to him soon, there wouldn't be much he could do to stop it from killing her.

Brent had long forgotten the days when he referred to the killer in human terms. In his mind, only a fiend from hell itself could do such things, this vile creature that stalked prey in the shadows for fear of being captured by the light.

Brent had camped outside Alyssa's duplex many times over the last few weeks, but the way he saw it, if he knew what the creature was doing, the visions probably worked both ways.

He went home, and stayed home. Unless she came back, his efforts were proving fruitless and ultimately left him helpless.

If she were with him, the beast would have to stalk them as a team, not when she was avoiding his calls, and asking him to leave her alone.

Originally, Brent had only gone into town to tell Alyssa that the beast was coming tonight, but she wouldn't have believed him anyway. He had decided to tell her the truth and he was glad he did.

At least this way, no matter what happened, she would know how he loved her. His clung to the hope that the last phone call he made would bring her back to him tonight, or at least before time ran out.

Casting one last look at the graveyard on the hill adjacent his bedroom window, Brent sighed deeply. The longing for youth was heavier than ever in this terrible time of his life, but he had to face the fact that Gram was gone... and she could never come back.

On Alyssa's request, he had read the diary and had not regretted it. Everything she had said of his grandmother was true. She had been a remarkable soul.

Also, while rambling through the attic, he found some old letters and finally understood a few things about this creature hunting the women in town.

He'd have gone to the police with his findings, but at this point, anything Brent did made him look more and more guilty. His anonymous tip to them earlier that the killer was after Alyssa had been logged. There was nothing to do now but wait, and pray she would come back to him. Now that he knew the identity of the murderer, he could discover how this rampage had ever become possible at all, find out why it was here, now... and then kill it.

****

Bending over the nozzle at the gas pump on the street corner across from Frawley's, Alyssa tapped on the window and waved at the kitten. The small creature stared at her out of the back window.

Lyssie whistled a happy tune. Pumping the gas, a light filled her heart for the first time in many weeks.

Brent had said he loved her, and better than that... the feeling had never been more mutual. Just the thought of being in his arms in a matter of an hour or less thrilled her almost more than she could stand.

Replacing the gas nozzle, she began across the parking lot to pay the clerk, and noticed a little brown Pacer pulling away from the restaurant.

"Whoever *that* tourist is... they're mighty busy." She murmured.

Trotting into the store, she picked up a drink, a candy bar and a can of cat food that you could just pop the lid off of with a pull-tab. By the time she headed for the cash register though, a line had formed. Seeing that it might take a while, she scooped up a newspaper to read while she waited.

Some old people in front of her began counting out pennies to buy lottery tickets and she groaned, quietly. The clerk, a fresh faced 20-something guy apparently shared Lyssie's enthusiasm and rolled his eyes.

Alyssa shrugged it off. She had waited two whole weeks. A few minutes wouldn't kill her, no matter *how* bad it agitated her.

Flipping carelessly through the paper, she settled on just reading cover stories. Reorganizing it, she was able to read the top half of the page first, and then the bottom.

She focused on the information about the killer. There were several stories about it to follow. This way, she'd be up to date if Brent started up. With no time to read them completely, she just glanced over gory details.

The number had risen to twenty now and, on a "*hunch*", they'd exhumed the body of a young woman who had originally been classified as a drowning victim. They found that she'd been the first victim... among those who were accounted for. The police suspected that there were more.

One of the last women to be killed was a real estate investment broker, in town scouting commercial property. Her car broke down the first day there and the best she could get until it came out of the shop, had been a brown Pacer that the shop owner loaned her. The Pacer was yet unaccounted for.

Lyssie's mind reeled. She had seen someone in a hat driving a brown Pacer the day she left Brent's farm. Later she had seen lights resembling that of a Pacer behind her, and tonight, only moments ago, she'd seen a brown Pacer leaving Frawley's...

"I *said* next!" the clerk rudely shouted at Alyssa as she was the only one left standing in the store, and hadn't seemed to notice.

Normally she would have chewed him out, but the brown Pacer came first.

Lyssie fumbled in her pocket for a twenty, silently doing the math.

'*$15 in gas, can of cat food, candy, diet drink... twenty should do it.*'

Oblivious to the newspaper in her hand, she started for the door but the clerk stopped her.

"You gonna pay for that?" He asked, pointing at the paper.

Flustered, Alyssa searched for cash. Tossing a five-spot on the counter she didn't even bother waiting for change as she darted for the door.

Sirens!

She looked across the small two-lane road at the restaurant on the other side, just as the sheriff's car pulled up out front.

Dropping her items on the ground next to the jeep, she considered ignoring it, but her sense of duty would never allow it. What if that thing got Frawley?

Her heart throbbed mercilessly as she bounded across the road. Bursting through the doors she ran straight up to the sheriff.

"Where's Frawley?" She screamed wild eyed and frightened.

In the silence that followed, everyone turned to look at her. The restaurant had been closing, so the only people there were the employees, apparently herded into a group by the police, and Alyssa scanned their faces trying to assess who was unaccounted for. The sheriff turned to her and patted her on the back.

"Now calm down gurl." He soothed. "Frawley's jes' fine. He was down to Bob's garage gettin' his car out from being repaired when this 'ere happened. He's on his way here raght now. We called down to Bob's the minute we foun' out."

"Found out what?" She asked, not recognizing her own voice as the words fell from her lips. The sheriff looked solemnly downward and didn't answer right away.

"What?" She asked softly, shaking him a little by his elbow.

Taking a deep breath, he took off his hat and scuffed his hand lightly against the top of his head. He watched quietly as they brought a body bag out on a gurney.

Alyssa looked back at the faces of the people assembled and began to count them... recalling the order in which they appeared on the payroll each week.

'*Savant*!' She thought, the name ringing through her brain like the end of the world had arrived!

"*Becky*? Please say it isn't Becky!" She cried.

All eyes were downcast, and Alyssa knew.

She thought over the events of the days past and realized that Brent had been telling the truth!

Her only hope now, was to get to Brent. Backing away from everyone, Lyssie stumbled out the door and made a break for the service station across the street... and her jeep.

Scooping up the groceries as she passed, she hopped over a small puddle that ran from beneath her car. She jumped in without hesitation in one fluid movement and dumped the items into the passenger side floorboard. Curled up comfortably in the seat, kitty showed only small signs of interest.

Seeing the small feline bought her a piece of mind. At least she didn't have to worry about it popping out of the back seat and scaring the hell out of her. Suddenly, she realized she hadn't inspected the back seat before getting in.

Screeching off to the side of the road, Alyssa grabbed the kitten from the passenger seat and sprang from the jeep. Rain began lightly pelting against the car, and she cursed quietly under her breath as she crammed the kitten into the front of her jacket.

She wondered as she zipped the jacket closed over the furious little creature, how she was going to see into the back seat. As the kitten scratched at her pocket, Lyssie could faintly hear her phone making electrical noises in there and remembered the flashlight app.

This came in handy on late nights when she was curled up with a good book and was too lazy to get up and cut on a light.

Frantically fumbling with the phone, she finally managed to get it to come on. As she snuggled the kitten closer with one hand, she flashed the light through the back seat cautiously with the other.

Lyssie reached for the door to the car, and carefully opened it so that she could slide the kitten back into the front seat safely. Slowly placing the cat inside, she eased the door back.

A groan escaped her as she looked down toward the back end of the jeep, where there were mounds of boxes, filled with her stuff.

Heading to the back of the vehicle, she lifted the window to the tailgate. As she dropped the tailgate itself, a box of old clothes spilled onto the ground.

"Oh for heaven's sake!" She fussed bending to scoop them up. Cramming them into an opened box, she quickly began picking through them, shining the light everywhere a person could possibly hide. Then a terrible thought occurred to her.

'What if he's dangling from something underneath the car?'

But that was silly. How could he hang onto anything under there and not be killed in the process? After all, she had been racing like a bat out of hell when she left the gas station.

Her aunt Edna's words echoed in her mind...

"Be sure of all things."

Swallowing hard, she pushed her now rain-soaked hair behind her ears as she bent to look under the car... prepared to face the worse.

Nothing.

Sighing gratefully as she headed back to the front of the car, Alyssa shined the light throughout the dark regions of the Jeep as she went. Stepping slowly back into the front seat, she locked the doors so that she could sit for a second and regroup. As the lights from her flashers pounded noiselessly against the wet pavement around her, she sniffed back a tear.

She was a nervous wreck.

With a moment to clear her mind of all the fiddle-faddle, she thought hard about Brent. She thought so hard that her head hurt, but before she knew it, she could almost smell his cologne. A faint smile lifted her features and she took a deep breath. By morning, she would be resting in Brent's arms, and this would all be far behind her.

****

Sheriff Griffin stood outside the restaurant staring in the direction that Alyssa's car had taken when she left. She had acted strange, but then he supposed most people did when faced with the reality that someone they knew had passed on… especially under these circumstances.

Grabbing one of his officers as he passed, the sheriff said, "Son. Get ahold of dis-pach, and ask 'em to call Detective Roberts from over to the next county. I got a feelin', this is something we're gonna need some help on. And did y'all get Frawley on the horn yet?"

"Yes sir." The young man answered, grimacing a little as the sheriff spit some of his tobacco onto the black top.

"What'd he say?"

"He's on his way, sir. Bob called a few minutes ago, too. He sounded upset, and the radio went fuzzy, so we don't know what he needed yet. Bubbas trying to get ahold to 'im now."

"Son… why's Bubba doing our job for us?"

"Aw hell, he was listening on the CB and came over uninvited. He's got Bob's number in his cell." The freckle-faced, red-headed police officer shrugged. "We figgered since the radios are experiencing interference, we'd let *him* call."

"Good boy." the sheriff smiled patting his officer on the back. "Let me know when y'all heah back from 'im."

The portly restaurant owner drove up while they spoke, and the younger officer trotted away with a slight "yessir" as he departed to do his duty.

"Frawley!" The sheriff called out cordially, hoping to keep the effects of the tragedy to a minimum for the old man.

"Thought you might as well know that Ms. Savant is no longer on the grounds, so yore more than welcome to walk through with me if ya like." There was a great deal of silence between the men before an answer could present itself.

Afterall, Frawley didn't care how cordial the sheriff was, he didn't like the idea of a walk through, whether the dead body was still in there or not. Gazing up at the top part of his building misty eyed and ill from the loss, Frawley's eyes fell on the windows on the front of the business. His own reflection stared back at him, as if he wasn't even inside his own body. Such helplessness overwhelmed him that he seemed an intangible spirit bound to earth by a cruel curse.

The weight of Alyssa's disappointment when she had left earlier, still lingered upon his rounded shoulders and he regretted the exchange now. Curiosity arose within him as to whether Alyssa had either done this to Becky out of spite, or had someone do it to her for the same reason. His gaze shifted uneasily over to the sheriff.

"Why should I go in?" He snuffed.

"Well…" Sheriff Griffin mumbled, struggling for the easiest way to talk the man into going inside with him. "You might be able to tell us something. We don't know what your restaurant is like back in the offices… and you do. If something were out of place, you would know.

"Look Frawley. I know this is hard on ya. Believe me, it ain't no easier for me to go in and see the little girl who grew up with my children like that. Come on. Won't you at least try? We have statements from everyone else… cept Lyssie."

"Have you tried her house?"

Sheriff Griffin looked at him curiously.

"No. She come by here though. Didn't she work tonight? I 'sumed that's why she was here. She was on the schedule that was hangin' by that time clock back yonder. She come in when they was totin' Becky out, and she left outta here just a cryin'."

The sheriff spit out the rest of his tobacco as he waited for the man to approach an answer.

Frawley seemed perplexed by something and the sheriff didn't like it.

"What's wrong, Frawley?" He pried. "She *was* supposed to work tonight wasn't she?" He asked, his laid-back, southern style evident as he squeaked out a faint disarming smile.

Frawley gave the matter a lot of thought before answering and he responded in the only way his heart would let him.

"If she was on the schedule then she was supposed to work. She was running late though, so I guess she must not have gotten here when she was supposed to. Technically, all she has to do is pick up the books anymore." Frawley hated lying, but he wasn't exactly lying either. He just couldn't tell them that Alyssa could possibly have done this, until he knew for certain that she had it in her to do such a thing.

****

Sheriff Griffin walked Frawley toward the door and as they were about to go inside, a loud screeching noise erupted behind them.

Wheeling around in the direction of the noise they encountered Bob, the mechanic, sliding into the parking lot sideways in a brown Pacer. Throwing the door to the car open, Bob hit the ground running.

"Sheriff!" He yelled as he jogged up to the two men. "I'm sorry I'm out of breath, but I hurried fast as I could to get here. This here's the car I loaned out to that real estate lady!"

The sheriff's interest peaked as he smiled at Bob.

171

"Where did you find that thing at boy? We been lookin' all over hell and half a Georgia for it."

"I *didn't* find it." He grasped at his side as he tried to catch his breath. "Someone brought it back."

Bob's obvious weight problem had gotten the better of him at this point and he bent over to rest his hands on his knees and breathe, his overhauls fluxing in and out with each breath.

A slow smile spread across the sherriff's cheeks.

Bob looked up at the sheriff, worry clouding his features.

"I hope you ain't mad at me for driving it over here," Bob said, his breath slowly returning. "but I didn't see it 'til uncle Frawley left. His car's the reason I was at the shop so late to start with, and I couldn't maintain radio communication tonight for some reason. I hope my drivin' it won't hurt y'all's investigation none."

The sheriff laughed out loud.

"*Son*! I'm so happy to see that car you could have shit in the front seat and I wouldn't have cared less. Why didn't ya jes call the restaurant?"

"I wanted to, but for some reason, the lines are down over here. I heard on the po-lice radio about the commotion, and got here fast as I could."

Sheriff Griffin grabbed another policeman as he went by.

"Get someone from the city to come tow this car in so's we can scour it for evidence linkin' it to them murders. Also, I want yuns to git dis-pach to call the telephone comp'ny and get somebody out heah' to check them lines." He barked pointing up to the phone lines, swaying gently in the wind, as if nothing had yet gone amiss.

"Our killer may'a been planning this for some time, and actually have some kindy access to telephone company information and procedures. Someone may'a seen sumpthin out that way too, so make sure whoever works the case gits out to the phone comp'ny and asks 'round."

"I'm on it." The officer replied taking his leave.

Patting the officer on the back as he walked away, Sheriff Griffin pulled his pants a little farther up onto his slightly paunch belly, and popped a Rolaids into his mouth before going back to walk the owner through his restaurant.

He stopped to grab a couple pairs of paper booties and some rubber gloves for their hands from the investigative team's vehicle on his way in.

"Gonna be a long night." He mumbled.

****

172

Frawley tread cautiously past the few employees who remained, and his skin began tingling. Poor, poor Becky... poor Alyssa if she was guilty of this!

His falling out with Alyssa could be the cause of all the mayhem and the tremendous weight it placed on him, nearly stole his breath away. He should have known better than to approach her the way he did.

As he proceeded down the hall, listening to the sheriff bark orders and talk to everyone, his mind went over the events leading to this night. If he had merely pointed out the mistakes, Alyssa would have pulled herself off of the duty, and probably appointed Becky to it herself. She was that shrewd and business minded. Frawley had treated her like an employee... and not a daughter. His first time ever doing it, and this ugliness may have come of it.

He had walked numbly through the restaurant, saying nothing and only shaking his head when asked if there seemed to be anything out of place. They finally came to the office. Sheriff Griffin turned to look at Frawley kindly before he spoke to him.

He handed a pair of gloves and paper booties to Frawley. He began putting his on while talking.

"This is where we found the vic-tim's bawdy. She had apparently come back heah' to close out the business day when he got her."

Frawley only nodded as the door came open and they stepped inside.

The Crime Scene Investigation crew had not come in yet and blood had not yet begun to dry, so not only did the office reek of death so foul that it made the poor man dizzy, the walls were colored with traces of vermilion.

Frawley swooned. Before he knew what hit him, he found himself sitting on the floor outside the office with Sheriff Griffin.

Stooping next to him, the sheriff was pressing the lid back onto a small vile of smelling salts, which he handed off to an ambulance worker.

"You okay Frawley?" He asked, taking a small Dixie cup of water from the officer who delivered it.

Frawley nodded. Though the sudden illness overpowered him, he was satisfied that this was *not* something Alyssa could possibly have anything to do with. As he began to drink the water, Sheriff Griffin looked up and a smile tilted the corners of his mouth upward.

A tall, handsome man of color drifted in and out of shadows through the hall, his camel colored trench coat going from gray to camel colored with each shadow along the way.

The sheriff greeted the man with a hardy handshake.

"Detective Rahbuhts. So nice to see you."

At the sound of social banter, Frawley rose to his feet, leaning closely to the wall for balance.

"This is Mistuh Frawley. He owns the restaurant."

Detective Roberts's warm light brown eyes moved unflatteringly over Frawley's chubby little body, and then up to his face. Upon having a good look at the man's features, Detective Roberts grinned. He could see Frawley's obvious terror and having the experience he had, the detective didn't want to complicate things for him.

"Nice to meet you." He smiled giving Frawley a hardy handshake. "It must be pretty bad in there huh?" He added as he leaned against the wall next to the portly man, and lit a swisher sweet.

"You can't smoke in here." Frawley remarked dryly, looking at the small cigarello.

Detective Roberts glanced up at Sheriff Griffin for support, but no luck. The sheriff only nodded in Frawley's favor as one of the forensic people came to get him and he took his leave.

"Sorry." Detective Roberts grunted pinching it off and quickly placing it in his pocket.

"I guess I didn't see a no smoking sign."

"That's cause yore leanin' on it." Frawley noted dryly.

Detective Roberts turned to look over his shoulder, then lifting an eyebrow to see he had missed it.

"So I am. I never go anyplace where I can't smoke unless I'm working, so I hope you'll forgive the err."

"Forgiven...*detective*." Frawley smarted, mocking a man of his station who had not even noticed the "*no-smoking*" signs throughout the restaurant. In an effort to fill the dead air, Frawley began to ramble.

"I only do it because insurance companies give businesses a break for being no smoking establishments."

"I never knew that. You can call me Jamal." The detective smiled.

"Frank." Frawley pointed to himself as if he were a caveman introducing himself.

"Nice to meet you!" he responded reaching out a firm handshake. "You don't have to go back in there Frank, but I will need you to answer a few questions for me. Okay?"

Frawley hesitated before nodding the affirmative. He hoped he could get around questions about Alyssa, and prayed that they wouldn't come up.

"I need first of all, for you to tell me who to contact... next of kin for Becky, that sort of thing."

"Becky had no kin. She was a widow. Her parents are dead and her dead husband's parents are dead. The only person she has left behind..." Frawley sniffled looking down at his feet.

He had to battle hard against the urge to cry as the realization of Becky's death swept over him for the first time, solidifying in his mind as a true and definite matter... not some phantom news story. The one survivor she had left behind, would always suffer her loss.

He answered with tremendous difficulty.

"Is her five-year-old son, Benjamin. He's with my wife right now. She baby-sits... baby-sat for Becky." he amended. Frawley looked into the detective's eyes with a cloud of water puddling in them.

"How am I going to explain to a five-year-old that his mother will never come home... never see him again... never... never..." Frawley sobbed into his hands. He couldn't bear it any longer. There had just been too much going on.

"Easy. Easy." The detective patted his shoulder. "One thing at a time Frank. Maybe if you just answer the questions and spare yourself the details, this won't be so difficult for you."

Jamal's voice had softened and become even, and Frawley relaxed a bit.

"Had Becky recently been arguing with anyone? A coworker, a boyfriend? The extent of the violence in this crime leads me to believe that this may have been personal, that the victim might actually have known the attacker. In order for someone to do this to a person, they would almost certainly have to be furious with them, and that's why we assume it's personal."

Frawley had been shaking his head 'no' the whole time the detective talked.

He would never admit that Alyssa might have a motive for killing Becky, and there just wasn't anyone else who could be angry with her.

"As I said before. Becky really didn't have much of a private life. She married one time out of love, and he was killed in a car accident before their child was born. She didn't date and stayed around here more than anywhere else."

"Maybe a customer then." Jamal pried, sensing an inner conflict, as Frawley's lips quivered and he instantly replied in the negative to most questions. "Did she have any regulars who stand out to you as unusually attentive, or strange?"

"No. Someone would most likely have known."

The detective raised a skeptical eyebrow at Frawley.

"Really Mr. Roberts. I don't know what your town is like, but I hire only people I know and trust. People who I have known for most of their lives. We're more a family than employers to our staff. This is all so senseless that it's mind boggling."

"Tell me about it." Jamal Roberts had been around the block a time or two in his day and could tell that Frawley was hiding something, but he could also tell that whatever he hid, was something he would probably never tell about either.

"Well Mr. Frawley, you're free to go if you like. I have to go do this whole investigative thing of mine now, but if you remember anything," He added flipping a business card from his coat pocket and handing it to Frank, "Call me."

Frawley started down the hall with nothing more than a nod when the detective stopped him.

"Oh Frank. Do you have a security camera in here somewhere?"

Frawley thought a moment before he nodded.

"Yes. But it probably won't help much. We generally only cut it on right before we go out the door at night. The last thing on it will probably be from last night."

"Is it timed and dated on the film?"

Frawley nodded and was beginning to turn away when a thought occurred to him. Jamal watched Frank stop... and he smiled.

He had gotten Frawley right where he wanted him. If he hired only people he knew he could trust, then why a security system at all?

"I know what you're thinking." Frawley's voice surprised Jamal and he let go of the doorknob to the office.

"What?" the detective asked quickly.

"I get an insurance break for security too."

"I never knew that." Jamal added stifling a chuckle. "Mind telling me where to find the camera so I can save a little time?"

"Behind the mirror on the door to the supply closet." Frawley watched the detective disappear into that awful room, and turned to walk toward the front of the building.

His wife would be worried sick about him. He should have been home two hours ago but then, he never *was* one for punctuality. Bringing a small cell phone to his ear as he made for the front door, Frawley sighed as he called home.

He thought about Lyssie and hoped that she would come out of this okay. He'd never expected anything this heinous to hit so close to home, but he guessed that maybe all of it was a little closer to home than anyone ever liked to admit.

End of Chapter Fourteen

Chapter Fifteen: Lights Out

Alyssa's jeep struggled up the steep foothills of the mountain. The rain worsened the ascent and she fussed to herself about it.

"Never a problem. Any other time this stupid piece of junk would run up this mountain without stopping to catch a breath, and *tonight* it wants to take a nap. Come *on* you stupid contraption!" She shouted slapping the steering wheel.

A car idled in a driveway as she went by and pulled out onto the road behind her. Under any other circumstance, this would not have bothered Alyssa but tonight, the matter rightly caused concern. Nervousness nagged at her, as she checked the lights of the car behind her.

"Thank God it's not a Pacer. Lights are too big." She whispered. Then she remembered the kind of car the real estate broker had driven and she looked again. "Nope. It's not hers either."

She smiled.

That car had been a late-model Cadillac, and this one had the lights of a newer vehicle. Continuing up the mountain, she complained every bit of the way that she hoped Brent appreciated her sacrifice. It was cold after all, and wet too.

The thunder rumbled the walls of the mountain, making Lyssie cringe. Immediately lightning ripped through the air like a tear in the fabric of nature. It magnified the fact that someone rode close behind her up the mountain road.

She crossed her fingers, hoping that whatever caused the jeep to sputter like it did would hold out until she could get to Brent's house.

Alyssa shook her long, strawberry blond hair, (which looked redder from the rain than blond), and some droplets of water came out, glistening across Kitty's back in the light of the dash.

She stroked the kitten, who had taken up a warm place beside her, and she smiled. She held no doubt that Brent would like the cat but as far as ol' Randy was concerned, she couldn't be too sure.

"How 'bout some music Ms. Kitty?" She asked turning on the radio. A great deal of static rattled the airwaves and Lyssie couldn't get a single station. Fumbling about with a duffle bag on the passenger side floorboard, she dug out an old Heart CD. All of her best CD's were in there and for the moment, she was glad to have remembered to put it up front.

"All right!" She cheered. "I haven't listened to this in ages! I thought I'd lost it!"

Quickly, she popped it in and skipped to the tune tickling her memory the most. As the music started, she felt a familiar smile part her lips when she heard the first line of her favorite song... "Wake me up with laughter. Wrap me in your arms."

She sang. She couldn't carry a note for long though, and decided to listen to the rest of the song in loyal silence. She hoped that every day of the rest of her life would be filled with laughter. She only hoped to wake every morning to Brent's love.

Completely enveloped in a serene feeling of security, she passed the mile marker that told her she had only a couple of miles left to go. With a sigh of relief, she glanced in the mirror to find that the car still followed.

The headlights on it penetrated the rain, but the vehicle stayed close enough to her, that they didn't interfere with her vision and ability to drive. She tried to think of all the families she knew who lived in the area, but the only one she could think of that lived past Brent's family... was her aunt Edna. Anyone else in those mountains dwelled there for privacy, and probably wouldn't think lightly of a visit this time of night.

Squinting at the lights of the car behind her, Lyssie tried to make out something familiar about it, but she couldn't. Completely foreign to her, the vehicle sparked no memory and she knew with certainty that it was not going to her Aunt Edna's.

Maybe it was someone coming to Brent for help... after all, she had sent that one man up there if anything went wrong with his pig. That must be it. This person was either on their way to Brent for help, or they were terribly lost.

Just as the thought formed in Alyssa's mind that it might be the killer, her car sputtered like a small creature pleading for air. She pumped at the accelerator, but it only stood to make the jeep gasp even more.

"This isn't happening." She fretted looking to the car in the mirror with fear. "Come on car. You've *got* gas..." Alyssa automatically glanced at the gas gauge to find that it now rested below empty.

"This isn't possible!" She shouted, banging furiously at the gauge with her index finger.

The engine died and Alyssa carefully maneuvered the vehicle onto the shoulder, which under normal circumstances wouldn't have been so bad. However, with the wet condition of the road and the car still going at least fifty miles an hour when it died, the power steering had quit working.

She had great difficulty getting off of the road with that other vehicle following so closely.

Likening the snatching of the steering wheel to grappling with a bear as it began to spin, she just managed to get over enough so that the car behind her went around.

She eased her foot onto the brakes, but found that they didn't want to work either. Closing her eyes for a second to think, she remembered that when the car was in a spin, you weren't supposed to turn the wheel contrary to the force of the car. So, when the brakes failed and the car spun, she had enough sense to go with the flow. She slipped the car into neutral, and it finally slid to a halt sideways in the middle of the road.

Lightning touched ground somewhere off in the distance, rumbling the jeep so forcefully that it frightened both Alyssa and Kitty. They jumped and shrieked at the same time.

Lyssie put her hand over her heart and caught her breath. She realized then, that she hadn't much choice in the matter. Having spun far enough down the road that she couldn't be more than a mile and a half from Brent's place, it looked like she would have to walk it.

Hopping from the car, leaving the door open, (she knew the cat wouldn't dare jump out in the rain), Alyssa bared down and began pushing it out of the middle of the road.

She didn't worry so much about someone wrecking her car, but she did worry about someone else getting into the same fix and getting hurt.

She pushed the car with all her strength toward the side of the road, and finally got it to move enough that she could jump in and guide it. Leaving the door open in case she had to get out and try to physically stop or start it again, she slowly steered the vehicle down the slope of the road, and over to a ditch. Once she got the car tilting sideways off the upside of the shoulder of the road, she cut on the flashers, and grabbed the keys from the ignition.

She glanced over at the kitten longingly. Hard as it was to leave the tiny creature, she didn't dare venture out into the night with a terrified feline. She patted the cat on the head softly, and climbed over into the back seat. Reaching into the back of the jeep, she lifted up a hidden compartment where she kept an emergency road kit.

There was a big flashlight inside, a lighter, some flares, and some fresh batteries. She plopped the batteries into the bottom region of the flashlight, and tested it to see that it worked.

Satisfied that she could use it, she put the flares into her jacket pocket, along with the lighter and started digging through a box for her raincoat.

The raincoat appeared to be missing, so she dumped her dirty clothes out of a 30-gallon garbage bag and before she knew it, she had a nice little raincoat.

"So much for showing up pretty and smelling like perfume."

She grimaced as she whiffed the smell of the dirty clothes that lingered in the plastic of the bag. Alyssa picked up her flashlight, and climbed back over the front seat where she kissed the kitten softly on the head and stepped out of the vehicle. As she glanced down to survey herself with criticism, she heard a car coming and stepped back to the other side of the jeep.

Peering over her vehicle, she could see a car coming from the direction she intended to go in, and discovered that this same car had passed her on the road earlier. She would know those head-lights anywhere, after the length of time she had fretted over them.

Ducking behind the jeep and lying flat to the pavement, Alyssa watched as the car passed by hers slowly.

She felt stupid.

She would just love to jump out from behind her car and shout "Could you give me a ride?" But she had seen too many bad horror movies end that way.

Relief arrived when the car went on by without coming to a complete stop. Somewhat convinced that it hadn't been the killer, Lyssie felt better, but angry that she hadn't stopped them. Tightening her grip on the flashlight, she thought for a moment.

Looking down both sides of the road as she lay on the steamy pavement, the fear of doubt clouded her mind. Suppose the killer found out she was going to see Brent, and wanted to catch her? Then she'd be a sitting duck on the road, but in the woods...

She turned to face the woods on the other side of the ditch that her car was parked on. Sighing, she rolled onto her back. Gazing wishfully back toward her jeep, as the flashers lit up the highway, she realized that as much as she hated leaving the light, it'd be a lot harder for a killer to catch her in the woods.

She had a great sense of direction. Besides, having grown up in the area and having ridden Brent's horses through the woods on a few occasions, her chances were better there. She sat up cautiously and started toward the woods, confident that this was the only way.

She would just have to make it. It wasn't so far away. She'd walked five times that on a good day at the ranch and if it weren't for the weather, she wouldn't mind the walk at all... but then maybe she could use it to her advantage, should the killer appear. No sooner had she penetrated the shelter of the trees, then the rain began to pound the ground like an angry waterfall. Alyssa was then thankful for the shelter of the woods. There wouldn't be half as much rain among them as there would have been on the road. She just had to keep her eyes open for fallen trees, flooding, lightning... and killers. Chuckling perversely, she began to trudge the long way to Brent's farm. If her memory served her right, about a half a mile ahead there should be a walking trail that came out at Brent's family's graveyard, which stood on the hill above both houses.

The lightning struck and thunder rattled the ground, but Alyssa was fairly confident that she could handle the elements. It was something *worse* than nature that worried her.

Standing on a leafy hill where she could look down onto the path below, she had made fairly good time... all things considered. As she picked her way down the steep hill to the walking path, she tripped on a stump that had lay hidden beneath the leaves and, finding the ground too slippery to regain her footing, she went tumbling down the hill onto the walking path. Here, she hit her head on a stone, and the lights went out in Georgia.

****

Detective Roberts had ridden back to the police station with Sheriff Griffin. His obvious height seemed even greater as he stood in front of a small television set waiting for Frawley's security tape to rewind. He smiled thinking that if Frawley's insurance agent knew how old the equipment actually *was*, they'd probably burn his policy. He chuckled trying to think whether it was worse that Frawley had old equipment or that Brion had the equipment necessary to utilize it.

Lightning struck ground up in the mountains and Jamal shook his head sadly. The thought occurred to him, that the life of that young lady had been struck down so prematurely.

The tape stopped.

Pressing the play button, he situated himself in the sheriff's chair behind his desk. He put his feet up, and took a long draw from his coffee cup before searching pockets for a smoke. He fidgeted about until he found one. It was a little smashed and damp from the rain, having been stashed in his trench coat, but he didn't care. Right now, his every thought was bent on taking a long relaxing drag.

As he put it into his mouth, he quickly realized that he had misplaced his lighter and, taking a deep breath, he rose and went to the door.

"Yo Griffin?" He yelled across the crowded office, his booming voice rattling Griffin's officers.

"Yeah?" The sheriff shouted back.

"Got a light?"

The sheriff reached inside one of his deputy's shirt pockets and yanked out a lighter, which he readily threw across the room to the detective.

Jamal winked smartly at the boy whose lighter he tucked in his own pocket after lighting his Swisher Sweet.

"Thanks kid." He chuckled puffing away, and waving to the sheriff before retreating toward the office to finish the review.

Brion Griffin headed for his office at a trot. He wanted to get Jamal situated before he began his task load for the night. If the detective kept busy doing his own job, the sheriff had a better chance of getting *his* done. Entering the office, he smirked, throwing Jamal's dress shoes off his desk.

"Ah have some paper work 't file, and Turner is going to let me use her desk since she's bout to get off tonight." Sheriff Griffin offered. "The office is all yores for now, jes keep yer smelly feet off'n my desk, Rahbuts. Holler if ya need anything."

Jamal merely nodded as his portly friend headed for the door.

"If anything happens, I'll let you know. We ain't careful, we might get wet tonight after all."

"Too bad it's gotta be in the rain. Huh frog man?" Brion replied.

"Them was the days Mistuh Toad."

They laughed.

The two of them had earned those names together as children and the memory of it never left them. Sheriff Griffin smiled, shaking his head at the inference, and he went back to finish the conversation he'd been having with officer Donald, prior to Jamal's interruption.

"Where were we, son?" He asked the young cop.

"What an asshole." Don remarked about the detective taking his lighter.

"Asshole, yes. Incompetent, nevah. If they's something important on them tapes... he'll know it. Now let's go get some bad guys, son. I got a feeling we're in for a long night."

****

Detective Roberts sat back down at the desk and put his feet up as he watched the slow tape. It rolled almost endlessly with nothing moving about in the office and, finding himself quite bored with it, he decided to fast-forward through the nighttime part when no one was even working. He took his eyes off of the screen to tap out and pinch off the end of his Swisher, but only for a moment.

Upon looking up, he discovered that something was going on.

The blurry image of a woman looked as if she were trying to cut off the tape, but didn't know how. He stopped forwarding and watched as Becky attempted to turn off the camera. She clearly fussed about something, but the audio wasn't obviously working, so he didn't know what.

Then, over her shoulder, Frawley appeared in the doorway. She seemed to pretend to have cut the camera off to keep Frawley from finding out that she didn't know how to operate it.

Jamal watched as the girl left the office, and Frawley sat down to count the money for the register. Nothing out of the ordinary yet. It was truly a God send that this girl hadn't known how to operate the camera... even if he couldn't hear anything.

Jamal found himself forwarding the tape here and there to get down to the nitty-gritty of the situation. He had been at it an hour when he found Alyssa waltzing into Frawley's office.

"Whoo!" He smiled at the young beauty. "Now we're talkin!"

Leaning back in his chair, Jamal watched Alyssa's expressions change in rapid succession from one emotion to another. Then he watched her go blank, as Frawley talked with her.

He would have spared no measure to find out what that old geezer said to hurt her so badly, that it showed with such obvious effect. A once vibrant, gorgeous lady had been reduced to indifference, hurt, and then... she got mad. He saw the fire jumping around in her eyes as she stood up. Alyssa nearly oozed anger.

Pausing the tape, Jamal rushed to the door where he could look out into the station house. As he glanced from desk to desk, he saw Sheriff Griffin's face nod up a bit above the backside of a computer, his glasses reflecting the computer screen in front of him.

"Griffin! Come here! I think I got something."

With no hesitation, the sheriff leapt from his chair and ran quickly to the office. By the time he arrived, Jamal had run the tape back for him.

"Watch." He said as he started the tape to the point where Alyssa entered the office.

Sheriff Griffin watched as she entered the room, her spirits seemingly light as a feather.

She wore a smart grin on her face, and the sheriff found himself smiling.

"You know her?" Jamal asked.

"Used to date 'er aunt in high-school. The name's Alyssa Johnson. Why?"

"Watch." He insisted. "You have any idea what this girl does for Frawley?"

"She does the books." Griffin replied watching her expressions evolve.

He too wondered what Frawley had said that wounded her so deeply, but as far as linking Alyssa to the murders, the thought never once entered his mind.

"What's this got to do with th' price o' rice in China?"

"What if she did it?" Jamal offered.

"That's ridiculous. 'Sides. You know yerself that you can't do nothing to her for being mad at her boss... that kindy thing happens all the time. This doesn't show me anythin' to do with Becky."

"Let's just watch it anyway. I sure would like to know what old Frank was saying to her."

"You and me both." Brion agreed.

Forwarding until he saw Becky re-enter the office, it seemed to Jamal that she was getting ready to close out for the day. She'd gotten the ledger from the drawer and placed it on the desktop, then arranged the adding machine and register receipts in order.

"Who is this?" Jamal asked pointing to Becky.

"Y'all know who that is." Sheriff Griffin answered quietly.

"I thought you said this Alyssa person was supposed to do the books?"

Sheriff Griffin nodded.

"I think it's time I had a little talk with Frawley."

"I'm goin' with yuns." Brion added, grabbing his raincoat from the rack, and slinging it on.

The two were on their way to the door of the station house, when Don brought a file the sheriff had requested.

"Thanks" the sheriff smiled. "Jes' put it on mah desk." As he watched the young officer walk toward his office, he caught sight of Bob, the mechanic, out of the corner of his eye. Sauntering over to the desk where Bob sat, filling out a report he asked:

"What are y'all doin' heah this time a night?"

"Some damn fool dun stole *my* car now!" he shouted.

"What?" the sheriff asked, leaning over to read the report. "That's right. Uncle Frawley took me back to the shop so I could close up, and when I went out back to the station, I found out *my* car was gone."

"All right." Sheriff Griffin frowned. "Yawl got the license plate number on yuns?"

"It's all in the report." Bob answered, yawning. "Could I just get a ride home? I'm awful beat and I don't wanna call Uncle Frank to git me."

Looking over to the other side of the room, Sheriff Griffin waved to a female officer.

"Erma." He said as she walked up. "Take pore Bob here home, and see that his wife understands that it's mah fault he's out so late. Tell her I'm sorry. Kay?"

Erma smiled as she led Bob to the door. The minute he'd left the room, Brion Griffin turned to one of his officers and handed them some paperwork from the mechanic's file.

"I wanna APB out on this plate, and I want yuns ta litter the C.B. and airwaves with it. Somebody somwheah knows where this car is, and ah want ta find it... yesterday!" He shouted. As the sheriff turned around to face Jamal, Don called to him from the doorway of his office.

"Sheriff. You gotta see this."

Donald stood in the doorway, his face ghostly pale, his red hair seeming duller in the dim light of the station house, and he held the remote to the VCR in his hand.

Jamal and Brion nearly knocked one another down trying to be the first in the door to the office. Reaching the office first, Brion had to shake Jamal from his back as they collided on the other side of his doorway.

There, in suspended animation on the screen, Becky appeared to be working on the ledger, and some dark ominous figure loomed from behind a curtain in the background.

"Hang on to yore ass sirs." Don said as he started the video.

"I'm going back to work. I saw most of this when I first came in, and I couldn't take it twice if I wanted to.

Not wanting to see anymore carnage than necessary, he trotted from the room, making doubly sure to close the door behind him without looking back.

On the video, as the door closed a beast leaped from the curtains behind Becky.

Both of their jaws dropped in horror as this hideous thing grabbed Becky in such a hold that if she had moved, he could snap her in two pieces.

He seemed to be growling something into her ear. It was a man of some sort, but one big ugly... weird looking man.

Becky's trembling fingers reached out for the telephone and she glanced right into the camera as she dialed the phone.

"Wait." Sheriff Griffin asked. "Pause it. Can you see what numbers she's a dialin'?"

"No dammit. She's on the other side of the phone. How are we supposed to find out who she called for this creep? The recipient of that phone call could be his next victim, or even his accomplice."

The monstrously huge man spoke into the phone first, then he made Becky hang up and dial again.

Brion Griffin shook his head solemnly as he looked into the sweet fearful eyes of a woman who would never again see the light of day.

The perpetrator tightened his grip on the woman's neck as she spoke, and she seemed to carefully word her sentences.

As Becky returned the receiver to the cradle on the phone, so awful was the carnage that ensued, that they had to turn off the tape. The sheriff staggered around to the back of his desk and sat down, placing his elbows on the top it, his head in his hands. He squeezed tightly at his temples in an effort to clear his mind of the terrible thing he had just seen.

"I'm sorry you had to see that sheriff." Jamal murmured politely, knowing in his heart how hard this would be on everyone. "Maybe if Frawley had security systems for something other than insurance reasons, this wouldn't have happened."

At first Brion was offended by Jamal's remark, but then he thought about it, and had a terrific idea.

He called Frawley.

"Frawley. This is Sheriff Griffin. No. It's all right. There's nothing serious right now. I just had something I wanted to ask you about."

"All right." Frawley whispered after checking to see that Benjamin couldn't hear him. "But make it quick. I can't afford to say anything in front of the boy."

"He doin' okay?" Brion asked.

"Oh a lot of cryin right now, but the wife's lovin him up. We'll work this thing out. What can I do you for, Sheriff?"

"You got caller I.D. down to th' restaurant?"

"Sure. Not only is it considered a security device by my insurance company, but also if someone calls to order out and gets disconnected, I can call 'em right back."

"Will that thing work tonight while the phone lines are down?"

"Yeah. As long as it's plugged in."

"That's all I needed t' know Frawley. I know yore busy so I'll let yuns know what's going on tamorrah. I ain't got time to get a search warrant, so would you mind too terribly bad if I went back to the restaurant and had a look around?"

"Be my guest." Frawley whispered again. "I'll see y'all tomorrow Brion. Good night."

"Night Frank."

"Are we goin to the restaurant?" Jamal asked walking toward the door.

"You know it." Sheriff Griffin walked out into the office and found another officer fiddling with papers and trying to look busy for the boss.

"Son. We gotta get a look at that phone system out at the restaurant. Have we got anythin' from the nerdy kid yet?"

"No sir. I haven't been able to reach him. But one of the guys said the telephone company had a man out to the restaurant having a look around at the phone lines. Apparently they're down."

"Good." The sheriff answered. "Get ahold of their dispatcher, and tell 'em to radio that fella to wait. I gotta get down there to 'im and asked some questions."

"Yessir." The officer called as Brion Griffin and Jamal Roberts made for the door.

****

The telephone technician waited in his truck, the rain still pouring down his windshield when they arrived. Knocking on the window, the sheriff motioned for the guy to let the glass down.

"Yessir?" He shouted above the thunder. "What can I do for y'all?"

"Was the lines cut?"

"Yessir. They was. I been telling this old man out here for years he needs to upgrade, but he won't listen. Every time a rat farts near one of these lines I have to come out here. They could have cut them old things with a pair of rubber scissors."

Looking around he realized it was just as he expected, most of his guys had gone and that skinny kid from IT never showed up.

"Do you know anything about his actual phone?"

"The landline with push buttons on the deck and the puke green spiral chord from the 80's?"

Jamal busted out laughing.

"That's the one." Sherriff Griffin replied with a smart look at the detective on the side.

"Yeah. I know the model. He's had the thing since the caller ID window was the latest tech device. Cheap bastard just keeps replacing parts rather than buying a new one."

"That said, laughing boy over here and I ain't tech-savvy. We need somebody to help us get some info off from it. Would ya mind having a look at it? I know it's late, but it might help us find a killer."

The technician nodded, slipping his ball cap on and zipping up his jacket.

He hopped out of the cab of his truck and shook hands with the two men.

"Name's Jason" He raised his voice above the thunder to make sure they could hear.

"I'm Brion, this is Jamal. Thanks for doing this, but... I'm gonna warn ya, that even though crime lab has been out chere and took care of much a the mess, it's most likely still mighty bad in there."

The man nodded.

Griffin rounded up the last couple officers and they carefully preceded Jamal and Brion into the restaurant to make sure the coast was clear. As they entered, Jamal turned to Jason and asked:

"If someone cut the lines... someone might have seen them do it, right?"

"Not necessarily." Jason put in. "The lines here are old and they run to the back of the restaurant. There's not much light back there so theoretically, anybody could have cut the lines and maybe *no* one would have seen them."

Both men nodded as they came to a halt in front of the office doors.

Sheriff Griffin turned to Detective Roberts, who was putting on exam gloves he'd lifted at the station.

"I'll go in to the supply closet first and see if I can find some Lysol or something to kill the smell. You guys should wait here."

Jamal disappeared into the room, and the Sheriff turned then to Jason.

"The problem is that the killuh made a call from this office, and that happens to be the last call made on this phone before the lines were cut. In order to keep him from killing again, we have to find out who he called. They may be in great danjuh."

"No doubt." Jason added in astonishment, still stunned by the fact that he currently found himself wrapped up in the most serious event of his life.

Opening the door carefully, Jamal motioned for them to come inside. As they entered, he offered Jason a pair of rubber gloves, which he readily took. The telephone repairman had to work hard on not looking at the blood. He focused on the telephone and started toward it.

Kneeling down on the floor, he leaned over the unit, still lightly spattered with blood.

Despite the gruesome situation they were presently involved in, he smiled when he realized someone had their thinking cap on while using the phone last.

"This is great." He said looking up at Sheriff Griffin. "It was set to record the last conversation on the answering device. Real sign of genius of the part of the person who actually did the calling. You won't have to even look up the number."

Jamal and Brion smirked at each other and said at the same time… "He must get an insurance break for having a fancy phone!"

Jason pressed a couple of buttons on the answering machine, and before they knew what happened they were listening to a conversation between Becky and Alyssa.

"She must be heading up to Edna's house." Brion Griffin muttered. "Jamal. Go to the car and radio dis-patch to see if Alyssa Johnson has arrived on her aunt's farm yet, and if she has, tell her to batten down and stay put!"

Jamal was out the door with nothing more than a nod, and the sheriff looked at the telephone man.

"Thanks son. You may have saved this little girl's life."

"Wish I could have helped earlier then." He added looking around the room at the macabre marks of violence that spread around them like a wall of death.

"We all do." The sheriff answered, patting the young technician on the shoulder, as they made for the door.

****

As they came across the parking lot, the sheriff thanked Jason and waved to him as he pulled out into the dark street. He turned toward his car, where Jamal sat half in the passenger side, talking on the radio to the girl that ran the switchboard. He looked up at Griffin with hope dancing around his brown eyes.

"Bubba just called the station. He passed Bob's Kia sittin' on the road way up in the mountain a while back, and had stopped to check it out. He couldn't find anyone in the car and when he heard the APB, he called the office on the C.B."

"Have we got his twenty?"

"Dispatch. You got a twenty on Bubba, honey?"

"Yes sir." She answered curtly. "Bubba Honey says he's a little farther than a mile from Dr. Price's house."

Though Detective Roberts chuckled at her candor, the sheriff's brow furrowed.

"Jamal, tell them to patch Bubba through to this radio. Station 14."

Running around and sliding into the driver's seat, he grabbed the handle, waiting to hear Bubba's voice.

"This is Bubba Bear. Got them ears on sheriff? Come on."

"This is Sheriff Griffin, Bubba Bear. What's your situation? Over."

"Well I seen this Jeep Cherokee sitting on the side of the road and Bob's car out here, so I figured he was helping out Miss Johnson... only ain't neither one of 'em here. I got back in the truck and heard the APB on the radio. I figured seein' as how I was here, I might ought to call. Over."

"That's a copy Bubba. Can you be a little more specific about your twenty?"

"Uuuh... I reckon I'm about half a mile past mile marker 126. Not far from Brent's place. Want me to head over there and have a look? Over."

"Don't you do it Bubba Bear. They's a killuh in Bob's car. We believe that he wants Miss Johnson, so we want yuns out of it. Copy?"

"You got it, good buddy. I need to get home anyway, but I'm keeping my ears on in case ya need anything. Copy?"

"That's a copy, Bubba. Out." The sheriff radioed headquarters. "Let me talk to my Shandra." He asked.

Brion looked over at Jamal. The detective's face was alight with amusement, a chuckle caught in the back of his throat.

"Shandra's a sweet gurl." Brion defended himself. "I used to date her grandma in highschool".

"Shandra." He said as her cheery voice bounced over the radio. "Find me what ya can on anyone who 'scaped from mental hospitals in the last year to five years, who might fit the description I want you to get from Donald. He saw the man on the tape and can help you out on it. Check also prison escapes and releases, and then cross-reference with victims fitting this MO in other Georgia / Alabama counties. Got that?" He asked.

"10-4 Sheriff."

"Good Girl. I think Detective Roberts and I are gonna need some back up at mile marker 126 on the mountain road toward Dr. Brent Price's place. Better send an ambulance and the coroner too…just in case. Can you do that for us?"

"Yes Sir." She answered, quickly beginning her duties.

"Well Mistuh Toad…" The sheriff remarked as he glanced at the rain pelting down on Jamal's legs, still stretched from the inside the car. "You ready for a wild ride with the Frogman?"

Jamal grinned at his old friend. The two of them had worked together dozens of times over the years, but neither of them had made reference to it since it first happened, until tonight.

They had been caught at Toad Bottom Creek with a couple of girls in the tenth grade. All four of them had been covered in silt and slime, were wet from head to toe for more reasons than just creek-bed frolicking and should have been in school.

It took them four weeks to wash all of the silty green out of their hair, and people had been calling them Frog and Toad right up until graduation after that.

"Might as well." The detective chuckled. "You'd have to be a frogman to survive the mountain in this weather."

"Well then get them long legs in here, ma friend, we got work to do." The sheriff grinned, and they were off to save the day.

****

Dizziness moved Alyssa to open her eyes. Moaning, the pain jolted through her as she lifted her head from the rock she'd hit it on. Gently touching the knot on her head, stickiness alerted her that she'd also lost some blood. Her eyes strained against the rain and the night to see.

She remembered how she had arrived here and what she had been doing, so she figured she couldn't be too badly hurt.

Rising, in an attempt to reach a sitting position, her neck began to throb and pinch in places she never knew existed. As she rubbed at her deltoid muscles, she began to wonder how long she had been out for. She hadn't a watch on to know for sure. She pulled her phone from her pocket hoping by some miracle she had finally gotten service, but the battery was completely dead. One thing was certain... the rain had gotten worse, and water ran all over the path like a small, muddy creek. That would slow her down, as it would camouflage the way.

"Gross." She muttered looking down at her jeans and her new white Reeboks, now fairly ruined. Carefully rising to her feet, Alyssa slung some of the mud from her clothes, and wrung some of it out of her long hair. Waiting only a moment to get her bearing, she turned in the direction of the farm and began the walk toward Brent's.

Her feet sank in the soft dirt and walking took great effort. She had twisted her ankle pretty badly in the fall. Still she pressed on, holding her head at a downward angle to keep the wind from stinging her face. Now that she tread over the path, there weren't as many trees to shield her from the storm.

Lyssie hoped like crazy that the killer would pick a better night to try anything. She was in no mood for it tonight. She chuckled at herself, muttering...

"Like I would be in a mood for it any other night. Must be the knot on my head." She growled.

Stopping for a moment to regain some of her strength, she bent, and then looked back the way she had come. Part of her wished she had stopped that car now. It would have been nice to be in Brent's arms instead of being wet and dirty on a back woods trail in the dark.

Then, hearing a heavy crunching noise in the leaves on the hill above her path, she turned to see if she could tell what it was. Dizziness returned, but she would not let it hold her.

Her mind lingered for a moment on the day that she had seen something running around in the woods on the outskirts of Brent's farmland, and her heart danced. The adrenaline pumped through her at the speed of light.

Standing up straight, she looked again in the direction the sound had come from, to find nothing there. She shook her head one more time, softly so that she wouldn't grow dizzy.

'*All of this crazy talk has got me to hearin' things.*' She thought.

Then it occurred to her... 'what if Brent really is the killer, and he's leading me out here to kill me?'

Alyssa only pondered the possibility for a second before deciding that if he *was* the killer, she'd sooner be dead than to live her life wondering about it. She might as well get this over with. Suddenly, the light in her flashlight began to fade. It grew dimmer faster and faster, until it quickly went out.

"So much for pink drummer bunnies." She fussed "I must have been out for quite a while." She muttered as she jammed the flashlight into her jeans pocket.

Continuing always in a forward movement, she went slowly. It took every bit of reserve energy she had left to continue in her quest to find Brent and set her life straight. Just when she felt she couldn't go another inch, a light fell down into the trees. She knew the place well. That glorious light stood on the edge of the graveyard, which separated Brent's home from his mother's. She tried to trot, but it came out more like a hop skip and jump to the property line now that her heart fluttered with excitement. Standing at the edge of the graveyard, she gazed tearfully down into the valley.

Brent's house nestled itself against the night like heaven come to earth. Darkness lurked from the windows, and it appeared that he had given up hope and gone to bed.

As she began down the hill, a pair of big, hairy hands closed around her throat so tight that she couldn't scream, try as she might. Though she fought as much as her tired arms and legs would allow, she couldn't do much more than flail about like a fish out of water.

Struggling with the unseen, Lyssie found herself dragged back into the dreaded woods, an action that went against every fiber of her soul. However, once she found herself back among the trees, the grip eased a bit and she got free enough to bite into the hands of her captor. As the grip retracted, the assailant let out an inhuman shout of pain, while she stomped its huge foot and began running. She ran so fast and frenzied that she thought her poor little frame would just crumble apart.

Her heart raced around her chest so hard it hurt, and she had to work to keep her breathing under control. The sound of heavy footsteps plodded along swiftly behind her and he outmatched her for speed. Leaping from the trail into the nearby shroud of trees, Alyssa quickly dove into some underbrush for cover. It never stopped coming.

Knowing that he had seen where, approximately, she'd left the trail, concern haunted her.

Still, she had been a good way ahead of him, so he had no way of knowing how far she'd gotten before hiding out.

A grey, misshapen foot soon passed the bush where she knelt for cover. He stopped so close that she could have touched him.

Alyssa's heart beat so loud that she just knew he could hear it. Refusing to panic, she sat perfectly still.

Though her visibility factor remained unknown to her, she would not chance giving herself away. She didn't even breathe. Her face ran red, and then purple from the lack of oxygen when the man must have finally decided that maybe she had gone farther than he thought, and started in the other direction.

Alyssa waited until he was out of earshot, then exhaled slowly. Before she got all of the breath out, those hands grabbed at her waist and pulled her up out of the bush.

He had come up behind her to keep her from being able to struggle. At the thought being caught, rage rampaged through her so hard that she almost forgot she was mad at the attacker too.

Reaching carefully to her back pocket, still not having been able to see the assailant, she snatched out the flashlight.

Finding herself momentarily free of his grasp as he got resituated, Alyssa spun around, and whacked the unsightly creature smack across the face with that flashlight as hard as she could. She leveled him and the moment he fell to the ground, he immediately began scrambling to get back up.

Alyssa held the flashlight askew and bashed at the man again and again with it.

Finally catching the flashlight, he fought with her to get it away.

Alyssa kicked, fought and clawed with all her might, but could not overpower such an inhuman thing.

Just when she thought she would die, a gunshot exploded in the night, which brought both she and the killer still for a moment.

"Get off her punk... and I might let you live to stand trial." Alyssa pushed at the man, whose impending size and weight nearly crippled her. Rising slowly off of her with his hands in the air, the killer turned to see Bubba holding a sawed-off shotgun on him.

"Don't even think about it buddy. If I missed... the spray would cut you in two." Evidently the thing could reason like a man. He knew that Bubba would never fire if there were some chance he might shoot Alyssa.

"Miss Johnson. I'll hold him. I want you to go for help." Alyssa was dumfounded. "Now!" Bubba shouted.

As the words leapt from his lips, the creature attacked him.

Bubba screamed, the monster growled and Alyssa remained paralyzed by her own fear.

"Run! Run!" Bubba shouted as the thing lunged at him and began to pound him into the ground.

"Get Brent! The sheriffs on his way! Run! *Run* Lyssie!"

Alyssa tore herself away from the sight of Bubba being beaten and began running as fast as her tired legs would carry her down the path.

Driven by the echo in her head that repeated over and over again: "Run! *Run* Lyssie!" she moved faster than she had ever run in her life. The light at the graveyard began inching toward her once more and she struggled to reach it. It was as if she were running in slow motion. No matter how fast she went she just couldn't get there quick enough.

Almost to the clearing that would put her in the graveyard, victory began to appear imminent, when the thing leapt from the trees onto the path in front of her.

"Oh *Shit!*" She cried, just before screaming at the top of her lungs, and he dragged her yet again off into the night.

End of Chapter Fifteen

Chapter Sixteen: Light Among the Night World Shadows

Lightning hit somewhere, and a tree fell. Brent sat straight up in his bed, sweating terribly. He wasn't sure what he had dreamed but whatever it was, it frightened him.

Standing, he stretched the kinks out of his back and went to the window so that he could look out at the night. A prayer lingered in his heart that Alyssa would reconsider this vendetta and return to him. He looked up, knowing that there wouldn't be any stars on a rainy night but he would have given anything to have seen just one to wish upon.

His gaze then trailed down to the graveyard. There, through the sheets of rain sliding over the glass, he saw a woman of small frame waving and jumping up and down under the light in the graveyard. After rubbing his eyes, Brent pinched his arm to make sure he wasn't still in the throes of a wild dream.

He looked again.

This was really happening!

Reaching for the jeans that he left over the back of the rocking chair, he slung them on in a hurry. It was time he got to the bottom of this.

He wasn't ten years old anymore, and he *wasn't* dreaming. His grandmother stood out there, waving at him to come there, so he would go.

He got the pants on without taking his eyes off of her and ran down the stairs, stopping just long enough to sling his flannel shirt on, but didn't bother taking the time to button it. Dashing out the back door, he picked up an ax in case this was some cruel ruse to get him out into the night without any protection.

Brent ran outside and started up the hill toward the woman flailing about for him to come to her. He found it hard to maintain his footing in the slick mud as it ran down the hill from the graveyard, but determination for the sake of his sanity drove him onward.

Reaching the pinnacle of the hill, he arrived just in time to see his grandmother disappear into the woods. He couldn't believe this was happening. He held out his hand to feel the rain, and then looked back toward the woods. This *was* real!

Moving as swift as his legs would carry him, he made for the trees until he heard a blood-curdling scream emanating from amongst the them.

"Lyssie!" He screamed above a clap of thunder, knowing immediately that the killer had her. How he knew it was her, was something he didn't understand and didn't care to analyze.

Racing into the thicket, darkness overtook him and the shadows became strangers in the night. The screams continued, but he couldn't get a bearing on her.

He turned one direction and then the next, calling to her in the darkness, then the unthinkable happened. The screaming stopped.

At this moment, the luminescent glow of his grandmother appeared ahead on the trail, as if leading him to Alyssa. Brent hadn't time to second-guess the reason he saw these things, he just had to hope for the best and went after the glowing presence.

His feet plodded heavily into the mud, sinking in with each step.

Wielding the ax and ready for battle, he hurried among the trees where his grandmother had just been, but found nothing.

Crouching close to the earth, he closed his eyes and listened carefully to each sound, feeling cautiously to every living thing around him.

The ax felt strong in his hand as if it were an extension of his body and his other hand rested softly in the mud. A tremor pushed at the ground, and he opened his eyes to see where it came from.

Squinting at the shadows of the night-world around him, Brent prayed for some semblance of sound that would lead him to Alyssa.

'*Come on Lyssie.*' he thought. '*Any other time you'd be squawking like black bird in the field... give me something now.*'

He concentrated as he gazed into a puddle of still rain water and waited for the next tremor.

****

Alyssa panted and gasped for air under the hairy hand that covered her mouth so tightly, she couldn't even open it to bite him. The thing had its legs wrapped around her like a vice and try as she might, she couldn't even squirm without him tightening even more. It was like being held helplessly doomed in the coils of a python.

She thought she heard Brent for a second, but then it was gone. She stopped squirming for a moment so that there wouldn't be any noise. She had to know that he'd found her.

Had he called her name?

Of course, he had... that's why the thing was trying so hard to hold her down and keep her quiet. Utter uselessness overwhelmed her. She could have rattled like an empty wagon any other time, but right now she couldn't even offer a squeak to help him find her.

Alyssa still listened intently for Brent, when she caught sight of a glow moving swiftly and silently among the trees. Her eyes widened over the restrictive fingers on her mouth, as she realized what she saw. She had seen it before... at the foot of the bed Brent slept in at the Biggmann Ranch. She now knew this was Brent's grandmother, Eliza Price.

Apparently... the assailant could see it as well, because he caught his breath and the second that Alyssa felt the slight flex of his fingers, she bit down until she could feel bone.

The creature wailed loudly, turning loose of Alyssa only for a moment. It was more than she needed.

Scrambling to her feet she snatched one of the flairs from her pocket, lit it, threw it into the air and ran as quickly as possible with her injury. She nearly got away, but the thing grabbed her sprained ankle, and she couldn't bare the pain.

She cried out and as she did, the monster slapped her to the ground, knocking her unconscious.

****

Brent heard the commotion in the cold stillness of a forest that shudders at the appearance of man, and smiled cunningly as the puddle he had been monitoring rippled.

"That's my girl." He grunted, jumping to his feet and tiptoeing in the direction from which the light had come.

The flair had burst into the top of a tree, illuminating a path to her location, but the glimmer faded in the rain before he managed to reach them. He'd heard Alyssa shriek though, and blood rushed to his head. He'd kill that bastard if he had in any way hurt her.

A cool mist filtered in through the trees and though it was fairly cold, sweat ran down Brent's nose.

He stripped off his jacket, perching it on a bush so that it looked as if he were standing on the other side of it. His well-formed muscles glistened with rain, as he began to hunt the hunter.

Ducking behind a tree, Brent scanned the terrain for any sign of movement, or unnatural placement of things. Broken leaves, limbs... something, anything. The woods had grown deadly silent and aside from the chilling rain, there was no noise where he crouched. He worried that Alyssa might already be dead. The silence was too great, and it overwhelmed him.

Apparently, this thing was not completely human, and it seemed in its natural way in the woods. It wouldn't have much trouble locating him in the darkness. It had only to find the place where there was some absence of sound, and he would locate Brent.

He began making animal sounds as quickly as the thought formed in his mind. He had been around animals enough that he could imitate a myriad of things. First his katydid ... then his owl. He made a scurrying sound in the grass in front of him.

The malice of this menace seemed to breathe all around him and the lack of movement had Brent paralyzed.

He closed his eyes, clinging tight to the ax and made up his mind that he would find Alyssa and just get the hell out of there alive.

As his eyes came open, he saw standing before him, the glowing apparition of his grandmother. He wanted to scream or say something to her, but the sound caught in the back of his throat. He could not compromise Alyssa's safety for any reason. He squinted at the floating angel to block the glare. A very warm and secure feeling crept over him, and he smiled.

The apparition put a finger to her lips and waved him on. He followed unquestioning and silent in his determination to save the only woman he could ever love. Following diligently, he continued surveying the shadows to be sure that the killer didn't lurk among them. He didn't have to look directly at his grandmother as she went, because the aura from her body ever so lightly lit the greenery around her as she drifted like a cloud through the trees.

Brent had an inexplicable feeling of confidence as he followed and soon, he arrived in a small clearing, where he found himself gazing down at Alyssa on the ground.

"Oh no." He breathed as he knelt down beside her to check her pulse.

"Thank God." He whispered. "She's alive."

His grandmother had gone, so he lay down the ax and scooped Lyssie up into his arms in an attempt to make for the house. Lifting her from the ground, he turned around and was met with the most forceful blow of his life.

A man loomed there: freakish in his size, and frightening to the eye. At least seven feet tall, he had terrible scant red hairs shooting from his pores and teeth that he bared with a snarl.

He smacked Brent to the ground with a short grunt, and then leapt on top of him as Brent carefully rolled Alyssa to one side.

The creature held Brent fast to the ground, and snarled like a wild animal into his face.

Closing his eyes, Brent concentrated. Suddenly, his body didn't exist. He found himself looking down onto his own face... seething with hatred for the one who had everything he had wanted for himself... the one who took his very normal life from him.

The thoughts of the creature puzzled him so, that he almost forgot what he had been trying to do. He concentrated on bringing to mind images of his grandmother... powerfully good images.

She had been the one truly good, pure thing Brent had ever known besides Alyssa, and the monster man didn't seem to have a bond with Alyssa like he had with Eliza. Neither he nor Brent had any difficulty thinking of her.

As the thoughts of her smiling on a warm summer day spilled across his mind, the creature lifted his weight from Brent for a moment.

He shook his head and cried loudly in octaves that might wake the dead. Brent wouldn't falter in his determination. He had to stop this thing and this was the only way he knew how.

Once he had it off guard, he hit it square across the jaw with both fists, and then Brent was able to get to his feet. The man-beast had long frightening claws for hands and lashed out, cutting Brent across the chest. He staggered backwards, but regained his stance. He refused to be beaten by this inhuman thing. Brent bobbed back and forth. He had fought a few fights in the boxing gym outside his university, and he knew how to stick it to a man. Dodging the next swing, seeing as how the animal merely figured that if something worked once... it would certainly work again, Brent took his chance.

Leaping with his swing, he swung in with a left uppercut that rocked the beast back onto his heels, his balance in jeopardy.

He snapped to quickly though, and jumped forward from the fall, rolling both of them to the wet earth, and landing on Brent's chest. He pounded Brent's head repeatedly against the ground. Banging his fury away on the frame of his helpless victim. The creature continued to wail away at Brent, until he was not able to fight any more.

He lay lifeless looking, a little blood trickling from the back of his head. The creature sat atop Brent staring with almost human pity, as if sorry for having been forced into doing this to him. He whined, and pushed a little of that sandy colored hair out of Brent's face. So, like his grandmother was he.

****

Alyssa rubbed at her cheek, and almost didn't want to attempt getting up. Weariness beat at her mind with such veraciousness, that she couldn't see straight. As she sat upright, she found her vision blurry to the point where she thought she saw three Brent's with… with… with three monsters on his chest!

At the very thought that Brent might be dead, Alyssa found her eyesight jump back into place... that's when she saw it.

A small ball of energy assembling from sparks the size of fireflies at first. Then a floating apparition appeared, equal to the one she had seen before when she had kept a vigil at Brent's side that long night that seemed an eternity ago.

The woman smiled at Alyssa, and pointed at the ax that Brent had put down in order to pick her up. The apparition put a finger to her lips, and Alyssa could see a tiny tear sparkle down its cheek. Reaching quietly for the ax, in a time that seemed forever to accomplish, Alyssa noted how the apparition placed a supportive hand upon the shoulder of the beast who now seemed to be weeping over Brent's lifeless body.

The creature's visage lifted upward with a look of tortured anguish and seeing this from her vantage point, Alyssa almost felt sorry for it. She could see the side of its long, lop sided face, and it seemed to whimper at the vision of Brent's grandmother. She shook her head slowly from side to side, as if trying to tell the creature that everything would be all right.

Alyssa looked upon Brent's still body, and swallowed against a lump of agony in her throat. He was probably dead, and this… "thing" had done it.

Rage flooded through her with such force that she thought her anger would burst through her body, and shoot out of her eye sockets in the form of laser beams.

She thought about all of the innocent women who had died for his twisted pleasure, and it was everything she could do not to scream at him out loud, and tell him just what she thought of him. Pulling back that ax, she aimed for his brain, training her sights on the top of that warped head of his. As the ax fell, her anger caused her to lose her bearing, and it came down between his shoulder blades. The beast wailed like a screaming Banshee and Alyssa, *so* unprepared for failure, was beside herself.

She would not leave Brent.

The image of Brent's Gram had faded the moment she swung the ax. The beast loomed before her like the reaper himself, coming to call upon the soul of the poor little farm girl, who loved a human with the strength of a god.

She stood, shoulders back, chin out, staring into the eyes of the thing that held her destiny in his hands, and she did not fear him. If Brent was dead, she didn't want to go on anyway, but she would go fighting. The creature growled and roared into her face like a bear, but Lyssie didn't flinch. She refused him the right to experience her fear. Enjoying the demise of his victims drove him to killing and if he murdered her, she would allow him no pleasure from it.

The thing, looking more like a man now than it ever had, naked and vulnerable as his gray skin faded in and out of shadows before he stopped, and stared at Alyssa as if looking into a mirror. He was dazed by her will and waited for a reaction to spur him on.

She got a clear ringing in her head, then heard faint whispering, and closed her eyes. She felt the beast leaping toward her, then a gunshot... and a yelp like that of a big dog. As the body hit the ground before her, the tremble of the earth almost caused her to stagger and fall down. Opening her eyes, she discovered that though blood had been spattered over her, it belonged to someone else, and she was still in one piece.

Looking then, up to where she could hear a round of cheers resounding through the trees, Alyssa saw Sheriff Griffin standing beside a man in a long tan trench coat.

There were a few other men too, who had rushed up the hillside to look down into the clearing. She instinctively glanced down to the figure of the beast that lay upon the ground, and a pang of pity charged through her like a knife.

The beast had something human behind those eyes, and she could only guess what torment he had suffered to drive him to this.

Rushing to Brent, she knelt over him sobbing, finally able to allow herself the liberty of real tears. The sheriff came and crouched next to her, patting her on the shoulder.

"Scoot over." He whispered. "And I'll check him out."

Lyssie scooted to one side, and allowed the sheriff and his men to crowd around Brent. She didn't even know how to check a temperature, much less look for signs of life, and check pulses. She rose, gazing down at the creature that lay lifeless upon the ground, and the sheriff came up behind her.

He tapped her softly.

"He's dead... isn't he?" She whispered through worried tears.

"He's fine." The sheriff grunted, giving her a professional hug, patting her on the back a lot.

"He's probly gonna have a headache for some time to come, concussion and all... but he'll be fine. He's still unconscious though. We really should be seein' to you. The county EMT's think you may have a nasty knot on yore own head."

Lyssie rubbed at the initial bump she had gained from her fall, and the blood had mixed with the rain enough that it was not quite as sticky as before.

"It might have been a problem before my adrenal glands got a crash course in panic, but it's barely more than a bump now any way."

"Still." The sheriff re-iterated. "You should have it looked at."

Alyssa glanced over at the ambulance at the other end of the clearing. It'd apparently had enough room to drive up the walking path from the mile marker, and she could see them lifting Brent into it... when she remembered Bubba's sacrifice for her.

"Have y'all found Bubba's body yet?" She almost whispered, half embarrassed by the notion that someone she barely knew would die trying to save her.

"We found him all right, but he ain't in no body bag yet. Bubba's a good ol'boy. He never goes anywhere without a pistol. He says he shot the thing in the belly, but it must not have hurt it too bad." He added eyeing the dead man-beast.

"Anyhow. Bubba's fine. Matter of fact, if he hadn't crawled back up onto the highway and flagged us down, we might not have made it to y'all in time. Now." He smiled back at Alyssa. "Let's go see about that bump on yer noggin."

"Do you know who he was?" She asked worriedly as she was walked to the ambulance.

"Who, the man-thing?" He asked as Alyssa nodded simultaneously. "Not yet. I sent a detective friend of mine back to the station a while back, and I'm sure he'll come up with something soon enough."

"Will you let me know when you find out?" Alyssa queried with genuine concern.

Sheriff Griffin eyed her curiously before answering the affirmative and stuffing her into the back of the ambulance where the paramedics could have a look at her. She sat down on a small bench next to Brent, and bent her head forward from where she sat, so that the paramedics could have a look without too much difficulty from the other side of the vehicle. She found herself gazing down at Brent's angelic face. Oh, how she wished he could take her into his big strong arms, and tell her that everything was going to work out okay. She didn't even care if he said he loved her any more, as long as he could show her... it wouldn't matter about anything else.

"Ouch!" She barked slapping the paramedic's hand away for rubbing a sore spot on her head.

"Good reflexes!" He grinned pulling his hand back. "I think you could just probably put some ice on that later, and you won't have any problem... however." He emphasized as she seemed to get happy too fast. "I strongly recommend a follow - up with your primary care physician. Those abrasions should heal fine with a little Neosporin." He said reaching across Brent's chest to touch at the scratch marks on her cheek. As his hand moved over the gurney, Brent's hand snapped up and caught it tightly.

"Watch it." He smarted pushing the hand away. "She bites."

"Tell me about it." the Paramedic laughed as he stepped away from the couple to let them be alone for a moment.

Alyssa gingerly reached over and ran the back of her hand around his face, stopping only when Brent held it, and kissed it. Her body begged for a big warm hug, but she knew by the big blood-stained bandages around his chest, that she had better not. Her eyes watered as she thought of how she had almost lost him.

"Look here." He soothed placing his hand on her cheek. "Everything's gonna be fine tomorrow. See if I'm not right."

Alyssa began to sob.

"I thought I lost you."

"I'm a little harder than that to get rid of I'm afraid."

"I noticed." She chuckled through the tears that trickled down her nose. She leaned over and prepared to kiss Brent, when someone at the back entrance of the ambulance cleared his throat. Both Alyssa and Brent looked up to see Sheriff Griffin and that man in the trench coat standing there.

"Oh Brent! Nice to see yore still with us. I have a little information I think would be interestin' for y'all."

"What is it?" Alyssa asked, her voice quivering with worry. Brent held tight to her hand.

"This is Detective Jamal Rahbuhts from the next county ovah, and he's dug up some pretty strange information on this killuh." Sheriff

Griffin nodded to let Jamal know he was free to pick up where he left off.

"I found out, after pulling a few strings in Hotlanta, that this man..." noticing Brent and Alyssa's puzzlement, Jamal added: "Yes he is a man... sort of. Anyway. He was a mental patient at Mother Mary Asylum and Wellness Clinic in Atlanta up until about a year ago. It's his reasoning for coming here that is most peculiar."

"I think I can pick up there for ya." Sheriff Griffin remarked sadly, not enjoying the need to recount such painful memories. "I used to date Brent's grandmother long years back,"

Jamal laughed, "Is there *any* woman in this county over the age of forty that you didn't date in high school?"

"Ha ha…it is to laugh." Brion retorted. "but I lost her to my best friend."

The sheriff's face told the tragic story almost without words.

"Eliza, Brent's Grandma, started getting love letters not long before Janet was born, from a man name of..."

"Hans Luft." Alyssa put in.

The sheriff, Brent *and* the detective were all three surprised by her sudden intuition, and Jamal checked his notes to verify the information. He was still puzzled when the sheriff asked her:

"How did you know that?"

"I found Brent's grand mother's love letters from him in the attic right before I moved back into town."

She noticed the downcast look on Brent's face and added: "Sorry."

Brent just shook his head "no", for her not to think anything of it. He had known that much about the man too, and looked to the police to unravel the rest of the mystery.

The Sheriff continued to relive the tale.

"Anyhow. The boy was 'bout eighteen when he showed up a selling insurance, and Eliza and Hank was good 'nuff to take him in. He raped Eliza, and was soon after shipped off to jail. He sent them letters from the jailhouse.

"Once he served his term, we all worried he might come back. But he didn't serve it. He broke out, and by then Eliza had a new baby on the way. I come this way to check on them when we got the news bout Luft's escape, but nevuh could find anythin' threatenin' in them letters he had sent. So by law, back then, they wasn't much I could do.

"They was no such thing as "stalkin'" back then neitha, so far as the law was concerned. Well…

"I did make it a regula' habit to check on them two, and it's a good thing. One night, I went out there to find the barn on fire and Eliza trapped inside. She come out of it with minor smoke inhalation, but Brent's grandfather had been killed by the man prior to the fire.

"He had beaten Hank to death with a sledgehammer and when Eliza caught him, he knocked her out, and set the barn on fire with them inside it. Latuh, Eliza helped us lay a trap for him, and we caught 'im. Now it was no secret that Hank was impotent."

Here, the sheriff paused and raised an eyebrow to Brent as he processed the information.

"You mean this thing is my *grandfather*?"

"Well then why does he *look* like that?" Alyssa questioned, disbelievingly.

"Partly because he was burned pretty good in the fire himself, and partly because they had to hold him in a hospital while he awaited a court date. This *"hospital"*, was layin' the groundwork for genetic experimentation back then.

"I reckon they used him as a sperimental guinea pig or something. In the late nineteen fifties, to mid nineteen sixties, all kind of places was tampering with genetic stuff.

"A'course, prison was the best place to find humans to 'speriment on, and lots of times them tests went bad. They wasn't many folks to live through it, but the ones who did, was usually bad violent and crazy as a loonie burd.

"Some Catholic churches, actually took on some of the successful experiments in a program they called "Asylum", even though they didn't zactly approve of the idée of men playin' God.

"These *"speriments"* were nursed to as great a level of health as humanly possible, and then maintained by a sisterhood over the years, until government funding stopped, and the churches had to find refuge for the genetic victims. Sad..." he added, pointing across the clearing to the creature. "I never thought for a minute that this mighta been a man."

"Me neither." Jamal added solemnly. "I did talk to his doctor this evening though. He escaped while they were transferring him from his original asylum to a new one about a year ago and once he got out, he had nowhere to go but to Eliza."

"It looks as if any woman who remotely reminded Hans of Eliza was in extreme danjuh." The sheriff said with a sigh. "that's why he'd been after Lyssie here. Nobuddy looks so much like my Lizzie as she does."

He looked sternly at Brent.

"I guess we can keep a lid on this if ya like, but we might have ta hose Bubba down to keep 'im from selling to a tabloid."

Both Alyssa and Brent laughed, which brought Brent a shock of pain and a heavy breath that burned his muscles.

"That's all right." Brent smiled. "I never was one for hiding anything."

He looked at Alyssa sympathetically.

He knew how wrong he had been to ask her into his life, and then shut her out and there would be no more secrets in their relationship... no more deception.

"Besides," He added "It might help people to understand just how serious stalkers are... I mean, I know this is like, the *worst*-case scenario ever, but you get my drift."

"Yeah. We get it." Jamal smiled at Alyssa. "And boy will your friend Bubba be glad to hear it... he was scratching out his ideas on a screen play in the last ambulance that left."

While the policemen shared a laugh, Brent spoke up.

"I'm kind of glad y'all are here... because I want someone to bear witness to the vow I make here, tonight..." Looking at Alyssa, and taking her hand in his he asked: "Alyssa Johnson... would you give me the pleasure of your company, as my wife for the rest of eternity?"

Alyssa was too happy to cry, and *way* too happy to restrain herself. She threw her arms around his neck, and answered: "With all my heart! Forever and a day..."

As her arms squeezed at his neck, Brent grimaced, then smiled and hugged her tightly despite the pain.

"On a God Given Grant Lyssie."

A tingle ran through her, as she squeezed him tighter with the hope of never being apart from him again.

"I love you." He whispered.

Alyssa allowed a few tears of joy to crease her eyes, then let go.

Brent sighed with the relief of not being restricted anymore, but would miss holding her the way she deserved to be held until he was out of the hospital... at which time, he would take great pleasure in making every *day* of her life the *happiest* day of her life.

End of Chapter Sixteen

Epilogue:

Brent stood at the counter slicing the tomatoes and tossing them into the salad for their family picnic.

The thought entered his mind that he hadn't seen Gram's ghost since the night he and Lyssie defeated the terror in the night. While he didn't mind so much, it did make him think.

He smiled with pride as he snapped the plastic lid on the Tupperware dish containing the final ingredient for a successful salad. Placing everything into the cooler and basket, he walked it out to get ready to leave.

He tossed the containers into the back of the new minivan he and Lyssie had bought after they got married, and headed back toward the house.

As he passed the barn, he grimaced, half expecting to have one of those bad feelings he used to have all of the time; but this was a new barn and a new day.

He built this barn. It was not the barn his Gram had built from insurance money that came with the policy Hans Luft sold her. When the frightening images didn't come, a satisfied smile crept across his face.

He went in the front door, walked through the house and out onto the back porch, where Alyssa had told him she would be when he got everything ready to go. He stood for a minute, his hand perched on the doorknob, and anticipation swept up his spine just like it had the day he and Bubba, his best man, went out it together on Brent's wedding day. He didn't think any one-day in his life would ever top that day, but it had.

Bravely turning the knob, he stepped out onto the porch in the beautiful mid-morning sunlight. Blinded by it only for a moment, he then he looked over at Alyssa.

He had married the most beautiful creature in the world and it seemed even more so today. She sat, feeding his son, Bradford Michael Price, now six seeks old, and Kitty slept lazily over Lyssie's feet. Brent smiled, as Alyssa looked up at him. She emanated a love that virtually glowed from the pores of her skin. She was so in love with him that he could scarce believe it at times.

Suddenly, he realized why he *hadn't* seen Gram. He had everything she had ever hoped he would have in his life now, and that was good enough for both of them.

The End

Made in the USA
Las Vegas, NV
17 August 2024

93969386R00122